HEART
of the
SUNGEM

JESSACA WILLIS

Heart of the Sungem.

ISBN: 978-1-7339925-7-2

ASIN: B08B4YV5VP

Front cover design by Luminescence Covers.
Editing by Sandra Ogle from Reedsy.
Proofreading by Kate Anderson.

Book published by Jessaca Willis 2020.

Jessaca Willis
PO Box 66574
Portland, OR 97266
https://www.jessacawillis.com

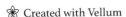 Created with Vellum

For all of the "Sinisa's" out there
who have fought to overcome their darkness.
Keep fighting.
You are worth it.
You will <u>always</u> be worth it.

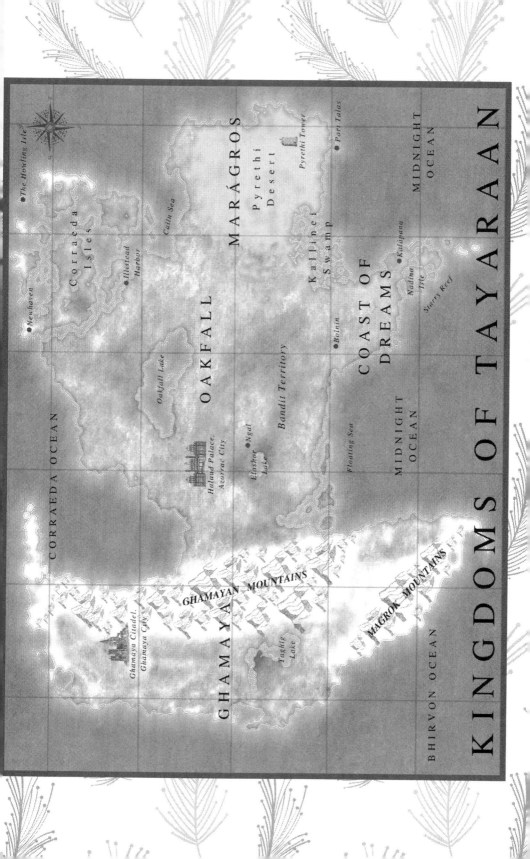

BOOKS IN SERIES

REAPERS OF VELTUUR

Assassin Reaper, Prequel

Soul of the Crow, Book 1

Heart of the Sungem, Book 2

Fate of the Vulture, Book 3

ESCAPE THE PALACE

SINISA

Left behind in the steaming bathhouse, I watch the king's rotund belly float above the waters. The aacsi unlatches from its parasitic bite. It skitters across the dead king's face and clambers back onto the stone floor, twisting to face me, ready to lunge.

Baring my teeth, I step toward its challenge with my arms out wide. "Go ahead. I dare you to taste the flesh of a Reaper..."

The taunt fizzles on my tongue like a torch dipped in water. I'd nearly forgotten that I am no longer a Reaper. Despite failing to save Acari, death does not linger beneath my skin anymore. If I truly wanted to kill this aacsi, I'd have to use force—the heel of my boot, some other blunt object, or whatever it is that the mortals use to kill.

The problem is that killing this creature now wouldn't bring Acari back. It would only make me a Reaper again. Once more, I would forget everything I'd learned about the Reapers, about their crows, about the Guardians; I'd forget about Acari and Gem, and the promise I'd made to look after her.

Becoming a Reaper again is not an option.

Shuffling backward, I move slowly, hoping that the aacsi will ignore my initial challenge. It blinks at me for a moment, the tentacles around its mouth twitching and dripping with saliva. But to my great relief, it pivots and crawls away, wedging itself between the stones lining the walls.

I hold my ear up, listening to see if anyone screams when they cross paths with the aacsi now roaming the Halaud Palace halls. None do. The people outside go about their cheerful and busy day as if nothing has changed, as if the Festival of Wings will continue on as planned, as if their king isn't already dead.

Once they discover his body, I'm fairly certain the palace environment will change. For me, where I stand in my Reaper tunic, it might even become hostile.

I head for the bathing house door and yank on the iron handle, surprised when a girl with a horse's mane of hair nearly falls into the room.

"Where is he?" Hayliel asks. She straightens to the tips of her toes to see past me and into the dim bathing house. When she finds no one following behind me, she steps aside so that I may pass. Her eyes pool. "W-where is Acari?"

"He's in Veltuur now," I say sharply.

The statement is meant to cut through her to get her off my back so that I can move on with my life. But despite the fond memories I have of my time in the gloomy forest of the underrealm, lounging beneath my familiar and twisted tree, when I utter the words, they stab my heart unexpectedly.

I couldn't stop Acari.

I couldn't save him.

He, of all people, shouldn't be in Veltuur.

And yet, he is.

He killed his father to save his sister. He did what he had to do just like I had done all those years ago. And although I *could've* saved him if I had been a moment sooner, now there is nothing else I can do for him. He is in Veltuur, and I am here in Oakfall, in Tayaraan, the mortal realm, left to pick up my life from where it last left off.

I blow past her.

Outside the bathing house, the courtyard is alive with servants and guests. They notice me in my Reaper red instantly, horrified by my presence and what it might mean for them. Few glance at the runes on my forehead, though they don't get to look at them long enough to draw any conclusions because I keep moving. I can't stay here. Once the king misses whatever activity had been next on his schedule, someone will come looking for him. They'll discover his floating corpse in one of the deep pools, but they won't find Acari standing over him, nor the aacsi that he'd unleashed. All they'll see is a girl in Reaper's clothing and a king slain for no reason.

I can't allow them to find me. Reaper or not, the people would demand justice for losing their monarch. Kings, queens, and other royalty are normally exempt from a Reaper's contract, unless they are in poor health or they've committed a crime so atrocious that they are to be publicly executed.

But Acari's father was neither unwell nor a known tyrant. The people will uprise when they hear of his death. If they find me beside him, they might imprison me and demand to speak with someone from the underrealm. And of course, now that I am no longer a Reaper, I wouldn't be able to faze away, nor would the Councilspirits come to free me. I would be locked away forever, or at least until I faced what would most certainly be an unfair trial and they sent for a Reaper to execute me.

What a miserable existence to return to after everything I've endured.

Balling my hands into fists, I march down the pebble path, away from Hayliel's silent whimpers, and head toward the secret passage that, if memory serves, is just down the next corridor.

Only a few steps into my stride though, Hayliel chases after me.

"Where are you going? Are you going to save the prince?"

I falter, if only for a second. "No. I already tried that, and clearly, I failed."

She jogs in front of me, prepared to stop me with a gentle grip on my shoulders, but she recoils before her skin meets my tunic. Apparently, even she still sees me as a Reaper.

Her hands fall to her waist instead.

"But you're going to try again, right?" she asks, staring me down. "You said that you did what needed to be done to end your service with the underrealm, which means you yourself know what it takes to...to change back. You can help him."

"No, I can't. The underrealm and the Councilspirits will shelter him until they're ready to send him out to claim his first soul, but even then, I'd have no way of finding him. They send Reapers to every corner of Tayaraan, to every kingdom and small village between the Magrok Mountains to the Corraeda Isles. I doubt they'll be in a hurry to send a former prince back to his own kingdom any time soon."

Clutching her skirts, she raises them higher to try to keep up. "Then where are you going?"

The memory replays in my mind: Acari unleashing the aacsi onto his father, the king thrashing in the dark waters until the Wraiths finally came for them both—one to become a Reaper in flesh, the other to have their soul trapped inside a crow. But just before they were taken to Veltuur, just before Acari would forget everything he'd ever known, I did the only thing that I thought a good friend could do.

"To uphold a promise," I tell her.

"Gem?" she asks. "Is she still with the Guardians?"

Her astuteness surprises me, but I answer both questions with a simple, "Yes."

Hayliel's silent for a stretch of time, long enough for us to make it to the corridor I need. The painting concealing the hidden passage, completely inconspicuous to the unknowing eye, hovers on the wall. In a few short strides, I reach for the gilded frame. As I shove it aside, I catch a glimpse of the guard just up ahead, the one I saw during my first visit to the palace when I thought my mark might be in a garden and he wouldn't let me enter.

As he strides to meet us, I notice that he looks just as he did the last time our paths crossed: his thick brows are permanently set downward, his beard groomed to a point, like one of the very conifers growing in the courtyard behind me. Given the various leather straps and drapes of fabric he's bundled in, I'm surprised he's as swift as he is to reach us.

Though, he loses points for stealth.

"Captain Borgravid," Hayliel says in greeting, sounding relieved to see him.

The man gives no indication that he feels the same, nor that he's even heard her. When his gait slows, he only has eyes for me, and they are aimed at my runes like daggers.

I shift under his scrutiny.

"Where is Prince Acari?" he demands.

Out of the corner of my eye, Hayliel's lip begins to quiver.

Without extra time to spare on a full recap of the events that unfolded, I give the painting one final shove and say succinctly, "He killed his father. He's a Reaper now. And if you don't mind, I'd like to get out of here before I'm blamed for it."

I expect a litany of questions, but when he asks none, I take one step into the tunnel on the other side of the wall.

"And what of the princess?"

Inching backward, I peer over my shoulder. "What of her?"

"If the king is dead, and if Acari is...gone, then the Oakfall throne is without a ruler. Acari said the princess is still alive. It makes her the rightful heir."

"Wasn't she kept a secret? The people of Oakfall don't even know she exists. Why was that again? Oh, right, it's because the Law of Mother's Love prevented her from legally living past infancy." I pause, ready to push forward again, when I'm struck by another, equally compelling argument. "Her own father sent a Reaper to kill her. You really think making her queen would remove the target from her back? Even with the protection of a Guardian, someone would take matters into their own hands."

Borgravid's brow furrows. "A Guardian?"

I roll my eyes. "Nevermind."

"It doesn't matter," Hayliel says, fidgeting with the frayed piece of cloth knotted at the top of her head. "Gem is the king's heir, and the people respect bloodlines more than anything else. Besides, as queen, she might be able to change the law."

I'm fully prepared to argue otherwise. These people clearly don't understand what it's like to be hated, loathed to the point of feeling uncomfortable wherever you go unless you're in the shadows. They think that the people will turn a blind eye to Gem's cleft lip, and sure, maybe some of them would, but not all. There would be a few who wouldn't be able to get past it, stuck living in the old ways, following traditions they don't even know the origins of.

My eyes shift to the sound of chainmail and leather boots stomping down the next corridor. My time here is up.

Unwilling to waste any more of the valuable seconds I have left arguing for what I already know to be true, I lie instead. "Okay. I'll make sure she returns. But I have to go, now."

"I'll come with you." Hayliel reaches for the jagged opening, hiking her skirts to step over the ledge and into the secret passageway.

I'm too surprised to know what to do, but thankfully, Borgravid acts instead. With a firm hand on her shoulder, he pulls her back. "That would be unwise. A king has just been slain; the prince is gone. If the palace also finds a fleeing servant—"

"Me? It's not like they could think I had anything to do with his death. I would've become a Reaper."

"There are other crimes they could accuse you of. Perhaps you were the one who summoned a Reaper here to claim his life."

"I-I wouldn't..."

Borgravid releases his grip and lets Hayliel's horrified imagination warn her against following me.

She steps back, her head down, and as I plunge into darkness, someone pushes the painting back into its place, closing the passage behind me.

2

THE PIT

ACARI

One of the robed Councilspirits leads me to a stone chamber. They extend their arm, a bony finger protruding from the wide, red cuff and, without words, they tell me to enter. For a moment, I want to do no such thing. I want to ask what's inside and why they've taken me here, where the other Councilspirits have gone, and why I can't seem to remember anything before a few moments ago. But when I see the layers of stains and splatter caked throughout the Councilspirit's robe, giving it a deep red hue that could have only come from one thing, I go in without asking my questions.

A chilling draft blows past me, and I don't need to turn back around to know that the Councilspirit has disappeared, but I do, surprised to find a lumpy stone wall in place of the entrance I'd just walked through. No sign of a door, just smooth, ancient stones sealed together in concrete.

For a fraction of a second, fear tugs at me. I am trapped. I am alone. But the feeling quickly dissipates like the fog beneath my steps before it can become anything more than a fleeting moment. This place, it's doing something to me. What, I don't know, but I can feel it, like centipedes crawling inside my gut, which should make me creeped out, but instead, I stare at the ground to where my feet disappear, letting a forceful calm press into me.

After a few deep breaths, my gaze travels higher, up the midnight trousers tight against my thighs and to the crimson tunic cinched in leather at my waist. There's something familiar about this tunic, even though it feels foreign draped over my skin. It's possible that it's just familiar because it's the same outfit all the Reapers wear, but I get the nagging suspicion that there's another reason.

A memory blinks in my mind, a girl wearing a similar red garment, accented by leather boots, and flowing, umber hair.

Caw!

The crow's call distorts the image, and my attention is drawn back to the present, to the dais where the bird is perched. Its chest is puffed, its beak pointing so high in the air that it looks regal. Perhaps when I selected my crow, I inadvertently allied with the king of crows.

"Maybe that's what I'll call you: King."

The bird stills as I make way over to it, shrinking beneath its self-important demeanor with every step, until I'm standing in the center of the room alongside it.

"Welcome"—a man's voice echoes from above—"to the Pit of Judgment."

I crane my neck back as far as it will go, looking past the abyss flies floating overhead, to the robed figure above me. I recognize him, the thin, spindly man, as the same Councilspirit who greeted me in the forest when I'd first arrived in Veltuur.

The rest of the Councilspirits come into view then as I rotate below to see them all. I count six in total, but judging from the empty throne, it's safe to guess that there are likely seven.

"Why have you summoned us to tribunal, Leumas?" one of the female Councilspirits asks. Her screeching voice grates against my eardrums like glass on glass.

The spindly man addresses her. "Because these are worrying

times, Nymane. A king stands before us, and only one other time in history has such an occasion occurred."

I glance at the crow, thinking that maybe I was right and they are referring to him and his royal standing with the birds I've taken him from. They *have* to mean him. I mean, I am no king. If I know nothing else, I can feel *that* much in my blood.

The bird ruffles its feathers, glancing at me sidelong—if birds can do such a thing.

"He's not a king. He's a Reaper," Nymane snaps, leaving no more room for me to deny who they're really talking about.

I try to stand straighter, to present myself as what I think a king might embody. But within a few seconds, my back is already aching from the effort, and when I catch my crow staring at me—who I'll have to name something else since we can't *both* be King—I feel his judgment and I sink back into my relaxed posture.

"We should send him back to the forest, where he belongs," Nymane continues. "So that he may await his first contract and fortify his allegiance to Veltuur, like all the others."

"Or," Leumas says, pausing dramatically. "Perhaps we return him to Oakfall, so that he might take his rightful place on the throne."

"The throne? He killed the king. He committed treason. The mortals will abolish any claim he once had to ruling the kingdom of Oakfall."

The Councilspirits start arguing amongst themselves, their voices a cacophony of roaring magroks. It's clear they are divided. Most oppose Leumas' proposal, but two are quiet enough that they seem willing to at least hear his argument first. For some reason, that worries me more than the fate Nymane is suggesting for me.

"Do I have a say in this?" I ask shyly, silencing them all.

Nymane quirks a thin brow, her skin seeming to crack with the effort it takes for her to force a smile. "By all means, *Reaper*. Tell us how you'd like us to determine your fate. You, who has no knowledge of how you came to be here, or what your duties are to Veltuur."

"Uh..."

The sweetness of her tone confuses me. It bares more likeness to a siren's song than that of a mother's lullaby. My mind might be foggy, but I'm fairly certain I understand my role here quite well. Veltuur has already whispered it to me: I am a Reaper, and it is my job to collect souls to help them make their way here. She's right though. I *don't* remember much from before, but that almost makes what I'm about to say matter all the more.

"Okay. You said I don't remember my mortal life, and honestly, that's true. I'm not sure why. Is that normal? Do all Reapers go through that?" At the sight of Nymane's eyeroll, I move on. "Anyway, if I was a king, I have no memory of it, and I have no real compression for it—*compulsion* for it. My duty is to Veltuur now, and I will gladly step down from any—"

"Thank you, dear Reaper, for your selflessness," Leumas says, saving me from myself with a gentle, albeit rotten smile. "Your loyalty to Veltuur does not go unnoticed, but I'm afraid Nymane is correct. This decision is above you." He signals to another Councilspirit. "Bhascht, would you be so kind as to remind the Council of what happened the last time a king became a Reaper and abandoned his throne?"

The largest of the Councilspirits stands, skin engorged and fetid beneath his robes. When he draws his hood back, I see that his face is swollen too, bloated and veiny like he could pop with the slightest touch of pressure. He can't even pry his eyes open when he speaks.

"In the Age of Divinity," Bhascht begins, his voice like the dying breath of an old man. "The king of Ghamaya slew his brother for an affair with the queen. When Veltuur claimed the wicked as Reapers a few score later, the king disappeared to the underrealm. His people revolted. Blaming the other kingdoms who had spoken out against his brutal act, they murdered countless innocents."

Nymane scoffs. "That was before the mortals knew of the Reapers. They weren't yet aware that committing murder would indenture them to Veltuur, and so they weren't aware that their king was serving the underrealm. Things are different now."

"Ah." Leumas signals to Bhascht to take his seat, addressing Nymane alone. "And what happened after the mortals found out? Did order return to Ghamaya swiftly?"

Nymane snarls, baring teeth like a wolf's fangs.

Leumas answers for her. "It took an entire century before the kingdoms of Tayaraan saw any normalcy, a few centuries more before peace and calm returned to Ghamaya. The mortals may know of Reapers now, but do not fool yourselves into thinking they are capable of rational thought and adaptability. Losing the king of Oakfall, and then his only living heir, will create chaos.

"The Reapers serve Veltuur by way of balance. Under normal circumstances, they counter life with death. But perhaps *this* Reaper"—he points one slender finger at me—"can do more than that. Perhaps he can ensure balance in other ways, by remaining in his throne."

"And what if you're wrong?" Nymane snarls. "What if they won't accept him? He committed treason. He's a Reaper. They won't allow him to sit on the throne."

A careless flick of his wrist. "Then he returns to Veltuur like any other Reaper, and we let the mortals figure out who to put in his place." Seeming every part a frail and dying man, Leumas lowers himself back into his throne carefully.

"They would choose their princess," Nymane hisses. "In fact, they can choose her now. There is no reason for this Reaper to live his days in the mortal realm, Leumas, and I'm sure the rest of the Council would agree with me. What you propose is unnecessary and reckless, and contradicts the very way of our being."

Of the Councilspirits I can see, all nod. Except Leumas. Steepling his fingers, he bows over his knees to think, and it gives me enough time to piece together the story they're telling. They say I killed a king and became one myself, which can only mean that the man I killed was my father. Any princess they're speaking of would have to be a sister of mine.

I let the knowledge sink in, mull it over like a steaming mouthful of stew, but whatever familial sensations I expect to come next, none do. I feel no love for the family they speak of, no sense of belonging or loyalty. I don't know this princess, nor this king; I have no memory of them, and frankly, I'm not sure I care to. My guess is I killed the king for a reason and likely knew I'd be leaving behind my sister to sit on the throne. I doubt I cared much for either of them.

Leumas looks up, addressing everyone again. "The mortals know not of the princess, and the Guardians will keep it that way. She is a Prophet, after all, and they have laws preventing her kind from surviving. Besides, if they *were* to find out she was still alive, they'd soon discover that a Reaper had failed in her execution. They'd start to understand more about us than they should. I trust that none of you want the secrets of Veltuur escaping, hmm?"

Silent nodding all around the chamber.

"We need young Reaper Acari in Oakfall. Only there can he best serve Veltuur."

The Councilspirits fall silent, the only sound puncturing the room the soothing buzzing of the abyss flies above. One of them shines more brightly than the others, I notice, and as it floats around, I catch Leumas eyeing it too.

"Very well," Nymane says at last. "The Councilspirits trust your judgment on this. Reaper Acari will serve Veltuur from his place on the throne in Oakfall. However, his duties as a Reaper must come first."

"Of course," Leumas says, inclining his head.

I don't know whether to be relieved or feel defeated. I have the sneaking suspicion that being king was never something I wanted. Then again, I'm not sure living my days in the grim and desolate forest of the underrealm was likely on my list of ideal lifestyles either.

Nymane leans over the podium separating her from the chasm. Her onyx eyes burrow into me. "You are to report to Veltuur every morning before dawn. You are to complete your contracts promptly, and only once you have finished may you return to Oakfall. Understood?"

My voice feels too shaky to test, despite whatever protests are clawing at the back of my throat, so I simply nod instead.

Beside me, the crow throws its head back. It squawks over and over again, and I'm almost certain it's laughing at me and my unwanted fate.

I am to be king—a Reaper King—and I have to admit it sounds like a joke to me too.

3

OUTCAST

SINISA

I ball my hands into fists when the hundredth person jumps out of my path, frightened by my red tunic. Veltuur has a sick sense of humor to spit their former Reapers back into Tayaraan in the same exact place where they committed their crimes, wearing the very garments that mark them as murderers in the eyes of mortals.

"I have runes!" I snarl at one man in particular, pointing to my face for emphasis.

When he scrambles even farther away from me, it takes me a moment to recognize where his fearful gaze has traveled. It's one thing to see a presumed Reaper walking around the kingdom with runes on her forehead, but entirely another to discover unfamiliar markings on her hands as well. The runes that decorate my fingers like petals of lavender are unlike any that he or anyone else living here has ever seen.

I lower my hands self-consciously, tugging my sleeves as far down as they will go to conceal as much of the intricate designs as possible, but at least I learned a valuable lesson: if people are afraid of Reapers, they're even more so of Reapers with unknown runes like mine. No one seems to know about the Guardians, nor the markings we bare. But even if I started screaming that I am a Guardian from the nearest rooftop, these mortals wouldn't listen. They're still too afraid of me, too afraid of death and what lies beyond this life.

After what I uncovered about my own crow, I suppose they have a right to be.

Turning down the next street, I find the worn sign I've been searching for, an image of a spool of thread and a sewing needle, etched into the wood, but fading with each passing year.

"Welcome to Taylor's Tailor," sings a cheerful man when I enter. "How may I—"

He gasps when he finds me standing in the doorway. Like all the others, his eyes first bulge at the Reaper red I'm wearing, then to my forehead, though he doesn't give himself enough time to consider that my runes mean he has nothing to fear from me.

"Flightless bird! No. Please, I'm not ready to die."

I roll my eyes. It's always the same thing with them. *I'm not ready to die.* Like anyone ever is. Even the majority of people I'd met on their death beds weren't *ready* to die. They'd simply had no choice. Just once I wish someone would come up with something a little more original when they spotted me coming their way.

"I'm not here to collect your soul. I'm not even a..." Before I can finish the sentence, I kill the words. Maybe I can use this to my advantage. After all, I don't have much else to barter with. No rupees, nothing to trade. Being a Reaper might be the only thing I have. "I'll let you live, but I need something from you in return."

"A-anything," the man pleads. He throws himself to his knees, a plume of dust wafting up from the floor where he lands. "I'll do anything. Just please don't hurt me."

Glancing around the shop, I eye the different types of fabric. Some soft, some rough, but that's about as far as my knowledge of linens goes. I've never had a need to understand such things. As a Reaper, we were given the one outfit—a single red tunic that I think might've cleansed itself every time we fazed in and out of Veltuur. And before I was a Reaper, sure, I'd eyed the beautiful gowns I'd glimpsed the high ladies wearing here and there, but other than that, my wardrobe had consisted of the few tattered items that the orphanage had provided us.

"I need some clothes," I tell the man. "Something suitable for travel that will help me blend in with the others."

He peeks up at me, uncertain, his chin all but resting on the floor still. "T-that's all?"

When I reassure him it is, he uses the stool beside him to get back on his feet. I would've offered him my hand if I thought he'd have taken it. Perhaps once I'm dressed more suitably though, maybe then I'll have an easier time of interacting with people.

"Right away. I have just the thing in the back."

He disappears behind the partition, returning a few moments later with a pile of green and brown garments. I recognize the colors as the ones of Oakfall instantly. It's the same colors Acari had worn when we'd first met, even if the tailor's fabric is obviously of lesser quality. But even though the bodice he holds up for me to see is hemmed with a feminine shape, the brown stitching dull compared to the golden thread that had been sewn through Acari's doublet, it's still too painfully familiar to look at.

My stomach sinks as deep as the Pit of Judgment.

The tailor begins unfolding the chemise, then the petticoat to match the bodice, but I'm suddenly uninterested. I can't imagine wearing any of it without feeling like I was flaunting Acari's absence and my failure.

"Do you have anything else? Anything that's not that color?"

The tailor's hands falter. "Well, no. Nothing ready. These are Oakfall's most popular shades. If you give me a day or two, I could—"

Growling, I yank the clothes from the man's bony hand. "It's fine."

I storm past him, ducking behind the cloth that separates the back room from the rest of the store. Trembling, I set the outfit down on a stool and undress. I can hear the tailor trying to figure out what he should do, if he should insist I leave his personal quarters or just leave me to it. As he paces, it seems he decides to do the latter, likely too afraid that opening his mouth will remind me that he's still alive.

When I reemerge, dressed in trousers that are as brown as cow pies and layers as stifling as the sun, it's without so much as a thank you or a farewell as I cross the room back toward the main entrance.

I brace myself for the cruelty that awaits me on the other side of the door, but then I remember that all of that is behind me now, discarded on the dusty floor in the back of the shop. Once I step through this door, no one will ever again mistake me for being a Reaper. I'll be seen as a mortal—I *am* a mortal.

But if that were true, then why does it still feel like a lie? Why do I still dread opening this door and seeing the way the people will look at me? Why do I miss the feel of my Reaper tunic, the fabric that was as soft as a snowfur, and fit me more perfectly than anything I ever remember owning?

With a deep, invigorating breath, I reach for the door. To my great displeasure though, just as I'm about to swing the door wide, a familiar face peeks through the transom window.

I yank the door open, letting Hayliel stumble inside. "What did I tell you about staying at the palace?"

"Y-you said nothing," she stammers. "Borgravid suggested I stay behind."

Scowling, it takes me a moment to recall that she's right. Though I thought I was going to have to insist she stay at the palace, it was in fact Borgravid who spoke first.

"You weren't supposed to see me," she says timidly. "At least, not until we reached the Guardian encampment."

If I hadn't seen her until then, I would've been even more upset knowing that she'd been able to tail me for that long without my knowing.

"What are you doing here?"

She pushes herself off the floorboards, nods politely to the tailor, before patting the dust from her skirts. "I want to help. I might not have promised prince Acari directly, but I am just as much obligated to ensure his sister's safety as you are."

Groaning, I push past her and into the crowded streets. A few of the denizens who had seen me enter the tailor's clamber out of my way, but others—*most* of them—hardly notice me. They carry on about their day, women holding the hands of their children as they walk toward the marketplace, men carrying lumber for construction of a nearby building. And though I should be relieved to finally be rid of their putrid tongue lashings and hateful glares, I don't.

I feel like a wolf walking among sheep, eager for the hunt and yet, not one of them is running. Does it no longer matter that I killed a man when I was just thirteen? Does it matter that I failed to save their prince?

"Leave me alone," I say to Hayliel when she pops up beside me. "I don't need you."

"I never said you did. I have no doubt that with all of your... experience, you are plenty capable without me." This time, when she reaches out to grab me, she doesn't falter. Her hand latches around my wrist, soft and warm, and I tense. It will take some time before I am used to physical contact again. "I am not here because I think you need my aid. I am here because I want to do right by Acari and Gem."

Sighing, I rub my forehead, surprised once more by the raised skin of designs I find there.

I look upon Hayliel like I'm seeing her for the first time. She's clearly had a much different life than I have. While I was stuck spending my most formative years in an orphanage, she was polishing the palace floors and sleeping on mattresses stuffed with feathers. Growing up in a palace, whether as a servant or not, she likely grew up with every privilege I never had: people she could trust, food that wasn't likely to have been scrounged from nearby gutters.

Even with Acari gone, she could've continued living that life of comfort and security, but instead, she chased after me. I see it now, the quiet sense of duty she carries about her, and it's obvious that no matter what I say, she will continue to follow me, and she won't rest until she's with Gem.

If that's really how she feels, then we may be more alike than I initially thought, and perhaps she deserves to know the truth.

"Acari is gone," I remind her. "The only person worth protecting now is Gem. You know that, right?"

Thoughtfully, she nods.

"And you also know that I have no intentions of returning to the palace with her."

Hayliel opens her mouth to protest, but presses her lips shut and casts her gaze to the ground. "You...you really think someone else would come after her?"

Nodding, I tell her a little bit about the life of a Reaper. "Every month we received a handful of new initiates that way, people who couldn't abide by their neighbors, family, and friends trying to break the rules. For as much as mortals hate Reapers, I think they hate people like Gem even more. You'd be surprised how many are willing to kill in the name of justice."

"They wouldn't." At first I think it's because she's so frightened for Gem that she can't see logic, but then I realize, like many of the mortals, she's more terrified of the thought of ever becoming a Reaper. "Who would want to do that to themselves?"

I level her a look, one that explains more than words ever could, that I, of all people, know just how desperate mortals can be. Some things are worth becoming a Reaper for. It's as simple as that. And you never know what will make someone cross that line until their toes are right on top of it.

"All right," she says finally. Understanding flickers behind her eyes, and I know she's thinking of Acari and the decision he recently made. That, or she's just remembered she's talking to a former Reaper. "I believe you. We can't bring Gem back because it wouldn't be safe. Believe me, I don't want anything to happen to her. I'm not even sure I want her knowing what her brother has done..."

That makes me scowl. "She'll have to eventually."

"I know, I know." Hayliel swallows, steeling herself to stone and making the tears that were threatening to fall evaporate. "But we'll cross that bridge when we get there. For now, where do we go next?"

I glance around the street, searching for my bearings, but truthfully, I'm not as familiar with the outskirts of Azarrac City as I am the few streets that I used to play on as a child. I'm not sure which road will lead us to Ngal, only that one of them will.

"Do you know how to get to Ngal?" I ask.

She beams. "I do. My sister lives there with her husband and children. I visit every once in a while, often enough that the journey is quite familiar to me." And then with sudden realization, she asks, "Are the Guardians in Ngal?"

"Not exactly, but they're close." I stretch my hand outward in invitation. Both of our eyes linger on the lavender designs there. "I'll follow your lead."

"Sure, but one more thing first?"

My head rolls when I turn back around to face her. "What now?"

Her amused smile takes me by surprise. "I was just hoping to know the name of my travel companion."

4

AVENGE THE KING

ACARI

Smoke billows around us as my crow and I are swept out of the Pit of Judgment. We float through the air like we're riding storm clouds, rolling through an endless night sky. Every now and then I try brushing some of them away to see what lies beyond them in between the mortal and underrealms, but they only dissipate once my feet meet solid ground.

The air becomes denser, not like the thickness of being surrounded by smoke as I just was, but the heaviness of steam and heat. A dark room fills in around me, with only the light of a few squat windows to offer any view of my surroundings.

But as I notice the black pools I find myself standing between, I'm overcome by a sudden sense of familiarity once more.

I see the girl again, the one in Reaper red.

Her hair is like smoke and her eyes are like night. But this time I also see the runes on her forehead, making her distinctly *not* a Reaper, and I'm even more curious about her, how I know her, and why she seems to be the only thing I can remember from before.

I remember her standing right here, right before me...but I can't remember why.

At the sudden whispering floating between these walls, the

memory fades away yet again, and my awareness shifts to the rest of the room and the people in it with me.

"It's the prince," one of them says, breathless.

"He's a Reaper..."

"You don't think he—"

"Prince Acari," says one of the many guards in the room. He steps in front of me, all squared shoulders and rigid posture.

I can tell from his positioning that he's trying to block my view of whatever is behind him. Without being too obvious about it, I sneak a glimpse past him, finding a few guards huddled over one of the pools, though I can't see what's inside it.

"What are you doing here?" the guard before me commands. Not *asks*, commands, like I'm some lowly beggar. If I was any king, I'd do something about such disrespect, rather than shrinking in his presence.

My crow spreads its wings, leaps into the air, and flies over him. It lands near the pool that the other guards are working over. This time, I can't resist the temptation and I jump to the side to get the view I wanted. The guard in front of me is waiting for that though, and so he steps with me, but not before I see the naked man being dragged out of the dark water.

"What's going on?" I ask.

The guard crosses his arms and repeats himself more emphatically. "What are you doing here?"

I'm about to stand down, intimidated by his stature and stance, when I see the others exchanging looks with each other. Perhaps it's like the Councilspirits said: the mortals here expect me to fill the role as their new king.

"Is that how you speak to your king?" Admittedly, there's less strength in my words than I'd hoped for, making me lose my bravado almost instantly. "Sorry, I'm trying to figure things out. Who are you?"

Before the guard steels himself, I see pain flash in his dark eyes. "You don't know me..." He straightens, shaking off his previous line of thought. "Captain Borgravid, Your Majesty. One of your most loyal guardsmen."

"And who's that?" I ask, pointing behind him, even though I'm fairly certain I already know.

"The king. Your father. He's been slain."

Curiosity spills through me. I want to see the face of the man that should be so familiar to me and imbedded in my memory but isn't. I want to see how I did it, what method I'd used. But like before, the moment I try to look past Captain Borgravid, he doesn't allow it.

I frown but ask the next thing on my mind. "No one's exposed— I mean *disposed* of him yet?"

Captain Borgravid squints at me, pained. "May I speak with you? In private."

I see no reason to refuse his request, and so I give him a noncommittal shrug.

"You three—" he points at some of the guards huddled near the entrance. "Search the grounds for the loose aacsi and contain it. It can't have made it far."

"Yes sir."

With Borgravid in the lead, the other guards scrambling behind us, we exit the bathing house, my crow gliding closely overhead. There are just as many curious eyes watching us in the courtyard though, so instead of stopping there, the captain continues toward a towering temple at the center. Everything looks so strangely familiar here, like I'm walking through a long-forgotten dream, that it's difficult not to want to linger. I suppose it makes sense though. If the king was my father, it means I lived here too. I just wish I had memory of it.

We slip off our shoes and enter the temple.

Inside, the place is empty, but he waits until I've closed the door behind me before he speaks.

"Why are you here? Why have you returned?"

"I already told you, I'm the king now," I say, starting strong, though by the time I finish, I'm less certain. "Aren't I?"

Caw! Caw! Caw!

Borgravid grunts and folds his arms again. "What kind of king kills his own father?"

Surprised by his knowledge, I don't have the forethought to deny it. "Your guess is as good as mine." Instead, I shuffle through the room, rounding one of the benches to take a seat beside the pillars beaded in gold. "All I know is I was sent to claim my place on the throne. The Councilspirits didn't want the kingdom of Oakfall to be without a monarch."

"And what makes you think that a Reaper, let alone a treasonous one, could be crowned king?"

Abashedly, I smile up at him. "Because one of my most loyal guardsmen is talking to me instead of shackling me up?"

Borgravid sighs heavily. When he takes a seat beside me, the entire bench rocks. He leans over, elbows to knees, stroking his thick beard as it dangles between his legs. I recognize the pensive moment, see the questions swimming in his mind, but I have questions of my own and I ask them before he gets the chance to launch into his.

"How did I do it?"

He peers over his shoulder at me. "You unleashed an aacsi on him, one stolen from the Forbidden Garden where I was supposed to be stationed." There's accusation in his tone, though it sounds more directed at himself than anything.

"An aacsi? Like, one of those weird bugs that spits out parasites? I had no better way of killing my father than that?"

He barks a cold, bitter laugh. "Given your family's history, it was a fitting death."

The crow caws again, bouncing up and down like it's a petulant child demanding our attention.

Borgravid twists farther around, bracing himself on the back of the bench to watch it. "What's wrong with your bird?"

Grimacing, I glance a sympathetic eye toward it. "I think it was meant for greater things than following a Reaper around."

The crow stops squawking. Ruffling its feathers in a gesture that almost looks proud, it launches into the rafters above us, disappearing into the darkness. I don't think it's left entirely though. First of all, there's no smoke. But more notably, I can *feel* its eyes on me like a brand.

"Greater than serving a king?" Borgravid scoffs. "I doubt any other bird has been granted such an honor." Wide-eyed, he catches himself, glancing guiltily to the statue of the Divine Sungema. "Aside from the Divine Altúyur, of course."

Neither of us say a word for a while, basking in the silence. I think about what I've been sent here to do and wonder if it's even possible. Nymane was right. A Reaper doesn't belong in Tayaraan, and the people won't want me here once they discover that I've killed one of their kings. Perhaps it would be best if my crow and I just returned now? Then again, I can't exactly outright disobey the Councilspirits like that. What kind of a Reaper would that make me? Maybe my crow knows that too, and it's just waiting for proof that we can't make this work before it fazes us back to the underrealm where we belong and—

"You really don't remember what happened?" Borgravid asks, his voice tired and heavy. He watches me from the corner of his eyes, still testing me, still assessing what he will do.

Maybe it's not entirely hopeless yet.

"I wish I did, but I don't. It's like everything from before is...is just gone. Like I didn't even exist."

"But you did," he says sternly.

"Yeah, I know. Obviously, I did. But I don't remember any of it."

Leaning back, he quirks an eyebrow at me. "You remember how to talk."

"Well, yeah...I guess I do."

"And you remember Oakfall, the palace, your home."

The suggestion gives me pause and I glance around the room. Though some of the details feel familiar, like the curvature of Sungema's wings, or the frayed edge of one of the maroon rugs, and the line of shoes at the doorway, as a whole it still feels mostly foreign to me.

I don't want to admit as much though. Whoever this man is, it's clear he remembers me, and I get the distinct feeling that he wants to do what he can for me, if I'm worth doing anything for.

So to get a better sense of him, I change the subject.

"How did everyone know I killed him? I mean, the aacsi technically did it, not me, but you know—" But it's then that it occurs to me that what he's told me about my father's death doesn't make sense— "Actually, I just made a good point. Aren't I technically innocent if some bug killed him, not me?"

Captain Borgravid eyes my Reaper tunic as if to say it's all the proof we need. "If you hold someone underwater, it's the water that fills their lungs, but it's still *you* who held them down. If you set fire to a barn, it is the smoke that suffocates the horses, and the flames that char their bodies, but you still held the torch."

The logic seems a bit fragile to me, but who am I to argue? Regardless of what I think is a worthy offense of Reaperdom, I've already been made into one.

"So how did they know it was me? Anyone could've brought an aacsi into the bathing house."

"They don't know. But appearing in a blaze of smoke freshly made a Reaper, materializing right beside your father's dead body will have surely roused their suspicions."

Sighing, I slouch farther into the pew. If the Councilspirits wanted to make this easy on me, they sure don't seem to be trying.

A new thought occurs to me then. "If no one knew it was me, how did *you* know? You even knew how I did it, but I don't remember you being there."

His brow sharpens. "I thought you didn't remember any of it."

"I—it's complicated. I'm not lying to you. It's like everything before today was just a cloud that's been blown away. But there are pieces that were left behind, I guess? I have this hazy recollection of me standing in the bath house. But...it's hard to really remember any of it. But I don't remember you being there."

Nodding, he sighs again and says, "Maybe it'll come back with time," before bringing his gaze to the golden statue of the Divine Sungema.

She stretches from floor to ceiling behind the altar, resplendent and blinding. Honey gold covers her from head to toe, limb to wing. Her hands are clasped at her chest as if she is grateful for everyone who comes to visit her.

Borgravid is quiet for a long time before he speaks again. "I knew because your friend told me."

My gaze snaps to the corner—*corners?*—of my eyes. "What friend?"

"The girl. The one who was a Reaper but now isn't."

I blink, wondering if he could possibly be talking about the same girl I've been remembering. She had been dressed like a Reaper, but the runes on her forehead had suggested otherwise. I just figured I'd been mistaken, that she hadn't had runes at all or that her clothes were different somehow from the traditional Reaper garb, but now, I might have my answers.

"Was she in the bathing house with me?" I ask. "When I killed the former king."

Borgravid frowns. "I believe so."

I blink again. She is the one thing I remember from my previous life. The two times I've recalled her, I never thought she would become more than a fractured memory. But now I'm told that she is a friend, a friend who helped me kill *the king* for crying out loud. She must be a *really* good friend to involve herself in something like that.

But the piece of information that surprises me the most is that she is somehow no longer a Reaper.

There is nothing I want more than to find this girl. I'm not even really sure why. I don't need to know more about what happened with the king, I don't even care about why she's no longer a Reaper —although, I'll admit, I am slightly intrigued. More than anything though, I just want to know who she is and why she had been there with me. I think there's a bigger story buried somewhere in there.

"Did she see anyone else—" I shake my head when I hear my embarrassing error, and correct it—"Did anyone else see her?"

"Some of the servants did, I believe. Why?"

Pressing my thumb against my lip, I chew on the slow grind of an idea forming.

"You liked me, right?"

He scowls at me. "I...don't understand."

"I just mean, before. We were friends, or something? Come on. Why else would you be having this heart-to-heart with me?"

With a wary eye, he nods. "I've known you since infancy and you have always had a good head on your shoulders and an even better heart in your chest."

"So, am I also correct in assuming that you want to help me claim my birthright? That you don't mind having a *treasonous king-murderer* on the throne?"

He crosses his thick arms, narrows his dark eyes down on me.

I shrink back. "Sorry. That was a terrible thing to say. I'm not saying I *am* a treasonous king-murderer—"

"But you are."

"Apparently...I just mean...I feel like I can count on you. Am I wrong? I'd rather know now than later because if I'm not wanted here then I'm sure the underrealm would gladly take me back, and I'd just like to know now before I try to get comfortable. But if you don't, then I understand, I just—"

He holds up his hands and I fall silent. "I will always be loyal to you, King Acari."

A rush of relief bubbles through me, even though the sadness reflected in his eyes nearly diminishes it.

"Great," I say quickly. "Good. That's...that's good to hear. Then, maybe you can help prove my innocence."

"But you're not innocent."

"No, no," I say, waving him off. "I know I'm not *technically* innocent. I may not have memory of killing the king, nor do I know why I did it, but I *know* I did. But the others, *they* don't have to know."

Eyebrows raised, Borgravid levels me with a suspicious glower. "What would we tell them?"

With a crooked grin, I rise from my seat. "We can just blame my father's death on the other Reaper. I'll say that when I arrived, she was here, and she had already killed him."

I'll admit, I feel a little guilty for even thinking of such a suggestion, but right now, I have a directive from the Council to follow through with, and my curiosities about *her* have to wait until I've secured my spot on the throne.

"And what do we tell the people about you? They'll want to know why you're a Reaper now too?"

Wincing, I say sheepishly, "That I tried protecting him? I fought the Reaper and killed her, and if anyone says otherwise, we deal with them later."

He shakes his head. "Your constituents are not as naive as you might think. If you fought a Reaper you would've likely died. You were not known for your prowess in battle."

Both of us retreat back into our thoughts. There has got to be a way to spin this to ensure it make sense.

Finally, Borgravid straightens. "A few days ago, you left the palace. It was unlike you to journey anywhere beyond the palace gates, let alone to flee without word or a guard. Your father searched all over for you, but no one knew where you were or why you'd left, except me and him."

Expectant, I raise my eyebrows.

"We can use that secrecy now to our advantage. We can spin a story of how you left because you were trying to protect your father. You were seen fleeing the palace with...with your sister, but no one knows that's who she was. We can tell them that she brought word that your father was in danger, and you set out to stop it."

Eyes fixed on mine, Borgravid stands, towering over me like one of the Councilspirits as they loomed atop the Pit of Judgment. "We tell them you were too late to stop the person from communing with the scripture worms and that a Reaper had already been contracted, but you still avenged the king. You killed the person who requested the Reaper, but in so doing, you became one yourself."

Nodding, I stand with him. "That's good. Since I knew I couldn't save him, I killed the person who sent a Reaper for him instead."

He bobs his head, once. The story is so airtight and perfect that I practically start skipping as I make my way around the benches.

But I don't get far before Borgravid's hand clamps down on my shoulder.

As I turn to face him, the crow swoops down to the bench beside us. Its claws click against the wood as it tightens its grip, listening just as intently as I am.

"Are you still worth following?" he asks, voice low and hoarse. At my surprised expression, he shrugs. "I, too, appreciate honesty and knowing in advance whether I've chosen the right ally."

My sigh is heavy and long. Not only can I not afford to lose his allegiance, but in just the few short moments that we've spent together since my arrival, I've already decided that I don't *want* to lose it. Whatever bond we shared before my Reaper initiation is still palpable now, even if I can't remember it. It's like translucent spiderwebs have woven our paths together, and even though I don't remember him, nor any of our previous interactions, I know he's a man I can trust.

Shrugging, I confess. "I think so. It's hard to say, since I don't really know anything about who I was before, and therefore nothing of my previous intentions for the throne. What I can promise you is this: I was returned to Oakfall because I am the rightful heir to the throne. I was told to fulfill my royal responsibilities, and if that is my job, then I have every intention of doing so."

Borgravid stares at me a moment longer. His brow twitches as he scrutinizes me, my words, the young man I was, and the new man he's deciphering.

Finally, he claps my shoulder. "Then perhaps you're better suited for the throne now than you ever were before."

5

WARM WELCOME

SINISA

By the time we reach Ngal, it's late enough in the day that if we continued through the woods now, we'd find ourselves wandering them come nightfall. After my last encounter with this forest after dark, venturing out there again, this time without my Reaper touch, is not a choice I'm eager to make.

"We should stay at the inn," I announce, gesturing to the familiar building ahead.

It's hard to believe that Acari and I were here just the other day. Even now, I can practically see the guards who tried kidnapping him and throwing him into the carriage, me threatening them to leave him alone, lest they face death. I wonder what we would've done if I hadn't still been a Reaper then. They feared me because of my touch. Without it, he would've been taken back against his will, and it's likely that neither of us would've learned of the ways to save Gem, and therefore Acari might still be walking the mortal realm this very moment.

"There's no need for an inn," Hayliel says, drawing me out from my dark thoughts. "Remember? My sister and her family lives here. She will provide us room and board for the evening. They're not too far away either."

The thought of willingly going somewhere where people will expect us to socialize instead of being allowed to retire to a private room appalls me, but I'm also not the one with any rupees to her name.

Silently squashing my protest, I allow Hayliel to lead the way. She wasn't exaggerating. Just a dozen cottages down, she veers from the uneven road and walks up to a door and knocks.

"Dearest sister!" a woman exclaims upon opening the door. She swings it wider, arms spread, and I see now that she is a near replica of Hayliel, only a little rounder in the face and waist. "We weren't expecting a visit from you until after the festival—"

Mid-embrace, her attention falls to me behind Hayliel. My breath hitches as I prepare for the worst, for the sneers, the spitting, the contemptuous glares that I've had to endure for years.

"Who's this?" she asks brightly.

I almost stagger, choking on my tongue.

"This is Sinisa," Hayliel answers for me. "She's a friend."

"Well, we can't have you standing out here while we have warm supper inside waiting to fill some bellies. Come in, come in."

She shoos Hayliel inside with a pat on her back then, seeing me hesitate on the doorsteps, she reaches for me and pulls me through the doorway as well. Inside, three copper-headed children race around the room, screeching and grabbing for one another. The youngest is maybe a year older than Gem.

When the kids notice they have unexpected guests, they halt abruptly to stare, all but the youngest. He sprints for his aunt with a roaring, "Auntie Hay!"

His mother is still closing the door behind us when she asks, "So, sister, what brings you to Ngal?"

Grunting from the force of the boy crashing into her and squeezing as tight as he can, Hayliel smiles. "We're headed...south."

A man with broad shoulders and the smelted stench of a black-smith appears beside us. Scowling, he looks between the lot of us. "South? That's not a destination."

The boy releases Hayliel, and she peers over at me worriedly.

We should've seen this coming. We should've known that her family would ask simple, understandable questions, and we should've been prepared with answers.

"Well," Hayliel begins, and I can already tell by the sound of her voice that I don't like where she's heading.

Fortunately, the young boy interrupts her, tugging on his mother's skirts. "Mama? What's wrong with her hands?"

Everyone in the room follows his finger to the hands I have tucked tightly at my sides.

"Oh," Hayliel says, a nervous giggle. "It's nothing to be afraid of. Sinisa is...she's unique."

"What do you mean?" Hayliel's sister asks.

The husband plants his fists on his hips. "Unique how?"

We exchange another worried look. I make it clear that we should *not* tell them anything about who or what I am. If no one knows about the Guardians then they'd have no reason to believe us anyway.

But Hayliel's eyes grow wider.

"No," I say. "Now is not the time—"

"It's all right. They're family." She rubs my arm before turning back to her sister. "This may be a little alarming, but I promise you have nothing to fear. Sinisa isn't a Reaper anymore, she's a—"

"A Reaper?" the husband snarls. His chest inflates, nostrils flaring like a magrok before a battle.

Hayliel's sister's eyes widen on me like she's suddenly realized I am slathered in pig's blood. With the instincts of a mother, she snatches her son and then Hayliel and pulls her into her arms, then calls to her other children. "Sybil, take your sister to the back. Don't return until we say."

Hayliel looks horrified in her sister's grasp. "That's unnecessary. I already told you, you have nothing to fear. It's a long story, but Sinisa is—"

"That creature will not stay here," the husband says, extending one callused finger out at me.

"Leave," the sister hisses.

She inches away from the door, her knuckles white from where she clutches her boy and sister. Once the entire family is behind me, I realize I can hear the children whispering in the back, the same song that's haunted me on all of my journeys through the mortal realm:

Reaper, Reaper,
Death's little keeper.

"She's not a—"

"It's fine," I say to Hayliel, acting like I am taking one for the team, when in reality I want to be inside that home less than even they want me to be. Slowly, I make my way back toward the door, open it, and tilt my head to the sheltered forge beside the house, cluttered with metals and tools of all kinds. "Is it okay if I rest in there then?"

"Sinisa," Hayliel says like a wounded animal. "You don't have to stay outside. I'm sure we can—"

The man behind her grunts, gathering his wife, child, and sister-in-law, before slamming the door in my face.

Outside, the streets are just as uninviting as I remember them. Even without my Reaper's clothes, I catch the wary eye of every passerby like they know exactly who I am—who I *was*—and I can't fault them for their distrust, just like I can't fault Hayliel's family.

If I had any rupees, I might try my luck at the inn again, anything to get as far away from this house, these people, and the guilt of my past as possible. In fact, I *should* leave. I needed Hayliel to show me the way to Ngal, but now that she's done that, there's no reason for me to stay and wait for her to get a good night's rest. I can find my way to the Guardian encampment from here; I don't owe her to bring her with me.

But if I learned anything from my separation from the under-realm it was how to spot and value loyalty. Hayliel and I might not be *friends*, and I might not owe it to her to bring her with me, but she left the comforts of the palace just to join me, to be there for Gem like I know Acari would've wanted to be.

We share an allegiance to a man who deserved far better than the outcome he received, and therefore I cannot leave her. If she wants to honor him and his quest to protect Gem, then who am I to stop her?

From the street, I glance back at the home, and notice the blacksmith quarters attached beside it. Taking care not to knock anything over, or bump into a particularly sooty pair of tongs, I sidestep around the anvil, slide between the worktables, and take a seat on the single wooden chair. I prop my feet and do my best to try to catch some sleep. It doesn't come easy though. The scent of burned ore is far different from the crisp night air of Veltuur. The sounds of the occasional carriage or cart rolling over the cobblestone road is unlike the ethereal quiet of the black forest I'm used to sleeping under. I tell myself I better get used to it, since this is the realm where I will now live out the rest of my days in.

Despite all odds, I actually do *finally* manage to doze.

The next morning, I awaken to the husband shoving my feet off the table with a long iron rod. "It's time for you to go," is about the best *good morning* I could have hoped for.

I rise, leaving him to his work, half expecting Hayliel to already be waiting for me outside, but she isn't. The sun has barely even risen. It doesn't take me long to figure out that she is still asleep, and that, unless I want to knock and risk the wrath of her sister, I'm going to have to wait outside until she is ready to leave.

A few hours pass, and Hayliel finally emerges through the doorway, rested and ready for the day. "Here, I brought you something. It's not much, but I snagged it from breakfast for you."

She hands me a single, fluffy idli, a paddy of rice steamed to perfection. My mouth waters so eagerly that, even without a chutney to dip it into, I barely notice the bland flavor. It's devoured before we've even left their street.

"I'm sorry about last night. I didn't think they'd—"

"It's fine," I say, clipped. "I'm used to it."

Hayliel grimaces. "Is that how people always treat you?"

I shrug away the memories that I've amassed over the years. "How else should they treat *Reapers, Reapers, vile, wicked creatures*?"

Not another word is spoken as I charge forward, taking the lead as we descend into the forest.

6

THE NEXT GUARDIAN

SINISA

J ust as I'd hoped, making our way through the woods that surround Ngal proves far less exciting and dangerous than the last time I came through here. During the daytime, the wolves are asleep, as are the firefurs that almost nearly got Acari and I killed.

It's also easier to navigate with the sun shining through the trees, and takes no time at all to find the encampment I fled from just the other day.

As we approach the front gate, my stomach starts to churn. I'm not sure what I expect from the people inside, the handful of faces I met only briefly a couple of days ago before fleeing from their hospitality, but surely, I'm walking into this with too high expectations. They could turn me away at the gate.

A man standing guard lowers his gray hood. Even in the daylight, I'm barely able to distinguish where Rhet's mulberry runes begin and where his skin ends, but I do notice the hint of approval behind his amber eyes, and although it calms my nerves, it doesn't mellow the static charge inside me.

"You're back. I wasn't sure you would be," he says, voice

booming compared to the silence of the woods. The approval in his
eyes fades when he notices who's missing. "Where is the prince?"

"Veltuur, I imagine," I say, trying to bypass the small talk.

"He did it then. He killed his father?" When I don't answer, Rhet
releases a long breath. "But you succeeded," he adds, noticing the
runes on my skin.

"Yeah, well, not completely, I guess."

Holding my gaze a moment longer, he jerks his head, nodding
for us to come inside. Grateful for the invitation and certainly not
interested in trekking all the way back to Ngal, we follow eagerly.
My eyes wander over the thatched rooftops, the fish being dried at
a nearby stall, the herbs growing in a small plot, and the array of
villagers I don't know.

None of those things interest me though.

"Where is Gem?"

Rhet grunts. "You should know."

"What does that mean?" I ask, exasperated. I've traveled a long
way to get here, and I'm already starting to think it was a mistake if
I'm going to have to put up with him the whole time.

But instead of giving me an actual answer, he just shakes his
head, slow and condescending, and waves at us to follow him
deeper into the village.

Hayliel leans over to me and whispers, "Who is that?"

"Rhet," I answer flatly.

"And...who is Rhet?"

"It doesn't matter," I growl, following after the man already
disappearing ahead. "Come on."

The village is small by any city's standards, but surprisingly
larger than it looks from the outside. Most of the huts blur together
as we walk by, all handcrafted from the same array of forest-floor
gatherings: fallen trees split into lumber, twine made from thickets,
door handles crafted from pinecones, rocks, and antlers.

When we pass the healer's quarters, I can think of nothing but
Acari. There's a heartbeat of a moment where I actually convince
myself that he is still inside, like the last couple of days never

happened and we never even left. It's such a tantalizing thought that I all but convince myself that maybe it's true. Maybe, if I were to walk through the door right now, I'd find him resting where I'd left him on his cot, with Gem still by his side.

"Sinisa," Rhet warns, but I can barely hear him.

If I want something bad enough, maybe it'll come to pass.

I walk to the tree-bark door and push it open.

No one is inside. Not the healer, not Gem, and certainly not Acari. But the room smells just as it had when I was here last—of oils, of yarrow and hyacinth—bringing with it a powerful, brutal memory of discovering who my crow really was, and the lies the Councilspirits had kept from me. I become dizzied by it all over again. The lightning buzzing inside me grows all the more powerful. As my mind reels to get a grasp on time and reality, I shuffle toward a table, leaning into it for balance.

It feels like no time at all has passed since Acari and I were last here, and yet, it also feels like forever. If he had just waited, I would've saved Gem on my own and he wouldn't be indentured to Veltuur right now. If I hadn't run out of the barrier, if I had stayed close while I was gathering my thoughts, the Council would've never fazed me back to Veltuur. I wouldn't have left Acari for Nerul to prey on, and I wouldn't have to be the one protecting Gem because she would still have her brother.

"Sinisa?" Hayliel says from the doorway. "Rhet's waiting for us."

"I'll be right there," I grit out, opening my eyes and blinking back to my senses.

As I stare down at the table, among the scattered herbs and tucked behind a mortar and pestle, there's a pouch that I recognize. I reach for it, glide my thumb over the worn leather, and feel the contents inside.

Hayliel clears her throat. "What is it?"

"It used to be Acari's." I drag the pouch off the table and hold it up for her to see.

In the dim light, she has to squint at it before recognition crosses her features. "I remember this. He'd take it with him to the

Forbidden Garden so he could store the memory leaves inside without anyone knowing."

"You knew about that?" I ask, surprised.

She nods.

The bitter sting of jealousy bites into me as I realize I wasn't the only one Acari shared that secret with. Why would I be? He'd only known me for a few hours, but I'd guessed Hayliel he'd known for years. I wonder if he let her use the memory leaves as well? Then again, I'm not sure she'd have much use for them. She doesn't seem like the person with any dark secrets locked away.

"You're right to come here to retrieve it," she says, her smile flickering with doubt. "The memory leaves are forbidden. I always told Acari as much. We shouldn't just leave them here where anyone could find them."

Before we leave the hut, I tie the pouch to a belt at my waist and assure her that we'll dispose of them as soon as we can.

Rhet's outside waiting for us, arms crossed over his broad chest. "Find what you were looking for?"

"No," I grumble, casting my disappointed gaze to the dirt.

We head deeper into the center of the village, to a structure of crisscrossed logs and beams, of freshly thatched roofing, a place where a collection of soft voices chant from inside. It's far more grandiose than any of the other buildings we've seen so far, and I have no doubt that it belongs to the leader of the camp.

We leave the light of day and enter the torchlit room, and I'm not surprised to find Aulow's orange ringlets inside. She sits among a circle of people, each of them muttering to themselves, all of them with their eyes closed. If the distinctive look of concentration didn't make identifying them as Prophets easy enough, the malformed limbs, discolored skin spots, and other unique distinctions would've done it. Many of my contracts as a Reaper were for infants and children like them, so seeing them together now ignites an instinct inside me, making me feel like I'm here to kill every one of them.

Fortunately for me and them, I now know the difference

between instinct and brainwashing, and I have no desire to continue fulfilling the Council's doctrine of killing Prophets.

I don't immediately see Gem among them, but before I can look harder, Aulow's green eyes open as if she senses our presence.

She beams across the room at me. There's a beautiful woman sitting cross-legged beside her with a brown patch of skin stretched over her cheek. Aulow pats the woman's knee, shares a brief and hushed conversation with her, before kissing the birthmark and hopping to her feet.

With arms wide, she greets us, pulling me in first. "Valiant. Vigilance. Victory. You did it. I knew you were ready." Glancing up at Rhet, she smirks. "I told you she would be our next Guardian."

I tense in her embrace, unsure of how to hold her in return. I try smiling and patting her shoulder, though I'm fairly certain that I look more like someone in pain than someone trying to show appreciation.

Aulow releases me and steps back, spotting Hayliel for the first time. "Hello. And who is this?"

"Hayliel," the former handmaiden replies. She pulls her skirts out wide and curtsies. "I've come to protect the princess."

"Oh?" Aulow raises an eyebrow at me. "Isn't that your duty?"

I squint at her, confused. "How did you know I promised that?"

It's only a second later that I remember that she keeps the company of people who can foretell prophecy, and so someone likely already told her I'd be returning for Gem.

"Promised?" Her brow twitches with amusement. "You are a Guardian. You didn't have to promise anything. It is simply so."

Despite my growing confusion, I can't express it in time for Aulow's next request.

"And what of our prince? Where is he?"

A somber cloud casts the room in gray. I've told the tale too many times already to be able to muster the strength to do it again, not if I'm going to have the energy to tell Gem once I find her. Meanwhile, Hayliel still can't stop the tears from forming any time someone so much as mentions Acari.

Thankfully, Rhet takes the lead this time, shaking his head, apologetically. "He made a choice."

I watch his words spear through Aulow like an arrow to the chest. Her cheerful disposition dims, the ever-optimistic incline of her head drifting downward. She searches the ground like she'll find something there that will make it all better, but when I look, all I find is dirt.

"But...how is that possible?" she asks at last, bringing her gaze to mine. "You saved the princess. You became a Guardian. He didn't have to—"

"I didn't get there in time," I bite out. My teeth clench so tightly against themselves that I fear I might actually break my jaw. I don't bother elaborating, confessing that I'd taken too long to realize what had actually mattered, that I'd spent far too long denying myself freedom and peace from my past, costing Acari his own.

I don't say any of it, but Aulow assesses me like she's heard everything, nonetheless.

She rests a hand on my bicep. "Patience. There will come a point when his paradigm will change. All seek peace. He will come around. He will figure it out."

As much as I'd love to believe that, I have my doubts. After all, if I hadn't met him, nor the Guardians standing before me, I would've never learned that the soul of my abuser had been trapped inside my crow for the entire duration of my Reaper life. Without that knowledge, and without Acari's friendship, I doubt I would've ever been able to make peace with what had been done to me.

"Well," Aulow starts, summoning her cheerful glow once more. "It sounds like you've had a long day and I'm sure you have questions about the Guardians and what it means to be one."

I'm embarrassed to admit that I had barely even thought about it. There hadn't been time to. After I'd reappeared in the orphanage, my only thought had been to rescue Acari. When that plan had failed, I'd needed to flee the palace and come here to uphold my promise. Though while we were traveling, I should've had ample time to think about it, I'd honestly spent most of the journey

wallowing and being angry at myself for failing Acari so magnif-
icently.

"Gem," Aulow calls to the group still sitting on the ground
behind her.

A black-haired girl bounces up. I don't know why I expect a
warm welcome, but when her curiosity crumbles to cautious
concern at the sight of us, my chest cracks. Gem stands, her muted
gray skirt already dirtier than the last time I saw her.

"I'll let Gem show you to her room. Two beds were already
readied for your return. Of course, we thought one of them would
belong to—" Aulow stops herself, glancing at Gem as she
approaches. "Well, I think the three of you have some catching up
to do. I'll leave you to it and hope to see you at supper around the
bonfire."

There's an unspoken agreement of silence between Hayliel,
Gem, and I as we make our way from Aulow's hut to Gem's. Whatever conversation needs to be had can be had from the privacy of
her quarters, where we will all have a cot to lay on after the
emotional tornado that is inevitably going to shred through each
of us.

All day I've been the one to tell the story. Just moments after
Acari had been taken away, I told Hayliel, Borgravid just moments
after that, and Rhet as well, so you'd think I'd be better prepared for
what is to come. But those had been condensed versions of the
story, ones where the people I was telling knew how to fill in the
gaps without needing me to spell the whole thing out for them.
Something tells me that this toddler will require more information.
And I think she deserves it; she deserves to know the heroic truth of
what her brother has done for her, what no one would've done
for me.

When Gem struggles to pull the front door open, I reach over to help. It creaks when I swing it wide and we all enter.

It's clear that Gem doesn't live here alone, as there are at least a dozen beds inside, but she guides us to hers, and points at two others that look freshly made. I take a seat at the edge of the cot that's lined up next to hers head-to-head, while Hayliel climbs onto the bed across the way.

Clearing my throat, I glance to Hayliel before I begin. "Your brother killed—"

"Your brother loved you very much," Hayliel interjects. She glares at me, appalled.

"Right," I say, trying to recalibrate, to search for the balance between coddling this small child and being brutally honest. But, truth be told, I've never had much luck with children, especially not little ones. "He did—love you. And because he loved you so much, he—"

"He did something," Hayliel chimes in again, apparently sensing my lack of tact even before I do. "Something that can't be taken back, even though I'm sure he regrets it. Something bad."

"Cari bad?" Gem asks, her eyes growing watery.

"No," Hayliel assures her. She rushes across the room and takes Gem's small hands into her own as she kneels at the girl's bedside. "No. Acari was good. He sacrificed himself greatly, and that makes him good, not bad, even if the choice was...in ways...a bad choice."

"Where Cari?" Gem asks, her voice breaking and shattering me along with it.

Although I admire Hayliel's skill, the way she is able to hint at Acari's crime while simultaneously proclaiming his righteousness, I can't help but wonder whether it's really what's best for Gem. She struggles enough with speech already, so I'm not sure how well she is able to comprehend this kind of runaround. Perhaps being direct might be more useful to her, even if it might also be painful.

After all, what is childhood without pain?

Hayliel's lip trembles. She bows her head to hide her tears, and so I, once again, say what no one else is willing to.

"Acari is in Veltuur." I make sure to soften my voice as much as possible. And, in an effort to make this unveiling of truth as quick as it can be, to limit the hurt she will feel, I tell her the piece of the story that we've all left unspoken. "You won't be seeing him again. None of us will."

At sunset, Aulow arrives at our door to accompany us to the bonfire. She seems more surprised that Hayliel and I are coming than she does Gem.

"Children are resilient," she says once Gem has raced past her and out the door toward some other children walking outside. "Adults, however, tend to need more time to rest and recover."

"Yes, well," Hayliel begins, standing from her cot and flattening the wrinkles from her skirt. "We also need to eat."

Aulow laughs. "True. Very well. If you insist, then come. Supper will be served soon."

We are the last ones to arrive, and so we take a seat at the outer edge of the circle, farthest away from the fire. Hayliel shivers beside me, however, I relish the crisp night air. It reminds me of Veltuur, a place that has given me comfort for years. Despite having my world ripped apart and the place I've loved taken away from me, I decide against beating myself up over relishing in this one small thing, and instead am grateful for the brisk evening.

The villagers pass each other bowls filled to the brim with a curry-orange sambar. Despite the knots in my stomach that continue to churn and coil, when I receive my bowl, my mouth waters at the scent of turmeric and tamarind, but it's the sight of okra, eggplant, and tomatoes that makes me crave that first bite like a predator on the prowl.

I savor the first spoonful. I take my time with it. But once I start shoveling the soup into my mouth, I can't stop.

Hayliel eyes me with bemused horror. "Do Reapers not eat?"

I wipe my mouth with the back of my hand. Still struggling to remember that I am no longer one of them, I almost begin by saying *we*. "They do. But a Reaper's diet consists mostly of meats. They can't eat living foods, and fruit and vegetables, well, even after they've been plucked, they remain alive for some time."

"You haven't eaten a single fruit or vegetable since you became a Reaper?" She pauses, a spoonful of food waiting at her lips. "What about once they're cooked? Aren't they dead then?"

I open my mouth to enlighten her on the ways of the Reapers that she simply does not and cannot understand, but I stop short when the logic of what she's saying hits me. She might actually be right. Honestly, I never tried to eat produce that had already been cooked. As a Reaper, you hear horror stories about the grotesque ways in which living foods will rot inside your mouth, but obviously it's not enough to deter us. Eventually, we all try it. Every single Reaper does. I guess it's a curiosity thing, and maybe even a sort of rite of passage.

Mine had been a delectable-looking mango. I came across it on an assignment to clear a forest—the mortals needed the lumber and they were too fearful to chop the trees down themselves and risk potentially killing any animals who might be residing in their canopies. Some even feared that axing the trees themselves would be an act worthy of Veltuur's attention. To be honest, I don't know. I never met a Reaper who served Veltuur because they harvested crops or stepped on and killed a blade of grass. The underrealm can be picky about the ways in which it defines life.

Before I had unleashed my power into one tree in particular, a low-hanging, perfectly ripe mango was dangling just within reach. My mouth watered the moment I laid eyes on it. Its tropical citrus scent summoned me forward. By then, I already understood how my power worked, and that no matter what, if I touched something living, my Reaper magic would trigger. But I wanted a taste. I couldn't help it. So I bit into the mango while it was still hanging from the tree, and I will never forget the way the peel rotted against my tongue, how the pulp inside melted into a mash so rancid and fetid that I vomited.

By the time my stomach had settled, and I'd pushed myself back up from where I was hunched, the entire fruit was black and fuzzy, and the tree it was hanging from was dying.

But Hayliel has my mind churning. Now I can't help but wonder what would've happened if I had tried my luck with fried plantains or baked pineapple instead. Of course, the only way that would've been possible was if someone else had prepared it for me, and mortals aren't typically in the mood for offering food to Reapers.

I imagine most Reapers had similar experiences, trying uncooked fruits and vegetables only to discover that what they'd been told about a Reaper's diet was true.

"I don't know," I say at last, chuckling at the absurdity of how long Reapers have gone without even trying a single cooked piece of produce. The more I think about it, the more my laughter amplifies into madness.

Hayliel's horror deepens, but eventually a smile breaks through. "You can be very strange."

I shrug, an act of indifference, though I feel far from unconcerned by such an accusation. Hayliel is right. Compared to the mortals I *am* strange. I didn't have a normal childhood, let alone adolescence. I became a Reaper at the ripe age of thirteen, and as one, I never had to worry about what I said or how I said it. I just spoke. Acted. Killed. I moved on to the next soul to collect without a second thought. Never once did I doubt who I was or where I belonged.

But now, seeing how easily Hayliel can point out my differences, it makes me wonder if I'll ever feel that sense of belonging again, that assuredness in purpose.

We spend most of the meal this way, Hayliel asking me questions about what it was like being a Reaper, and me doing my best to answer them. She stumps me a few times though, like when she asks me why Reapers don't have runes like everyone else, but I tell her that some things are just the way they are and always have been.

"Before you were a Reaper, where were you from?"

It's the first question she's asked me that isn't about my time in the underrealm, so it takes me a moment to recalibrate. That life feels like it was so long ago. My upbringing is not a story I've yet told since becoming a Guardian, but as I think on it, it comes out as natural as the moon rises and the sun sets.

"I spent a few years living in an orphanage in Azarrac City. But before that, my family came from Kalápana, along the Coast of Dreams."

"Oh, I hear it's lovely there. Is it true it's like the sea swallowed the night sky?"

Remembering the long days I'd spent there on the beaches with my friends, I nod.

"Why were you at an orphanage? Where is your family?"

Before the spoon can reach my mouth, it sinks back into my bowl instead.

"Oh, I've done it again. I'm sorry. That was an insensitive thing to ask."

"No, it's all right. I just haven't thought about them in a long while. Reapers don't retain memories from their mortal lives." Before that bit of information can make her spiral into dark thoughts about Acari's new life as a Reaper, and what it means for how little we matter to him anymore, I decide to give her the answer she requested, even if it is murky. "There's the story I've been told, and then there's what I think I remember."

"What were you told?"

"That my parents died in Kallinei Swamp on a journey north to trade some of my father's wares."

She looks up at me from under her lashes. "Did your mother accompany your father often on his business trips?"

"No."

"Hmm." Returning to her meal, she sips the steaming sambar and asks, "What's the story you remember then?"

"I was young. I was probably just having a difficult time accepting that they were gone but...I swear I can remember my father leaving for that trip. My mother stayed home with me, but the next morning, I was sent to my aunt's house and told to wait until her return a few days later. But she never came.

"Everything afterward is...hazy. I remember my father coming home. I remember him screaming and thrashing about, first at my aunt's and then back at our home. Everything was so dark, like we lived in perpetual night during that time. Then, a few days later, we traveled to Oakfall and visited Halaud Palace and...I don't have any specific memory of this, but when I think about that time, I feel like we were searching for her, for my mother. I don't know why we would go to Oakfall, and I don't know where my father went after, but, for a long time, I didn't believe either of them were truly gone. Even though the matron of the orphanage insisted they were and told me that it'd be best to forget about them, I still held out hope. As long as I could, anyways. But then that hope finally faded, and that's when I..."

I draw my gaze up from the quivering bowl in my hands to find Hayliel's wide eyes on me. My cheeks flush. Here I am, sharing my life story with someone I barely even know. How desperate and lonely am I in my new mortal skin?

"Nevermind," I say sharply, before spooning more broth into my mouth.

Gingerly, she leans closer, lowering her voice so that no one around us can hear. "Why don't you take some of the memory leaves Acari left behind? I...I never condoned his use of them, but he did say that they always helped him feel better. They gave him clarity whenever he was uncertain. Maybe if you took some you could learn the truth about what happened to your parents."

Blinking, I stare at her. I can't believe the thought hadn't already crossed my mind. The memory leaves *could* bring me the answers I've forgotten, the ones I've longed to know since the day my mother left. Even when my memories returned when the under-realm spat me out and I became a Guardian, they still weren't as crystal clear as I would've hoped they'd be. They rolled over me like the crashing waves of the ocean. There were so many that I had little time to focus on any of them. The second one ended, another began. From infancy to adolescence, memories of friends and enemies, of sunny days and stormy nights, it was all just a blur. And then, even once the memories finished coming, I still had no time to consider them because I had to rush off to try to stop Acari before he made a huge mistake.

But now, sitting here in the firelight, it's finally quiet enough that I'm able to consider it all. I remember the day I killed the matron's husband, all those years ago, the day I finally realized that my parents weren't coming back for me. Rather than living the rest of my days in constant fear of when my body would be used against my will next, I decided that the life of a Reaper was far more preferable to the life of an orphan girl, the life my parents had left me to.

What good would memory leaves do me now? Either my parents are dead, or they abandoned me. I'm on my own, either way.

"No," I say finally. "It would change nothing."

Hayliel chokes on a spoonful of spiced liquid. "It would change the way you feel. It could bring you—"

"I said no."

She stiffens. Her jaw hangs agape before she finally manages to fasten it shut. Slowly, hesitantly, she scoots back to her previous, safer distance. "I'm sorry," she whispers.

Fortunately, before the silence can become too awkward between us, Aulow addresses the village. From beside the roaring fire, she makes the announcements that I expect are common among villages like hers: she provides the people with updates on important events—like an excursion a few Prophets and Guardians will be going on tomorrow morning; she introduces some newcomers, me and Hayliel; and she requests a few special assignments for the following day.

When she's done, well after Hayliel and I have finished our

bowls, she leaves her place in the center of the group, wanders through the crowd and takes a seat next to me.

Aulow doesn't speak, doesn't do anything but watch Hayliel until she finally stands.

"It's getting late. I should find Gem so she can get some sleep. It's been a long day for her—for all of us."

Aulow nods her thanks. She waits for Hayliel to leave before turning back to me. "I expect you have questions about being a Guardian."

I snort. "Without knowing anything about them—*us*—other than we're former Reapers and that no one else seems to know about us, I'm not sure where I would even begin."

"Then let me start with what you already know. Only a Reaper can become a Guardian, but to do so is not easy. There is a price. All Reapers have a dark past, one that they largely live in denial from."

"You already told me all of this. In order for a Reaper to become a Guardian, they have to come to terms with the first murder they committed."

She inclines her head, deeply. "You remember well. You, Sinisa, severed your ties with Veltuur by releasing your crow, but you did so while you still had an active contract open. In doing so, you have bound yourself to another. You saved Gem from an unwritten death, one that likely would've come well before her true end, and now you are forever connected with her. You are a Guardian, in the truest sense of the word."

The thought of that sets my chest on fire. I spent years bound to my crow, and it took every ounce of strength I had to let go, to free myself.

"What would've happened if I released my crow when I didn't have any contracts? Would I still be stuck in the underrealm?"

She laughs, a bright and airy sound. "No. It doesn't happen often, but on the rare occasion that a Reaper finds peace while they are in between contracts, they still become a Guardian, just one with a different purpose. They are not bound to a single soul when they return to the mortal realm. The few who reside here spend most of their time ensuring that the barrier remains stable, and accompanying others on excursions to procure the endangered Prophets.

"This is where Guardians received their name. We are protectors, no matter what. As long as you live, no other Reaper can be sent to claim Gem's soul because you are already bound to it. It is one of the greatest gifts you can ever offer. Her only death will come naturally, at its projected end."

"What about her soul?" Although I'm no longer a Reaper, I've been one long enough to have developed an appreciation for the natural ways of things, for the balance that death brings to life.

"Her soul will be set free."

Taken aback by her blasé response, I scowl. Every Reaper knows what happens to souls if they aren't collected, and since all Guardians used to be Reapers, she should know full well that what she's talking about goes against the laws of nature.

"Souls need to be taken to Veltuur," I remind her. "Otherwise they accumulate in the ether, directionless and unable to be born anew in the mortal realm."

She sighs, crossing one leg over the other, hand resting on her knee. "When will you start to understand that nothing you were told as a Reaper is the truth? The only reason the crows eat souls is to remain at their Reapers' sides. They feed off life. As far as we can tell, once the souls enter a crow's gullet, that's as far as they go."

I try swallowing down my disgust. I'll admit, looking back on it now it should've struck me as odd then, that in order for the souls to travel to Veltuur they needed to be guzzled down by crows first. But that's the thing about the ways of the underrealm and the Councilspirits who run it. They make it all seem so natural. Never once did I doubt that what I was doing was necessary. I never had a reason to.

"So, all those souls I took, my crow just..."

Her gentle hand falls to my shoulder. "Don't worry yourself too much about them. What's done is done. The best we can do is hope that they were released when our crows were, but we cannot say for sure."

I'm silent for a while as the weight of it all sinks in. Five thousand souls. During my servitude, I claimed the souls of five thousand living creatures.

"Okay..." I say slowly, ready to move on before crippling regret can take hold. "What else can Guardians do then?"

"We can sense life, some more than others. Prophets, other Guardians especially."

"What do you mean we can sense them?"

She smiles. "When we're near another Guardian, we feel a connection to them. You have likely sensed it already, that buzz inside your belly."

The fluttering in my stomach seems to hasten when she mentions it. When we'd arrived, I just assumed it had been nerves, or a result of all of the excitement from the past few days. It should've dawned on me though, the way it grew stronger the closer we came to the encampment, and how any time I'm near another Guardian, my stomach somersaults.

"How is that helpful?"

Aulow chuckles. "Maybe it's not. But for some of us, it was everything. Being able to sense your kin, for some it reassured them that they would never be alone again."

Averting my gaze, I tuck a section of my hair behind my ear and fall deep into my thoughts. I can't remember the last time I didn't feel alone. Most likely it was years ago, before my parents died. Still, I've never before been bothered by it, and I'm not sure I'm willing to admit I'm bothered by it now.

Aulow continues. "There is more."

I drag my gaze from my lap to hers, finding her scarlet-drawn hands clasped together.

"As I mentioned before, you are now bound to Gem. Though you cannot faze from place to place with her aid, you can speak directly to her at any time, no matter how far away you are. You can communicate telepathically, if you haven't done so already. The last ability, you've already witnessed: you can cast a protective barrier around an area, one that rejects all members of Veltuur, including Shades, including Wraiths, and including the Councilspirits."

Yet again, I'm reminded that she, too, has a dark past. She only knows about all of this because she was once a Reaper who became a Guardian. I wonder what her story is, how she came to find herself indentured to Veltuur, how she freed herself from her servitude, how she became the leader of this village here.

"I'll answer your questions, if you'd like to ask them," she says, smirking.

"You can't—you can't hear my thoughts, can you?"

Another chuckle. "No, but I've had this conversation with many new Guardians, and they all start wondering the same thing right about now. It's hard not to, knowing what we know about the underrealm, about what it takes to secure yourself a place there, what it takes to leave."

Toeing the dirt, I glance at her sidelong. "So how did you become a Reaper?"

Her eyes are trained on mine, unblinking, unwavering. "I saved the woman I loved, and in so doing, let another die."

A hateful exhale escapes me at the injustice of it. She saved someone's life and still was condemned as a murderer. I protected myself and I, too, was taken away.

"How old were—"

But before I can ask her anything else, villagers gasp.

Hayliel's voice is among them. "Gem!"

I'm on my feet and shoving through the crowd before I'm even aware of it. When I reach them, Hayliel has Gem's head cradled in her lap.

"Somebody do something!" she shrieks, voice warbled like someone has their hand around her throat.

Gem's eyes are clouded white. Her body has become as stiff as stone, and all that I can think of is how I've already managed to fail her. I was supposed to keep her safe, not only because of a vow I made to her brother, but because I am bound to do so.

"It's all right," Aulow says, stepping in front of me. She takes a place on her knees beside Hayliel, brushing Gem's unruly black hair away from the bronzed skin that has already lost some of its glow. "She is receiving a prophecy. It'll pass. Please, everyone, it's getting late, and you all know how that first prophecy can impact a person. It's best we give her some space."

Most of the villagers leave. The ones who stay behind busy themselves with tasks, collecting the discarded bowls and plates, tending to the fire, and they make sure to give us all the space we need. The woman with the birthmark on her cheek approaches us once everyone else has cleared. She asks Aulow if she needs anything before she leaves us, returning not long after with a mug of something steaming and handing it to her.

I become transfixed with Gem's eyes. They're pale, as white as the moon, and the longer she's gone, the more I start to worry that, despite Aulow's confidence, she may never return.

I'm still staring straight into the whites of her eyes when she blinks. The sign of life both startles and relieves me at the same time.

"Gem!" Hayliel cries, throwing her arms around her. "You're all right."

"She is," Aulow agrees. She encourages Hayliel to release Gem so that she can gently slide her hand behind the child's neck and help her upright. "Bels?" Aulow says over her shoulder.

The woman with the birthmark comes forth and hands a mug to Gem.

Gem doesn't grab it though. There's bewilderment in her gaze as she surveys the area around her like a cornered fox ready to flee. Aulow takes the mug instead, nodding to the woman for her to leave, before speaking a few soft words to Gem.

"Would you like to tell us what you saw?" Aulow asks with a gentle caress to Gem's cheek once her pupils have returned to their normal sizes.

Gem swallows. She licks her scarred lip, her tongue pausing only briefly on it before she bites into her bottom one.

Finally, she looks up, eyes searching from Hayliel to me. "Save him."

"Save who?" I ask, exchanging a hopeful glance with Hayliel.

But Gem can't contain it, that hint at a possibility that neither Hayliel nor I have dared to think might be an option. Her words are breathless when she utters, "Save Acari. "

7

A GATEWAY TO VELTUUR

SINISA

"Is that what you saw? A prophecy about how to save your brother?" Hayliel inches closer to the child.

Gem frowns, eyeing her warily. It's then that I remember what Acari told me about her. How she's spent most of her life in isolation. As someone else who isn't accustomed to the proximity of others, I can relate to her hesitancy to have someone so close to her.

But despite her hesitation, she nods reluctantly.

The confirmation earns an ear-piercing squeal from Hayliel, who follows up with a gleeful bought of clapping before throwing her arms around Gem and Aulow both. "Yes! Of course we will save him. Just tell us how and we will do it. I promise. Right, Sinisa?"

Dumbly, I blink. I'm not sure what's more jarring, the idea that she would so quickly volunteer to work alongside me, or the sudden unfolding that Acari can be saved.

I keep telling myself that I've heard them both wrong, that there is no possible way for us to save him. After all, Acari lives in Veltuur now, and although it *could* be possible to save him, the odds of us ever seeing him again to be able to do such a thing are stacked against us. He'd have to be sent to claim one of our souls, but I think the Council takes great measures to ensure that their Reapers never interact with people they knew before their initiation. It's the only logical explanation I've been able to come up with as to why I never crossed paths with anyone from my mortal life.

As fearful as I am though to believe it can be true, to dare think that I can right my wrong and free him from the torment that is being bound to the person you murdered, I can't deny that it *is* possible. After all, was I not a Reaper just yesterday? Did he, and Aulow, and Rhet not save me?

Barely aware I'm doing it, I nod.

"Tell us, Gem," Hayliel says, whipping back around to face the child. She must realize she's still squeezing Aulow as well, because she finally releases them both and says with a little more resolve, "Tell us how to save him."

The girl pauses, her brow furrowing, deep in thought. "Save Cari," she repeats, giving the instruction like it is the most obvious and simple thing in the world. "No more bad."

Watching the joy bleed from Hayliel's expression, the hope that's sucked away from her like a mosquito is drinking away her optimism, I wince. Gem still hasn't earned her third language rune. Far from it. She's barely able to put a few words together, let alone construct a detailed recounting of events that happened only in her mind's eye. Whatever prophecy she just gleaned will be lost on her until her third language rune appears, or far longer if she forgets the vision before then.

I plop to the ground beside them and bury my face in my hands. I should've known better than to get excited about something that was so obviously impossible.

A hand pats my shin, and I look up to find Aulow staring at me, hopeful.

"What?"

Her smile broadens, despite the bite in my tone. "Do you remember what I told you, about being a Guardian? About the special abilities you and Gem share between you?"

Hayliel turns to me. "Special abilities?"

It's not until then that the realization hits me, but it's quickly followed by a healthy dose of doubt. "I don't know how to communicate telepathically."

"Have confidence, certainty, conviction," Aulow assures me. "It's far easier than one would think. You've likely done it by accident already. All you have to do is let your guard down. Listen for Gem, and you will hear her. It is innate for a Guardian, like a Reaper's connection to their crow."

"I couldn't speak to my crow."

Aulow chuckles. "No, not directly. Not even consciously. But you understood your crow on some level. We all do. You could sense what its calls meant, and you could even get it to do things without actually needing to tell it to."

I scoff. "You didn't know my crow."

"Perhaps not, but I've known many Reapers, and it has been the same for all of them. They didn't need to know the language of birds because they intuitively understood it. And I know the same is true for you too."

A scowl answers her, but it doesn't linger long. I do remember moments where I could've sworn I knew exactly what my crow was thinking, days when he was angrier and more depressed and I simply knew it. On some occasions, I even thought I could hear him say things, or at least guess at what he would've said, had he had human words.

By the time I've convinced myself I might as well try using that same intuition to listen to Gem, Aulow is already backing away to give us space and motioning me toward the girl still sitting patiently on the dirt floor.

She is still wobbly when she looks up at me, apprehension in her dark eyes. In them I see the reflection of the dying flames behind me, and for a moment, it makes her appear far angered than I think she's capable of.

"It's worth a try, right?" I say, smiling weakly. "For Acari?"

After some thought, she nods, and we both look to Aulow for further instruction.

"Gem, I want you to close your eyes. Remember the images the prophecy showed you, but also the emotions and the thoughts that came with it. Prophecy is more than just pictures, it is everything, and forgetting even one small detail could change the meaning of it all."

A student eager to impress her mentor, Gem bites her tongue and squints her eyes closed.

"Now, Sinisa, all you must do is listen. Not with your ears—you'll have to find a way to drown out the stridulating of the locusts tonight, and any other noises you find distracting—but listen with your instincts. Let your intuition guide you. If it helps, you may close your eyes as well. Behave as though you still have a crow." She throws her hands up before my expression sours fully. "I know, I know. Believe me, *I know*. Thankfully you are no longer bound to that creature, but for this exercise, it might help to pretend that you are. It will make it feel more natural since communicating with your crow is something you had been doing for years."

Begrudgingly, my eyes fall shut. I wait for more guidance, but when none comes, I realize Aulow wants me to focus on Gem, not her, and she likely won't chance interrupting any success we could find now that we've both begun.

When nothing happens, my frustration quickly grows. Squinting more, I force myself to focus as hard as I can on my mind, on whatever is supposed to be there that will allow me to access Gem's own thoughts. But all I find is blackness.

With a growl, I open my eyes. "It's not working."

"Don't try so hard," Aulow offers unhelpfully. "Close your eyes again. Forget your defenses. Free your mind. Focus on opening up to Gem, rather than digging deeper into yourself."

Feeling as ridiculous as I feel frustrated, I roll my eyes. Things were never this difficult when I was a Reaper. Using my Reaper touch to kill something, sensing what my crow was thinking, even fazing between the realms had come as naturally to me as breathing or blinking.

I'm not used to having to work for something like this, and I don't think I like it.

But I like the idea of being useless with my supposed talents even less.

Using Aulow's advice, I try focusing on opening myself up to Gem. I remind myself that sometimes with my crow it had felt like its thoughts were part of mine, especially if I had commanded something from it. I try to do the same now.

"Tell me what you saw."

In front of me, I hear her shift on the ground as she burrows into herself, just as determined to see this through as I am.

I ignore the insects buzzing throughout the woods, ignore the crackle of burning logs as the flames become cinders. The harder I listen, the more distinct the distant humming of conversations throughout the camp becomes, but I close myself to those as well.

Instead, I focus solely on Gem. Since my ears are unreliable, and my eyes closed, I let my other senses tell me about her. The wind blows on my face and one of my arms, telling me that she's sitting across from me at an angle and is so short by comparison that she's blocking only a little of the airflow. Beyond the turmeric and tamarind still tempting me with their aromas from the leftover bowls around us, I smell the lotus and lilies used in her recent bath, the salt staining her cheeks from crying earlier. I feel her presence by the rest of the emptiness surrounding me and I let myself lean forward toward her.

When our foreheads touch, sight bursts in my mind's eye. Images flood me, reminding me of what it was like to receive my orders from the trees of Veltuur, the vision a complex tapestry of fragments and details.

The first is an ocean that mimics the night sky, a galaxy of floating stars beneath the waves. But the vision is more than just an image. I smell the damp air of a cave, hear the mewling of a lost neko. My body is so cold that it's like I'm sitting in frigid water rather than on dry land.

The vision fades, replaced by another.

Sand pelts against my skin, in my eyes. I feel it in my lungs, but I trudge forward. My hands clasp an iron doorknob and I find refuge inside. That is, until I'm staring into my own reflection, one of horror and monstrosity.

But I can't peel my eyes away, not until that vision clears too.

A third comes.

My feet are wet, soaking in something lukewarm and grimy. I'm surrounded by every shade of green I can imagine. Jade and olive and sage. My hand grazes a nearby fern, the other traces over a tuft of moss on tree bark. I'm overcome by a sense of peacefulness that I know isn't real, like I'm walking into a viper's mouth instead of through a swampland.

There's a door.

Not a typical door made of wood with a frame outlining it and a handle to pull on, but a mass of darkness arched into the shape of a doorway.

The neko mewls again, and the darkness seeps out, black smoke reaching for me and pulling me inside.

My eyes burst open at the same time Gem's do. Hayliel is perched eagerly beside me, while Aulow is still a patient distance back.

"Well?" Hayliel asks. "Did you see him? Do you know how we can save Acari?"

Just like the assignments I received as a Reaper, the vision we shared wasn't explicit. No one said anything about actually saving Acari, nor were we given any instructions on what each of those images represented. But there's a deeper understanding conveyed through a vision, one that is intuitive in conveying specific locations, events, timing, and other information not explicitly stated.

I understand it all.

I know exactly what we need to do.

I know how we can enter Veltuur to save Acari.

"There is a neko trapped at the Coast of Dreams," I begin, listening to myself in disbelief. It's a legend that I grew up with, one that I never fully believed. "It's said to be able to grant access into Veltuur, but no one has ever entered the cave it's trapped in, at least none that have survived."

"But you saw it, in the prophecy, right?"

Reluctantly, I nod. "It'll be difficult to get to, impossible even. But yes, I saw it."

Hayliel's eagerness is unrelenting. "What do we do once we have the neko?"

"We take it to the gateway to Veltuur. According to the vision, it's in the Kallinei Swamp." I pause long enough to swallow, unintentionally drawing the sympathy of Hayliel. I shake my head. "It's fine. They died long ago."

"Who did?" Aulow asks.

"My parents," I say sharply. Then, not wanting to bear the focus any longer, I redirect the conversation back to what really matters. "The gateway in Kallinei is guarded though, by a serpent or something."

"The Deceptive Serpent," Aulow tell us. "It is a fabled creature, said to dwell only in the deepest depths of the swamp. It mostly keeps to itself, but every now and then, it breaches the surface, and if any mortal is nearby, they succumb to its deception."

"What's that?" I ask.

She shakes her head. "It's said it's different for all."

"How do we get past it?" Hayliel asks.

"The vision showed us going to Pyrethi Tower to retrieve some mirror there."

It's Aulow again to impart her wisdom on us on the matter. "The Mirror of Truth, another ancient legend built upon the stories of the ones who failed their quest in retrieving it. It is said to prey on your doubts, on the lies you tell yourself."

"So it's like the serpent?"

"Not exactly. The Deceptive Serpent makes you believe lies. The Mirror of Truth shows you what you've been denying yourself from knowing or facing. But I don't know for sure what that means, or why it has caused so many to enter the tower and never return. With no survivors, not much else is known about it."

"So..." Hayliel bites her lip. "We retrieve the neko and the Mirror of Truth, go to Kallinei Swamp, use the mirror on the

Deceptive Serpent, and then use the neko to open the gateway to Veltuur?"

Nodding, I add, "And once we're inside, we can find Acari, remind him of who he was, and convince him to make peace with his past."

Aulow's brow creases. "Is that what the prophecy showed you? You saving the prince?"

I shuffle through the images once more, scowling when I realize the vision ends at the gateway. "Not specifically...but why else would we go to Veltuur?"

She pinches her lips, gazing into the embers that cast a glow over her scarlet runes. "I can't pretend to know, but it is rare indeed for a Prophet to receive a vision that doesn't include another Prophet in need."

"No one else was mentioned," I answer before she can ask the question. Then, thinking more about the visions, I add, "Acari wasn't even mentioned or shown. All I saw was us getting into Veltuur, but it has to be to save Acari, right?"

"Prophecies can be fickle. They don't always mean what we *think* or *hope* they mean. And then, there are other times that they do."

"Well, whatever it meant"—I shift my glare down to my hands and to the lavender markings that spiral and coil around my fingertips and up my wrists, the markings that are supposed to make me a protector—"if we're going to Veltuur anyway, we might as well save Acari while we're there. I don't know why else we would go there, or what we would do once we're inside if we weren't rescuing him. It's possible saving him is exactly what we are meant to do."

Aulow nods, but I get the impression that she's not even really listening to me anymore.

Hayliel pushes herself off the ground. "Do we leave now?" It's clear from her expectant gaze that she's ready for only one answer, and it's not one I'm sure I should give.

Although I'm aware that the dying flames make the shadows under her eyes appear much darker than they probably are, I can't help but notice her exhaustion. I feel my own too, in the creaking of my bones and the aching of my legs.

"No," Aulow says. "You should wait until first light, when the other Prophets and Guardians are leaving. They're headed for the Coast of Dreams as well. Traveling with them will be easier than going alone. Besides, you could both use the rest before such a journey."

Eager as I am to get started, I sensed from the prophecy much the same. Visions, although vague in ways, are actually quite specific, and it seems like the one Gem shared with me wanted us to leave tomorrow as well.

Hayliel helps Gem to her feet, Aulow extending her hand to me. While the two of them start for the path to head back to our hut, Aulow plants a hand on my shoulder. She waits until they're out of earshot to speak.

"I didn't want to say this in front of the girl. It's clear how much she loves and misses her brother, and if this prophecy will allow you to save him, then I will be most pleased. But you should know that trying to save Acari while he is still in Veltuur will be challenging. It would be difficult even if he was in Tayaraan. Unveiling the secrets of Reapers and their crows is a sensitive and delicate process. If someone is not ready to hear it, they will deny the truth you are sharing. Often, when we try aiding a Reaper along their path to becoming a Guardian, we do so slowly. We give them pieces, small bites of information so as not to overwhelm them.

"Acari has not been a Reaper long. Although the argument could be made that his short time in Veltuur could mean his allegiance is lessened, I fear it will mean the opposite. He has lived little, in his mind. He has formed too few memories. He has not had the opportunity to witness humanity, nor has he had any experiences yet that might challenge his perspective, things that he may regret.

"The hold Veltuur has on him will be strong. If you are to get through to him, you will need the most compelling case. For you, it was the knowledge of who your crow was, and access to your former memories. It might not be the same for Acari."

I consider her words. Acari's father is his crow, someone who doubted him his whole life, while also expecting more from him than he could ever give. Though I understand their relationship was strained, and Acari was angry with him for sending a Reaper after his sister, to my knowledge the man never physically harmed him; he didn't violate his body and mind in ways that made him think that death would be better for either of them.

Aulow may be right. Finding out that his father is his crow might not be enough to persuade him to let go and move on.

"You have time to think about it on your journey," she assures me, walking me to the path. Before she departs in the other direction, she offers me one final piece of advice. "Just make sure you're asking yourself what will work for *him*, and then maybe you really can save him."

8

CROWNED

ACARI

S taring into the wardrobe makes me feel a little more like the king I'm supposed to be. Every doublet, jerkin, and robe are gold-trimmed and quilted, sewn together with the finest silks, satins, and brocades. As beautiful as the ample collection may be, to select any of them would make me feel like a traitor to Veltuur. But Borgravid and the Council have assured me that my greatest purpose today is to show the people of Oakfall that I *am* their king.

Before I can talk myself out of it again, I yank the first outfit I can grab from the hanger, an assortment of pale green, silver, and black. Cringing, I step out of my black stockings, pulling my red tunic overhead, and stand naked before the mirror. When I see myself like this, it's even clearer to me that I am no king, at least none that I envision when I think of the title. I haven't yet completed my transition into manhood, though some muscle mass seems to be filling in where my limbs have lengthened.

At least the scar across my chest and shoulder makes me appear more rugged. It's too bad it would be considered inappropriate to walk around without a shirt; I might've otherwise been able to intimidate some folks with a scar like that.

The knock at my door sends me scrambling for the nearest article of clothing. I press the puffy pair of knickerbockers against me, only covering the lowest section of my waist and the tops of my thighs as the door swings open.

"My Lord, I have come to escort you to the throne room," says Borgravid, bowing as he enters. When he straightens and sees me in all of my un-kingly glory, he frowns. "You're still not dressed."

I glance at the many layers of this single outfit alone scattered across my floor.

"Not even in the slightest," I admit.

He steps through the threshold without another word and grabs the braies first, tossing them to me. "Start with these."

I drop the knickerbockers just in time to catch them and waste no time shimmying into them to reclaim some sense of dignity.

"Where'd that come from?" he asks, pointing to my chest.

I glance down to my shoulder, eyeing the teethlike scar. "I don't know. It happened before. Was I attacked by a bear or something?"

Borgravid comes closer for a better look but stops enough of a distance away that I'm aware he still doesn't trust me.

"The maw is too large to have been a bear. It looks like wolf teeth to me. But you were never attacked by wolves. Unless it happened after you left."

"I thought you said I was only gone a couple of days?"

"You were. Perhaps Reapers heal quickly."

Piece-by-piece he throws the rest of the clothes at me, until I am standing tall in a perfectly tailored ensemble that reminds me of the sun rising over a lake on a late autumn morning. I top it off with a velvet cloak lined with sloth bear fur.

"Can we stop by the Forbidden Garden on our way?" I ask.

Borgravid frowns, leaning away from me, leery. "What purpose do you have there?"

Before I turn away from the mirror to eye him more closely, I give the moss-green doublet a final tug, making sure it's centered precisely the way I want it. When I'd first arrived—or rather, returned I suppose—Captain Borgravid informed me that my father had died the same way my mother and brother had: death by aacsi. When I questioned him later about how I'd obtained such a creature to do my bidding, he also informed me that the Forbidden Garden was the only place in all of Tayaraan where the aacsi can be found.

"Why don't you want me to go there? This is the third time I've asked, and you've denied me each time."

He straightens, looking more indignant. "The last time I let you inside, you killed the king."

"Okay, well, obviously I'm not going to kill the king now," I say with a crooked smile.

"It's forbidden for a reason."

I groan. "Yeah, but it was forbidden under my father's reign, not mine. Even if I decide to keep the law, I think I, of all people, should be allowed in. Don't you?"

He snorts. "Not on your coronation day. Especially not when you're already running late."

My sigh is the only indication I give him that I understand this is a moot point. We can discuss the matter later, after I'm officially the king and I can change whatever rules I want.

Calling over my shoulder to my crow, I extend my arm. "Come on, Sidian. It's time to go."

The bird squawks, and I still can't tell what it thinks of the new name. Personally, I think it fits pretty well—short for Obsidian—considering how the creature's wings still shimmer in certain lighting, despite being as black as ink.

Ultimately, Sidian swoops down from its perch atop the curtain and glides to my forearm.

"We'll continue this conservation later," I say, correcting myself only after Borgravid's silent chuckling. "*Conversation.* Ugh, has my tongue always struggled to form coherent sentences?"

"Yes," he answers, grinning at me fondly. It's the kind of look that is entirely uninhibited, like right now he's not a royal guardsman talking to the King, or even a mortal talking to a Reaper. In this moment, we're simply men, friends, and though I have no memory of what I've done to gain such rapport and trust, I appreciate it, nonetheless.

Reaching for the door, Borgravid draws it back and waves me through.

"Let's get this over with," I sigh.

We exit my chambers and head down the hallway. Instead of continuing past the Forbidden Garden that's just up ahead, Captain Borgravid veers us through the Hall of Altúyur. Each time I find myself in this room I become unsettled. Surrounded by the tapestries, of which are detailed depictions of the eight Divinities, I feel the weight of their scrutiny bearing down on me. This room glistens so brightly—the marble floors polished, the gilding on the columns, doorways, and the vaulted ceiling immaculate—that it's almost like no shadow can seep into this room, like not even a Wraith could penetrate its pristineness.

I try to distract myself and blurt out the first thing I can think of.

"This sister of mine, will she be at the coronation?"

Borgravid halts, boots screeching against the polished marble floor. "She's...not here. You took her somewhere safe."

"Where?"

He glances over his shoulder at me, one eyebrow raised to ensure I know just how stupid he finds the question. I'd almost forgotten. Apparently when I'd left the palace, it had just been me and Gem. No guard, no guide, just me following my instincts, I guess.

He starts walking again, and despite feeling like there's more to that story, I'm too eager to get out of the Hall of Altúyur to press him further right now.

The memory of the Reaper girl strikes me again though, fading the room to some distant place. She's standing in the bathing room with me, pools on either side of us, our hands outstretched.

Every time I recall the moment, I glimpse a little more than the last time, and this time is no exception.

This time, I see her lips parting, the concern and terror in her brow. Just as the dark shadows coalesce around me, her smoky voice follows.

"I will protect her!" she screams. "I will protect Gem!"

I don't expect that level of desperation from another Reaper, former or not.

"Are you coming?" Borgravid is standing in the archway waving at me when the memory fades.

It takes me a moment to collect myself. My instinct—no, my *desire* is to ask him where the Reaper went, to insist that he tell me everything he knows about her and where I might've taken my sister before I returned to kill my father. But shadows flicker just beyond Borgravid, down the next corridor. It's probably nothing, probably just a trick of the light or my own paranoia, but it's enough to remind me that the Council *is* watching, and I've been instructed to become king, not chase around some former Reaper.

This conversation, too, will have to wait when we have the privacy and time for me to ask him everything I want to know.

My subjects are already waiting for me by the time we reach the throne room. Borgravid leaves me at the entrance to take his place beside the other guards lining the path. They stand, as tall and sturdy as columns, as I make my way down the aisle toward the Master of Ceremonies. But as I walk, I am grateful for the barricade they offer between me and the rest of my court. I sense their uncertainty, their distrust, even their hostility as they glare at me through the cracks of my soldiers' arms. For a moment, I fear every one of them has seen through the lie we spun. Though Borgravid assures me that he convinced them all that it wasn't me who caused the king's death, but some disgruntled peasant who I, then, later murdered in the name of justice, but I have to wonder just how convincing he was. If he left room for *any* doubt, surely they would've realized how unbelievable it would be for the underrealm to sanction a Reaper to come anywhere near a king before his time.

But I hold my head higher, trying to embody the confidence that Sidian exhibits from its place on my arm. If I could have half of its conviction, I just might be able to pull this whole king-thing off.

I reach the Master of Ceremonies, half expecting someone in the crowd to start a revolt, but no one does. If anything, the silence in the throne room thickens, making my ears ring.

At the motion of his hand, I take to one knee and present my head to the Master of Ceremonies. He turns to a courtier besides him, holding a velvet pillow where the crown rests. It's a glistening, golden thing, a honeyed tangle of bramble vines and oak trees reaching for each other at the topmost point.

Gently, the Master of Ceremonies takes the crown from the pillow, holding it like it will collapse if he puts too much pressure on the jade-encrusted branches. He hovers it over my skull.

"Lords and ladies of the Court," he begins, voice raspy with age. "For millennia, the Halaud family has governed Oakfall under a just rule. Our kings have prevented drought, stabilized peace between our nations, our most recent even protected us from the dangerous aacsi that were overrunning our lands and taking the lives of many, including our beloved queen and crown prince."

A murmur ripples through the crowd. The people kiss their fingertips in honor of the memory of all those they have lost, and I realize too late that I should've done the same considering it is *my* mother and brother he is referring to. But just as I lift my head, the Master of Ceremonies glares at me to stay put, and continues.

"I stand before you today to crown our own Prince Acari Halaud, not with speculation of what he *may* do for us, but with assuredness that he will be more just, more selfless, and far kinder than any other king we've ever known. For it was he who sacrificed himself when a resentful peasant sent a Reaper after his father, our king. It was Prince Acari who tried to stop him from communing with the scripture worms. It was Prince Acari who, upon realizing the deed was already in motion, took it upon himself to avenge his father and our kingdom. It was Prince Acari who sacrificed his mortal life to ensure the peasant's crime would not go unpunished.

"I know some may be wary of having a Reaper for a king, but I for one doubt him not. He has proven his loyalty more than any other Halaud before him, and under his rule the people, our values, our way of life, will continue to be protected."

With my head still bowed, I watch his feet shuffle toward me.

"Prince Acari Halaud," he says to me. "Are you prepared to take your oath?"

"I am." My voice echoes throughout the room.

"Then speak, and let the Court and the Divine Altúyur who watch from above bear witness."

I bite my lip, hoping that I can keep my tongue in check so as not to embarrass myself. I've done nothing but practice these lines the past few days, using feedback from Borgravid to perfect my delivery, but not once during my iterations have I felt confident that I've perfected them yet.

Finding the same doubt behind Sidian's stare makes me glance away, all the more certain that I am most definitely going to blow this.

"I, Acari Halaud," I begin, throat already as dry as the Pyrethi Desert. "Second son of Renaudin Halaud, descendent to the throne, hereby promise to govern the people of Oakfall and the Corraeda Isles according to their respective laws and customs."

Not for the first time since I started reciting this oath do I sense the hypocrisy of me speaking these words. One of the most necessary and sacred laws of any country in Tayaraan is that its citizens shall never take another life. Not only am I a Reaper bound to do just that, but even before I became one, I had already killed.

Ignoring the murmurs that seem to echo the same concern, I trudge through the next part of my lines. "I will guarantee that law and justice will prevail in all of my judgments."

Impossible.

"I will preserve, protect, and defend the beliefs and teachings of the Divine Altúyur."

Doubtful.

For every vow I take, I fear I'm only giving my people more reasons to eventually be disappointed in me. No one can perform these duties perfectly, especially not someone straddling the two realms, two sets of obligations and principles.

But I recite every word, make every promise. Even the ones that I'm sure I will break as sure as I am that rains will flood Elashor Lake in the spring, I swear them to the people in this room, to the people of my kingdom, to the Councilspirits depending on me to maintain stability in Oakfall.

"That which I have hereby promised, I will perform and keep. So help me, Divine Quetzi."

Although the whispering has nearly reached a roar, once I'm done, the room silences. Eagerly, we wait to see what the Master of Ceremonies will do next. Although anyone could protest my coronation, ultimately, *he* is the only one who can deny me my crown.

He pauses, the crown floating over my head. Panic swells inside me. What if he doesn't crown me? What if I fail the simple task I've been given by the Councilspirits thus far? For a brief, shameful moment, I consider just sitting upright so that my head will slip into the crown *accidentally*. I've already said my vows, gone through the motions of tradition. What could they do but accept me then?

But before I can commit, the Master of Ceremonies places the crown on my head. It's large enough that it slides down to my brow, but I tilt it back to rest it at an angle, hopeful that I can get it fitted later.

"Rise, King Acari Halaud of Oakfall."

I do as I'm told, pride stretching my grin thin as I turn to face the people who have come to share in this momentous day. I bow to them, catching the crown just before it slides forward again. The people applaud, and though I want to bask in the glory of this moment, I realize the sound is slow, unenthusiastic.

Not a single person in this room is happy to see me crowned king.

"At least now he can request an audience with the underrealm," someone whispers from the crowd. "They'll only conduct investigations at the behest of one of the monarchs."

Clearing my throat, I try staying focused on the coronation and what's expected of me. Now that the crown is atop my head, the Master of Ceremonies makes quick work of fastening the Oakfall sigil to my shoulder, a silver bundle of daminila flowers, native only to Oakfall. Once he's done, as is customary, I turn my back to the crowd and walk up the short steps to sit upon the Throne of Wings.

Though the people of Oakfall honor *all* of the Divine Altúyur, they hold the most respect for the Divine Lorik of Bravery, the Divine Sungema of Memory, and the Divine Iracara of Compassion. As such, the Throne of Wings is an homage to those three in particular. It's a slender, modest thing, hand-carved from ash wood centuries ago and painted black. By far, it is the starkest thing in the entire room, perhaps even the entire palace, that is, it would be, if not for the magnificence of the backrest.

Hundreds of delicate feathers are etched along the three spires that form the backrest. Instead of black, they are painted with each of the three Altúyur in mind. The lorikeet and the sungem share some colors in common—a shimmering green, bright orange, and a color that could be mistaken for violet under the right lighting, and royal blue under another one. In between Lorik's and Sungema's spires is Iracara's, the Altúyur for which I am named. Though it is mostly black, as is the aracari bird, the shaft of each feather is yellow and the vane itself fades from black to the darkest maroon.

The applause fades as I settle into the colorful throne, and no sooner than I've claimed my throne do the people put me to work.

"What of the Reaper who killed your father?" cries another person, this one less interested in whispered wishes, but in appealing for justice. "When will you demand recompense from the scripture worms for their role in our slain king?"

Agreement buzzes through the crowd.

His request confuses me at first. What reason would I have to speak to the scripture worms, after all, when I can go straight to Veltuur myself. But then I remember that most mortals don't know the innerworkings of the underrealm. They presume that it's the scripture worms who decide where to send the Reapers because that's who the mortals communicate with when they need the services of one. They have no knowledge of the Councilspirits, and therefore have no way of knowing that it's the Councilspirits they should aim their outrage at.

Of course, since no one *actually* requested a Reaper to kill the king and therefore the Councilspirits never approved such a request, they'd *still* be casting their blame in the wrong direction.

But they don't need to know that.

Finally understanding the man's demand, I glance to Borgravid anxiously. He's standing all the way near the back of the room, unable to provide any counsel. Fortunately, he warned me this might come up. Though we told the people that I killed the man who sent the Reaper after my father, Borgravid feared that some of them might be outraged that the underrealm would allow such a thing to happen, being as such a thing is almost entirely unprecedented. Monarchs have been known to live long and prosperous lives. More than a few have earned the hatred of their people, and yet their deaths always came near the end of life, despite their constituents obviously having sent multiple requests for a Reaper to finish the job sooner.

We'd considered blaming my father's death on the made-up peasant himself, but then realized how equally unlikely it would've been that someone of low stature could've made it into the bathing house unseen.

The easier story to tell was this one.

More demands arise from the intimate crowd, warbling together until their voices are one great echo in the throne room.

With a raise of my hands, the room quiets. It's so instantaneous that it catches me off-guard. I don't think I've ever known respect or power like I do in this seat. Then again, I guess I wouldn't remember if I did.

My nerves begin to twitch, and the only thing I can do is clear my throat to hopefully try to settle them enough so that my tongue might stand a chance at speaking steadily.

"There will be no need to commune with the scripture worms."

Hushed whispers hiss through the crowd like a den of snakes.

I continue. "It is not for us to question the work of the Reapers. They kill those they are contracted to. That is the way of things. My father—"

"The way of things?" someone asks.

"Someone killed our king!" cries another.

"We can't let this stand!" bellows another.

The room grows boisterous again, and I can feel myself losing them.

I glance around, searching for someone who might be able to help me out of this mess, but all I find is my crow. Its stern, stoic nature is oddly reassuring. I would've expected it to join in on the chaos, but instead, it just stares at me, like it's trying to tell me only I can end their arguing. That might've made me feel more frantic if it had come from anyone else, but coming from Sidian—the king of crows—it reminds me of the power I have inside me, the power I've obtained simply by sitting in this throne.

"Silence!" The booming echo of my voice surprises even me, but the others practically cower in fear. "The underrealm will not be bothered by this! I dealt with the man responsible and that is that. My father is gone, but we remain. We have more important matters to focus on, so I suggest we do just that and have faith that those reigning over the underrealm know what they're doing."

The murmurs return, but none challenge me outright. It's something I think they'll abide by, but it's becoming abundantly clear they don't do so out of a sense of loyalty or love, but because they have to. I am their king, even if they don't want me, and they don't.

Frankly, the trees of Veltuur are more inviting than this place.

I nestle back into my throne. With the ceremony officially concluded, the people who so obviously loathe me start to clear the room, and as I watch them disperse, my only thought is that I desperately hope Veltuur will give me my first command, and soon.

9

A NEW QUEST

SINISA

Ditching the burdensome garments I haggled out of the tailor back in Azarrac, I slip into a pair of black trousers and a scarlet bodice that Aulow gave me. It still feels strange to have fabric tightly hugging my legs, stranger still to have so many layers and belts around my waist, but I am at least grateful for the color. Green was only bringing with it painful memories, and although I know red is not eagerly welcomed among the people of Tayaraan, that it represents Reapers and the threat they pose to mortals, I can't help that it's a familiar comfort to me.

I fasten Acari's pouch to one of my belts and stare at the cloth folded on the chair beside me.

I've saved the cloak for last, for it will be the hardest item to wear. In Veltuur, cloaks were reserved for Councilspirits and Shades. They were a sign of status and power, one that I had almost earned before giving it all up for a chance to save the prince.

Even if I had ascended as a Shade, it would've taken time to get used to the extra weight hanging off my shoulders.

I throw the cloak over my shoulders, fastening it in place, and leave the room and everything else behind me for good. To my surprise, the cloak makes me feel strong. Powerful. Like I ascended after all, only the title is different than I expected.

Just outside my door, Rhet tosses a wad of leather at me, catching me by surprise. "Put these on."

Confused, and slightly bemoaning the idea of having to change again, I unfold the garments to reveal two long gloves. "What are these for?"

He nods to the runes on my hands. "No one knows about the Guardians and we have sworn to keep it that way."

Before I can press him further, he storms away. Keeping the Guardians a secret seems absurd to me. Think of all the Reapers who would perhaps end their service to Veltuur if they knew it was a possibility to do so. But this isn't my camp to lead, and I am in no place to make demands.

Begrudgingly, I wiggle my hands into the leather, lacing up the sides before heading for the gate.

Awkwardly, I stand alone outside as the rest of our party says their goodbyes.

Aulow embraces the young woman, Bels, who brought tea to Gem after her vision last night. When they break away from each other, Aulow brushes a lock of umber hair away from the woman's face, tucking it behind her ear before leaning in to kiss the brown shape covering her cheek and temple.

Rhet walks past them, a father and son following close behind him. He addresses us all. "A Reaper will come tomorrow for the Prophet that Gilliame saw in his vision. If we are to make it to Kalápana in time, we must go now."

The rest of the group wraps up their farewells as he marches out the gates.

I wait for Hayliel and watch her sneak a glance over her shoulder, before spinning Gem in the air one last time. They've been like this all night and day, giggling and playing like they've been close all their lives, even though, according to Hayliel, they only briefly met the one time before. It confounds me how quickly they've taken to each other. A part of me, dare I admit it, might even be jealous, but I've become well adept at hiding such feelings.

When Hayliel finally sets Gem down, the girl's smile is so wide it lights up her whole face. They're not close enough for me to hear what Hayliel tells her next, but I see her point at me, Gem's eyes following, and while the young girl runs toward me, I feel compelled to straighten my back.

She stops abruptly at my feet and blinks up at me from behind shy eyes. "Bye-bye."

A grin tugs at the corner of my mouth, one that surprises even me. "Bye-bye, kid."

The eight of us—Rhet, Bels, the man and his one-armed child, a woman and her horse, another young woman who I haven't met yet, Hayliel, and I—leave without so much as looking back. We disappear into the trees. The farther away we get from the village, the quieter it becomes, and the more peaceful I feel, like I'm returning to my own sense of normalcy.

Of course, Hayliel seems averse to the idea of silence.

"Why isn't Aulow joining us?" she whispers to me. Considering the rest of the party is walking in silence, she's far from quiet enough to be unheard by the others.

Her question draws the attention of Bels, the woman with short raven hair and catlike eyes.

"She can't stand to be anywhere by the sea anymore," she says. "The smell of fish churns her stomach."

There's something about the way she says it that feels like she's leaving part of the story unspoken, but I barely have time to think on it before Hayliel continues.

"Are you Aulow's Prophet?" she asks, leaning forward to see past me to Bels. It's obvious from her lack of gloves that she's not a Guardian, but I get the feeling that Hayliel is more interested in making conversation than anything.

Bels' smile bows, a hint of mischief about her. "More like Aulow's *my* Guardian."

She and the young woman beside her, the one with shorn hair

that makes her ears stand out more than they should, erupt with laughter.

Hayliel and I exchange a look.

"My apologies," she continues, laughter fading. "I'm Belsante, and yes, I am Aulow's Proph—"

"Lover," sings the other girl in a grating, but somehow endearing tone. She can't be more than a few years older than me, and yet, her round features have a childlike appearance to them. "I guess we should all do introductions. I'm Rory."

"Hayliel," my companion says before clasping my shoulder. "And this is Sinisa."

The woman nods her shorn head at us both. "It's a pleasure. I'm Dethoc's Guardian." At the head of the group, beside Rhet, the man with the young boy on his shoulders waves without looking back. "That's Dethoc. The little guy on his shoulders is Gilliame, his son. He was one of the youngest Prophets we had, until yours showed up."

"Oh," I say, a little confused. "Is that a problem?"

"Not at all! I'm sure Gilliame loves having someone else his age around."

Hayliel leans forward again to speak to Rory on the other side of me. "They're both your Prophets? I didn't know a Guardian could save more than one. Then again, I don't know much about Guardians at all. It's all very new to me."

"Oh, no," Rory answers with a laugh. "Dethoc isn't a Prophet at all, and Gilliame isn't mine. He's Rhet's—or rather, Rhet's his. It's a funny story actually, how they all wound up tangled together. After Dethoc's wife—"

"Not now." Rhet's command rumbles in the air like thunder, terrifying even the woodland critters back into their hiding holes.

But not Rory.

She leans over, hand shielding her mouth, and whispers rather conspicuously, "When Dethoc's wife gave birth to a baby with only one arm, she had to summon a Reaper. Law of Mother's Love, you know? But she knew she couldn't live without her son, and she couldn't exactly kill herself and leave her family without a mom and wife either. So you know what she asked the scripture worms?"

Equally horrified and intrigued, Hayliel shakes her head.

I, on the other hand, have seen this story play out a dozen times before.

"She requested a Reaper to claim them all," I say. "Her whole family."

Rory nods. "Yep."

"That's horrible," Hayliel gasps, hand covering her mouth. "How could a mother do such a thing?"

"It's not as uncommon as you'd think," I tell her. "The law forces them to have a hand in the execution of their own children. I think they do it because, for them, the idea of living without their child would cause immense suffering, and rather than forcing that kind of pain on their entire family, they opt to have them all killed. Together."

Even more horrified now, Hayliel can't stop shaking her head, tears glistening in her eyelashes.

Rory shrugs, continuing the part of the story that she seems to deem more interesting. "With a request that large—a mom and her four children—they had to send the best of the best. Someone fortified and unwavering, loyal without fault. They sent Rhetriel for the job. He'd been a Reaper for...for decades. Had never once failed a contract."

I glance forward to take a better look at the man, but even knowing how Guardians are made, it's still difficult to picture him as a Reaper. Don't get me wrong, he's as cold and direct as they come, but ever since our paths crossed, I've sensed an unrelenting compassion inside him, one that would've been difficult to hold onto as a Reaper.

Then again, I forget just how much Veltuur takes away from those who are initiated. Like me, he likely lost that side of himself too while he was in servitude.

Perhaps, when we return from our respective quests, he might be able to talk to me about how to find that side of myself again too.

"So Rhet gets to the house, right?" Rory continues, exuding so much excitement she's not even whispering anymore. "And he actually kills the mother and their three older children first, figuring an infant will be easier to dispose of once the rest of the household is gone. But what he doesn't know is that the father is also home—he was supposed to be traveling to visit his parents for a fortnight or something, and so the mother hadn't included him on the contract.

"But get this. Dethoc comes home early. He walks in to find three of his children are dead, and Rhet standing over his wife's corpse. Somehow, he manages to escape with their newborn son— that's Gilliame. Even more impressive than that though, once Rhet finally and inevitably catches up to them, Dethoc actually convinces him to spare little Gil. He begs him not to kill his only son, pleads that no one should suffer what he's endured only to have it all taken away, and something just clicks for Rhet. It's not a memory yet—because we all know none of us had those while we were in Veltuur—but he gets the sense that he's had that conversation before, and something inside him just won't let him kill his final mark.

"He finds out later—once he's become a Guardian and regained his memories—that the reason that conversation felt so familiar was because he begged someone else not to take his only child away from him, even though they were dying of illness. The Divine Owlena works in mysterious ways, right?"

As we walk, my gaze still settled on the two men ahead of us, I catch the silent glances they exchange. Judging from Gilliame's size, I'd guess he was at least seven years old now, which would mean that at least seven years have passed since the incident. It's plenty of time to move on, make amends, and find forgiveness, and yet, Rhet still wears his guilt like a bag of bricks is slung over his shoulders, like it might as well have happened just yesterday.

Dethoc smiles sadly at the man and pats his shoulder.

"Forgive me," Hayliel says, shyly. "But I'm afraid I'm having difficulty following. So Rhet saved Gilliame, becoming his Guardian, but didn't he save Dethoc as well then?"

Rory shakes her head. "Nope. Dethoc wasn't on the contract. His wife thought he'd be away with family for a while. She figured by the time word would reach him of his family's slaughter, he'd already be surrounded by loved ones and that he, out of all of them, would be able to move on—he comes from a big family."

Hayliel's face contorts even more, trying to piece it all together. "Okay...so, since Rhet was Gilliame's Guardian, Dethoc stayed around."

"Right." Rory nods emphatically, pleased to see that we're both following. "He wasn't contracted to me until a few years later."

"But you said Dethoc isn't a Prophet. I don't understand how you became his Guardian?" Hayliel asks.

Rory rolls her eyes, but it's such a childlike expression that she doesn't seem irritated when she does it.

Rhet cuts in before she can answer, apparently having heard the entire story. "A Guardian does not have to watch over a Prophet. They can save any soul they are contracted to take."

It sounds recited, like he's had to give that response a dozen times or more. How many people has Rory blabbed this story too? I wonder how it makes him feel about it?

"Like Miengha," Rory says, skipping backward to put her hand on the blonde woman's shoulders. "She became a Guardian to a horse that some town had asked her to slaughter."

Miengha brushes her long, braided ponytail off her shoulder to eye the white horse beside her fondly.

"Avalanche," she says, voice flat and thick with a Ghamayan accent.

"Avalanche?" I ask, eyebrows popping high. "It sounds like there's another good story there."

Frowning, she says simply, "Not what you think. This one is wild and reckless. Anytime I let him run, havoc is left in his wake just like—"

"An avalanche," I say, a little disappointed.

"You will find more Prophet-Guardian pairs at camp," Rhet interjects before resuming his speech. "Because the Prophets call out to each other before a Reaper comes for them. For that reason, Prophets are more easily saved."

"That's how you knew about Gem?" Hayliel says with understanding. "She called to your Prophets for help and you came to her rescue."

Rhet nods.

Rory elaborates. "We would save others from Reapers too, but since the Prophets don't know when everyone will die, we focus on the lives they foresee us saving. The Prophets are always our first priority, but if we think we can help the Reaper transition back to the mortal realm, we do what we can to aid them."

"And that's where you're headed now? To save a Prophet, maybe a Reaper too?"

Rory's reply is hopeful. "If we can."

"That's very kind of you all, to risk your lives like this to save the others."

"You gotta understand, half of us wouldn't be here if someone hadn't convinced us we didn't have to kill for Veltuur."

Belsante speaks then, her voice low. "The rest of us wouldn't be here either, if our Reaper hadn't changed their mind."

Rory blows through her lips. "Like you ever had anything to worry about. Aulow was never going to kill you. The way she tells it, she fell under your trance the moment she laid eyes on you."

Belsante's smirk is victorious and proud. Beside me, Hayliel opens her mouth to ask another question, likely to hear the story of how Belsante and Aulow came to cross paths next, but she is interrupted by the sight of Belsante's face falling flat, her eyes flooding white.

"Bels!" Rory yells.

I reach out for her as she's collapsing, but pull my hands away on instinct, afraid my Reaper power will kill her. It's only after Rory and Miengha catch her, and Rory assesses me with sympathy, that I remember I no longer have a touch that will kill.

They lower Belsante to the forest floor, Rhet whistling for

Dethoc and Gilliame, who had become too lost in their own conversation to notice the rest of us, to circle back.

The raven beauty is just opening her eyes when they return.

Rhet looms over her, imposing and anxious. "Are they close?" he asks, already knowing that any vision she or any other Prophet has would involve saving a life.

Wearily, Belsante nods. "In Bolnin, at the orphanage."

I try not to flinch at the word that sounds so much like pain and terrifying memories to my ears. I'm sure there are orphanages that aren't run by greedy matrons and their predatory business partners, but I can't help but have any other imagining of the place Belsante speaks of. Considering the owners have summoned a Reaper to come and kill one of the children in their care, I can't imagine this place is much better off than the one I grew up in.

Rhet rubs the strip of hair growing along his chin as he looks out through the trees. "We won't make it to Bolnin until nightfall."

"Then we need to hurry," Belsante bites out. She reaches a hand up to Rory and, with her help, pushes herself back onto her feet. "I think we stand a chance at saving him if we hurry."

Shyly, Hayliel inches forward. "Save who?"

"Well, ladies," Rory says once Belsante is stable on her feet. Her grin broadens. "Looks like you're about to see this whole Guardian thing in action."

10

SHADOWING

ACARI

I t's only day three of the Festival of Wings, and it already feels like it will never end.

The first day was the traditional feast. Every household celebrates with an array of special plates: sambar and curries, samosas and pakora, and a variety of grilled and fresh fruits. Neither my father nor I attended the banquet held at our palace this year, but I'm told the tandoori chicken was exquisite.

Day two is the opposite. Whereas we gorge ourselves on the first day in honor of all that the Altúyur have given, the second day of the festival is meant for acknowledging that all resources are limited. It is a day of fasting and putting any leftovers from the previous nights out on the altars that are scattered throughout the kingdoms.

I woke up this morning so hungry I would've eaten my own pillow if a servant hadn't brought me some steamed rice and coconut balls.

Day three, however, marks the first of the eight days of devotion to each of the Altúyur. I'm not sure why we spend the first two days of the festival gorging ourselves before fasting; perhaps it's a way to cleanse ourselves for the remaining days of the festival, so that we can clear our minds and bodies to honor the Divine Altúyur.

Today the people celebrate the inspiration of the Divine Pecolock. The kingdom streets will be vibrant with music and art, dance and costumes, all for the Face of Pecolock carnival.

It might actually be exciting, if I wasn't meant to play a lead role in the culminating dance at night's end.

In my hands, a mask of deep blue and green shimmers. Feathers spread like wings from the creases at the eyes, and a beak covers the place where my nose would go.

I want no part of it.

"I told you already, I won't be wearing that."

The servant clutches the blue- and green-feathered outfit to his chest. "But, my Lord, it is customary for the king to dress as Pecolock during the festival. You are to inspire the entire kingdom during the ceremonial dance with the other lords and ladies."

Groaning, I eye the garment again, paying extra attention to the opening where most of my torso will be left bare, aside from the flashy sequins and feathers connected at the shoulders. "I'm going to look ridiculous in this..."

He bows. "You will look regal, my Lord."

Before I can reluctantly grab the costume from the man, an ominous voice purrs from the shadows. "Sorry to interrupt."

The servant and I jump. I twist around just in time to watch a black cloak emerge, the Shade crossing the room just to lean against the vanity.

"I am afraid your king has more important matters to attend to today than frolicking in the streets."

The servant becomes slack-jawed, glancing from me to the Shade, lip quivering. It takes me awhile to realize he's awaiting final orders, as he surely thinks that I, as king, reign over even this Shade. What he doesn't know is that in matters of Veltuur, I am almost always outranked. My crown warrants no power or privilege in the presence of a Shade.

I wave the servant away, and he drops the peacock costume to the polished floor, before excusing himself from the room eagerly.

When I turn back to the Shade, I bow, grateful for the interruption, but also mildly uneasy. "Do I know you?"

"My apologies. I forgot; you no longer know who I am. Allow me to introduce myself." He sweeps the hood away, revealing his ashen skin and bloodred eyes. I do not know how long he's served the underrealm as a Shade, but I expect it's a number nearing centuries. "I am Shade Nerul. I will be somewhat of a mentor to you for the day."

"Hi," I say wearily, focused more on what he'd said about me no longer remembering him. "How did I know you from before? You're a Shade, and no offense, but I was a prince. I'm not certain our paths would've likely crossed during my mortal life."

Teeth peek out from his lips, and though they aren't sharpened like a shark's, they might as well be for how menacing that smile is. "Shall we?"

"Shall we what—"

But the only answer I receive is one of smoke as we are whisked away.

Black barren trees appear around us, the ethereal haze that carried us to Veltuur dissipating into the mist that hovers just above ground.

"Am I to be contracted for my first...um...contract today?" I ask sheepishly.

Nerul puffs a single laugh. "Not yet, little Reaper. First you must be taught our ways."

"I already know the ways," I grumble, looking up to Sidian circling overhead. "A Reaper's duty isn't a secret."

"No, but there is more to it than you yet know. But your lack of understanding is nothing to be ashamed of. No one has shown you yet. You've spent your first days as a Reaper in the mortal realm instead of here with your brethren. You are not to be blamed for being behind, but that changes today."

Nerul steps over a gnarled root, hands clasped behind his back. He leads me through the leafless woods, passing thin trees and thick trees, fallen trees and rotten trees, as if he's searching for one in particular. They all look the same to me, but I follow him deeper into Veltuur's forest, certain that if I lose him now, I'll never find my way out.

When he finally stops, standing beside a thick oak with bark that's cracked like magma, he sighs contentedly, like a man walking through his front door after a long and arduous journey. I watch him reach his hand into a hollow I didn't see at first, and as he digs inside, I look at the other trees, only realizing then that they all have a hole like this one too.

He pulls out a splintered wood chunk, holding it out in his palm. It rests there on display, every inch of him unmoving and unnervingly silent. I stare at it for a moment, unsure of whether I'm meant to grab it. By the time I decide I am, just as my fingers reach for it, the wood ignites, a ball of flame in his hand. It burns through quickly, leaving nothing behind but ashes.

Blinking, he drills his fingers against his palm, letting the dark soot sift to the Wraiths below the fog. "This is how you receive your orders. Every Reaper has a tree, and every day your tree will tell you whose soul you are meant to claim."

I can't stop staring at his hand. "What just—How did you— Where do I—"

"Your crow knows which tree marks your place in Veltuur. Whenever the two of you shall faze here, it will bring you to your tree, to where your hollow awaits you."

"Can we go there now, so I know where it is?"

A lazy wave of his hand. "I'm afraid not. You won't receive your own orders until I've deemed you ready. Until then, you'll be accompanying me on mine."

"Okay," I say agreeably. Anything beats playing dress-up in the palace today. "Where are your orders sending us then?"

"Patience. We have a few more items to review before we set out. But, if you must know, once we're through, we will be headed for Bolnin."

11

TO SAVE A PROPHET

SINISA

S linking in the shadows, precision edging our every soft step, is a part of the job that I could get used to. As a Reaper, I never needed to rely on stealth. It didn't matter if anyone saw me coming because if they ran, I'd just faze to them again. And again. And again. Until I completed my task.

Things are different for us Guardians though, so very different, I'm coming to learn. In some twisted, backward way, if the people inside the orphanage before us knew of our existence and saw us coming to protect the child inside, they'd be outraged. The people of the kingdoms are nothing if not mindless sheep who follow laws. When the punishment for not doing so is to greet a Reaper at your door though, I suppose it's only understandable.

Rory holds up her hand, halting the six of us without a word. She waves Rhet and Belsante forward to check in one last time about the plan to extract the child Prophet.

"Are you sure you want to do this?" I whisper to Hayliel, to the terror that seems to have permanently etched itself into her expression.

With a clipped exhale, she steels herself. "I—I want to help. They say I can be useful."

My cheeks heat at the reminder of what they've asked her and Belsante to do.

Send me to kill another living being. Send me to claim their souls. Flightless bird, send me to break into an orphanage to steal a babe from its cradle at night, but don't ever expect me to be bait a man in the ways that Hayliel and Belsante are being asked to.

"You don't have to if you don't want to, though," I remind her.

"I know. I'll be okay. Rhet will be just outside if we need him. Nothing will happen to me."

I nod, realizing that, at least in this matter, she is far braver than I.

"Are you sure this will work?" I growl up ahead, drawing the attention of the three of them. The rest of the group are off with their own parts to play in this: Dethoc and Gilliame keeping an eye on Avalanche, while Miengha takes to the roofs with her bow and arrow, just in case.

It's Rory who answers me, the mastermind of this half-baked idea. "Believe me, Sinisa, this is the best plan we have, and it's not a half bad one. I grew up in this place. The brothers that run it entertained prostitutes all the time. When these two beautiful ladies wander in, asking for directions, they're going to pretend to be gentlemen and offer them a nice meal and a warm fire, and when they think the time is right, they'll try to get under their skirts." She looks to Hayliel and Belsante when she adds, "You girls will be able to keep them distracted for a long while before it comes to that though, don't worry."

"No offense, but," I say, casting an apologetic glance to Belsante. "Are we all just going to ignore the birthmark on her face? Mortals don't take too kindly to people with deformities, and they especially don't like when said people live well into adulthood because it means they've evaded the law for decades. We already know the men inside abide by the Law of Mother's Love; they already sent a Reaper to come and claim a child inside. We can't send a Prophet in there without putting her at risk—"

Rory flicks her wrist. "I told you already, I *know* these blokes.

They don't care what the woman looks like if she's willing to get on her knees for them."

"I appreciate your concern," Belsante says to me as she undoes the top few buttons of her bodice. "But I can handle them. Men are easy to ensnare."

When she steps forward to cross the street, Rhet clamps her shoulder. "Be careful with your charm. Remember, your job is to distract. Lay it on too heavy and they'll figure out you're conning them."

"Or," Rory adds with a wince, "you'll get them too excited and they'll skip the gentlemen act and go straight to being dogs."

Belsante shrugs out of Rhet's grip and rolls her eyes at the both of them. "Obviously I'm going to do whatever keeps their paws off me and gives you two the most time. But if cleavage is what saves this baby, then it's a weapon I am not afraid to wield."

Before anyone can warn them further, Belsante nods, summoning Hayliel to walk into the moonlit street. They loop arms, cross the road, and enter the building across from us.

"I guess that means we're up." Rory flashes me a smile and shifts the bundle of rope over her shoulder.

The two of us make our way across the road next, leaving Rhet in the alleyway in case Belsante and Hayliel should need him. I peer over my shoulder up to the rooftops to see if I can spot Miengha or the glint of an arrow tip anywhere yet, but Rory was right. The woman knows how to stay hidden.

We reach the side of the orphanage, a stony wall only two stories high. Sticking two thin strips of metal between her teeth, Rory reaches for one of the protruding stones and starts to climb. She scales the wall like a spider, like gravity bares no hindrance on her fortified grip on the smooth rocks. She shifts her weight on each foothold before reaching for another round stone with one of her hands. Each grasp she takes, I'm sure will be her last, that her hands will give, and I'll have to catch her before she falls and breaks her neck. But to my surprise, her fingers grip easily onto the round stones, like the pull of gravity has no bearing over her.

When she's level with a window on the second floor, legs spread between two footholds like she's in a lunge, Rory anchors her weight into her highest foot to free her hands. She grabs the thin strips of metal from between her teeth and starts working on the window. It pops open without a sound, and she casts an arrogant smile down at me before climbing inside.

I climb the rope that falls down afterward, using the stones to help, thinking it would be far easier than what she just did.

But by the time I reach the windowsill, I'm winded. My hands are raw from where they kept slipping. She offers me hers, also rough from gripping the stones, and hoists me into the room.

There are at least a dozen beds around us, some of them with more than one child tucked inside. I feel small, like I'm ten years old again visiting my own orphanage for the first time. I wish we could take them all with us.

When Rory finishes tying off the rope, she stands beside me, looking out over the sea of beds. We spot the corner with three cribs at the same time.

"Do we know which is his?" I whisper to her.

She levels me a look as we tiptoe across the room. "Should be easy to tell."

A board creaks beneath my foot and we both freeze. My heart pounds. I crane to listen to what's happening below and I hear Belsante's honeyed voice shift to plan B.

"I'd heard the men of this establishment were handsome, but no one told me how ruggedly so."

Rory and I exchange a worried look. I'm not sure what her experience is with men, but I know how quickly things can escalate from here.

We make our way to the cribs, standing over them and peeking inside. The babes sleep peacefully, without a care in the world or any knowledge that one of them may or may not survive the night.

But all three of them seem normal. Bundled in their blankets, it's hard to tell which of them might be missing a limb. Rory and I each claim a crib and begin gently unraveling the blanket around the baby inside.

"You've gotta be kidding me," Rory says, drawing my attention.

"What is it?"

She shakes her head. "All this, over one missing finger. Not even a full finger, just the tip of it."

Knowingly, I frown. "The law is law, and orphanages of all places have to abide by it. They'd be shut down if they were caught during an inspection for having a child with a malformity."

"I know. But it's just...it's so unfair."

I nod, helping her finish unwrapping the baby so that we can tie the blanket into a sling around Rory's neck. All of the handling rouses the boy though. He starts fussing, despite Rory's cooing.

A man's voice, distant but powerful, roars from downstairs. "What's going on here?"

Rory and I secure the baby inside just as Hayliel cries out.

I straighten, bounding for the stairs. Rory snags my arm as children stir in their beds.

"That's not your job."

"I have to go help her."

She pulls on me harder, dragging me to the window. Below us, I hear Rhet burst through the door, fists colliding with faces only seconds later.

"He can handle this. We follow the plan."

Reluctantly, I nod, but as Rory swings her leg over the windowsill and positions herself to begin climbing back down with the rope, a shadow shifts ever so subtly in the corner of the room.

It feels like liquid ice is coursing through my veins as I turn around to find what the Wraiths are thrashing for.

"Well, well, if it isn't Sinisa Strigidae, the traitor," Nerul sneers.

With a growl bubbling in my throat, I lunge for him, claws reaching to rip out his throat. As much as I've blamed myself for Acari's predicament, seeing Nerul now reminds me that *he's* to blame as well. When the Councilspirits summoned me back to Veltuur, he was the one to intercept Acari and plant the idea in his head like a poisonous slug, that the only way he'd free Gem was by killing his father.

Nerul did it to fulfill his Reaper quota.

He did it to impress the Councilspirits by telling them he'd recruited a prince.

He did it to spite me.

"Whoa," Rory says, drawing the syllable out. Still perched on the windowsill, she leans for me, yanking me back beside her. "Slow your magrok. You're not a Reaper anymore. Remember? They can kill you."

"But it's his fault," I grit out, rage bubbling beneath me like I am a volcano ready to spew.

But a fraction of a moment later, I realize she said *they*.

My eyes catch on the young man standing beside him then, the crimson tunic every Reaper wears, making them all look so alike. But this Reaper stands apart. I recognize the black hair that's swept over his head, the sun-kissed skin, the gentle, dark eyes.

"Acari."

Even though I knew what he'd become, it's still surprisingly upsetting to see the crow perched on his shoulder, the one he has no idea is his father.

To my surprise, recognition crosses him. "You're the Reaper, the one who helped me kill my father."

I stagger backward, surprised. But after a quick glance to Rory, finding her wide-eyed and shrugging, I return my focus to Acari. "I didn't help you *kill* your father. I was trying to save you."

Confusion twists his expression, but it barely has time to arrive before Nerul steps in between us.

"That's enough of that. What brings us the pleasure of your company tonight, Sinisa?" He pauses, clasping his pale hands in front of him. "Don't tell me you're working with the Guardians now."

The only answer he gets from me is a scowl.

"Come now," he says at last, stretching out a slender hand. "Give the child to me."

Behind me, I glance to Rory. The smirk she flashes is wicked and daring, aimed directly at Nerul as she pushes off the ledge. My heart nearly bursts from my chest as I watch her disappear, see the rope go taut half of a second later. I lean over the ledge just as she finishes sliding all the way before she darts across the street.

"You're too late," I say, sporting a wicked grin of my own. "He's lost to you already."

I turn back around just to watch Nerul steam.

He hisses when he steps toward me. "I will not be made to look a fool by the likes of you."

My smile fades a little at his approach, my mortality suddenly feeling far more threatened than I care it to be. I take another step backward, glancing again to Acari before I, too, swing my leg over the ledge. "It looks like you already have."

Before I start my descent, I see Acari thrust out his hand.

"Wait! Don't go!"

The words pin me in place like arrows. There's so much desperation in his voice, so much curiosity that although I know I should leave, I can't. I know I can't trust Nerul, but I *know* Acari. He's the type of person who wouldn't hurt a fly, the kind of man who chased after a firefur in the dead of night because he wanted to make sure it was all right.

But he's also not the same person I met. He's a Reaper now, with no memories of his past to help guide him.

"Silence, boy," Nerul warns.

But Acari heeds him none. He shoves past the Shade—a disobedience that I'm sure will not go unpunished, and one that is so uncharacteristically him that I can't help but feel impressed—and races to the window. "Why were you helping me? Why were you—"

Before he can finish the question, an arrow whizzes by my ear. It lands with a thud, puncturing his forearm and pinning it to the windowsill.

He screams.

Startled by it all, my hands slip. I fall out of the window and down the two stories, the entire time wondering what he was about to ask me, and whether or not I'll live long enough to ever know.

But just before I hit the cobblestone road, Rhet catches me.

"You good to run?" he asks, setting me down on my feet.

Though the fall was short and my landing far gentler than it could've been, the impact still ricochets in my joints, reverberating alongside Acari's agonizing wails. I nod despite this, aware that wasting another second gives Nerul a chance to intervene, and though I was invested in saving this child before, knowing Nerul is the one I'm helping to thwart makes me all the more eager now.

The two of us bolt for the alleyway without knowing if anyone is following but running like they are.

Before I turn the corner, before I disappear with the others behind a barrier impenetrable by Reapers and other underrealm inhabitants, I look over my shoulder one last time to find Acari hissing through his teeth, the arrow still jutting from his flesh.

Then I keep running. It's only once we regroup, once we are racing through the streets with a sobbing babe, do I realize the opportunity that I just let slip through my fingers.

Acari was here.

He was standing right in front of me, asking me what had happened, and I didn't tell him anything. I didn't *do* anything but run from him. I should've told him about his sister. I should've mentioned that his father is now his crow. I should've told him that Hayliel and I are still trying to save him.

Instead, I ran.

Once we're out of the town and in the safety of the woods again, I find Hayliel. We share our stories, her going first about how the man at the orphanage struck her and how fast Rhet was to barge through the doors and come to her aid. It's meant to make me feel better about her being put in that situation to begin with, but I can't help but notice that her cheek is still red, and it grows brighter still.

"You should've never been sent in there," I say to her, glaring across the way at Rhet as he, too, checks in with his friends.

"I'm fine," she says. "I promise. What about you? It sounded like you two weren't alone up there."

Shaking my head, I lower my gaze to my hands. "It was Acari. He was the one they sent."

She gasps, a dainty hand to her mouth.

"I just left him," I say. "The only reason we're going to the Coast of Dreams is to make our way to the underrealm so that we can talk him into leaving, and I just completely ignored the opportunity I'd been given to speed up all of it. I just abandoned him."

"You didn't abandon him," Hayliel reassures me. "Gem's prophecy says we'll save him once we get into Veltuur, remember? Tonight might've been part of that. Maybe you planted a seed, but it's not until we reach Veltuur that the blossom will be fully bloomed."

Numbly, I nod and shift my cape tighter around my shoulders. I glance over at her and nod to the dried blood on her lip. "What about you? How are you?"

She smiles. "You already asked me that." Her hand floats to the red bruise blooming on her cheek. "It still hurts, but I'm thankful Rhet came when he did. And it was worth it, if that's how we were able to save that small boy."

Her kindness draws a smile from me, one that I didn't even know was inside me.

At the edge of our camp, Rhet and Miengha talk among themselves, the baby pressed against her body in the sling. I didn't see when Rory passed the infant to her, but watching her now, the way she sways with the babe in her arms, the way she holds him like her arms were meant to carry him, it seems a natural choice.

When they're done talking, she walks over to us.

"Sorry," she says flatly, and I know instantly that she's referring to shooting Acari. "I didn't know who he was."

"It's all right. You did what we told you to do," I say, the words like traitors on my lips. "Are you leaving with the boy now?"

Never taking her eyes off the infant, she nods. "Your trip to Kalápana is not safe for a babe like him. With Avalanche's help"—

she nods to the white horse—"we should be able to make it back to camp before sunrise. I can keep a barrier around us until then. No Reaper will be able to approach us."

"And what if his Reaper comes looking for him?" I hear the worry in my voice; I know just how close I came to never having a chance at leaving Veltuur.

"You should know better than most," Miengha says. "If a Reaper should come for him, Aulow will determine whether or not they are ready for the path of the Guardian."

She says her goodbyes to us, leaving me to sit with the sickening understanding that not all Reapers are ready to become Guardians.

I just hope, by the time we reach Veltuur, Acari is.

12

DREAMING OF DEATH

ACARI

Nerul grabs the shaft of the arrow and snaps it. My arm jerks with the force of it, throbbing with another burst of pain. But it's when he grabs the sharp arrowhead and yanks the rest of it out of my arm that blinding agony burns through me. I cry out, dropping to one knee and nursing my arm to my side.

Blood spurts from the hole just above my wrist. I clamp my hand over it, wincing and wailing in pain again as I squeeze.

Every child in the room is awake now. Most cower from atop their beds, while a few charge down the stairs, screaming for their masters.

Nerul's fists are whiter than usual as he clutches his blond head. He thrusts his hands down with a terrifying roar, and smoke wraps itself around us, blacking out the room. The pain in my arm fades, the blood between my fingers drying before crusting away like pollen blowing in the wind.

By the time we reach Veltuur, my wound has healed completely, any traces of blood, gone. Without the pain to distract me, I'm finally able to reflect on everything that just happened, on seeing *her*.

Sinisa, Nerul had called her. I had thought she'd helped me kill my father, until she denied it. But if she wasn't there to aid me with his death, what was she trying to help me with?

When the smoke is all the way cleared, I realize someone is waiting for us in the fog.

"Councilspirit Leumas," Nerul says, falling to his knees in a bow. "Forgive me."

I follow suit, my knees landing on a soft, damp mound of moss.

Leumas hobbles closer, the hem of his red robes trailing behind him like a waterfall of blood. "What is there to forgive?"

"I lost the child," Nerul stammers. "Sinisa stole him from us."

With a flick of his hands, Leumas summons us to our feet. He pauses, staring thoughtfully out at the trees around us. "You have secured us many souls in your time here, Shade Nerul. It was but one child."

Nerul blanches. "But...Councilspirit...I have failed Veltuur. I should be punished."

With bored indignation, Leumas rolls his eyes. "If you insist."

A single clap of his hands summons the shadows that dance beneath the fog. They pool together, racing from all directions of the forest, until they've coalesced at Nerul's feet. I stagger backward as they climb up him. They reach for him, claws at the end of spindly, shadow limbs, and as they drag him into the nothingness below our feet, his whimpers boil into a maelstrom of agony.

All I can do is stare in horror at the flat ground that reforms once the shadows are gone and hope that I never have to be unlucky enough to warrant a visit with the Wraiths.

Leumas and I stand there silently for a moment, my gaze trained on the solid ground where Nerul had been standing. Suddenly, every caress of the fog at my ankles feels threatening, a warning not to take one wrong step.

"I look forward to seeing you tomorrow, bright and early," Leumas says, drawing my gaze to find that he's already a good distance away. "King Acari."

"Oh, w-will I be shadowing someone else tomorrow?"

"No, I am deeming you ready," is the only thing he says before disappearing into the gray.

The next morning, I awaken to something sharp tapping my cheek. When I peel my eyes open, Sidian is perched on my chest, pecking my face.

"You can stop now. I'm awake."

Ignoring me thoroughly, the crow continues.

Groaning, I throw the blankets off me, sending Sidian flying to a decorative knob at the top of my wardrobe. It's not a very subtle creature, and I take its hint begrudgingly, dragging my feet across the floor while rubbing my eyes.

This time when I draw back the doors, I don't have to rummage through the ornate clothes inside. My Reaper garments are all I need for now, and they're readily waiting for me.

Caw, Sidian warns.

I'm fairly certain, judging from its tone, that if I don't dress quickly, it'll faze us to Veltuur with me still in my nightshirt. That's not exactly how I plan to spend my first official day as a Reaper, so I hurry. It's a good thing too, because not a moment after I finish buckling my boots, the room distorts behind gray smoke.

The scent of moss and mist fills the air before the woods spring into view around me. When they do though, despite knowing that the trees go on for an eternity in every direction, I'm certain I recognize the one before us. It's a younger tree, far shorter than the others around it, but still wider than my torso. Its bark is still intact, unlike the one Nerul shoved his hand into yesterday.

This tree is mine. I can just *feel* it. Like it has its tree-hand wrapped around my heart and it's pulling me toward it.

I come willingly.

It only takes me a few steps to circle it, finding the hollow I knew would be waiting for me.

I take a deep breath and reach into the black hole. It's warm inside, like I've dipped my hand into a great maw, its breath heating my skin. All I want is to jerk my arm back, convinced the tree is about to chomp down on me, but instead I wait like I know I'm supposed to.

When the breath of the tree cools, leaving something that feels like a coal in my palm, I don't hesitate to pull my arm out.

A chunk of wood rests in my hand, not too dissimilar than the one I saw Nerul with. Just as the wood ignites, flames dancing against my palm with no heat, Leumas appears from the shadows.

But I am swept away into a mirage, one that so thoroughly surrounds me that it's hard to tell it's not real.

Strings of beads clack against each other dangling from a doorway.

A pot of water boils over the open fire. Bony, shaking hands take it away, and once it's cooled, they dip strips of cloth into its waters.

The air is fresh and salted, but even it can't fully mask the scent of fever and sick.

Then, abruptly, the scene fades. It's disorienting, finding myself in the dark woods instead of in that beach home, but seeing Leumas waiting patiently for me motivates me to act like I feel perfectly fine.

"Truly wretched day," he says with a blood-curdling smile. "I hope your first soul collection is a good one."

"How can you tell if it's a good one?" Looking at the charred embers in my hands, I rub the soot into my palm. "I think the person was already going to die."

"Ah, yes. The natural deaths. Pity." He frowns, looking out past the trees. "Unfortunately, they can't all be as exciting as the one last night, I suppose."

It feels like a test, like he's setting me up to ask him questions about the girl—Sinisa. Or perhaps he's filling the role as my new mentor now that Nerul is...indisposed. Either way, after what I witnessed him do to the Shade last night with a simple snap of his fingers, I'm not sure I want to test either theory.

I change the subject back to the matter that's quite literally at hand. "I was only given one vision, one assignment. Is that how it'll work every day?"

A knowing smile creeps up his hollowed face, a test passed, I think. "Your assignments are uniquely chosen every eve. Some days you will have many, other days you will have none. It depends on what the scripture worms bring us, and the natural deaths the Councilspirits glean through the ether."

"I didn't know that's how we got those ones. Will I ever gain the ability to foresee deaths like that?"

"I'm afraid not," he says curtly, transitioning effortlessly back to his instructions. "Once you arrive, once you find the soul you are meant to aid in its travels to Veltuur, all it takes is a simple touch, and their life will be yours."

The information is not new to me. In fact, I'm pretty sure I've known it all of my life. A Reaper's touch brings death; it is a widely known fact. Still, my gaze drifts to my hands like I am seeing them for the first time, and I swear as I watch them, I can see the smoke of death lurking just beyond my skin.

"Your crow will do the rest," Leumas finishes. "Once you're finished there, your duties to Veltuur are done for the day. You will find little time for relaxation now that you are king, but might I recommend you take advantage of your trip to the Coast of Dreams. I understand you've never been, and the sea is quite remarkable to gaze upon from that corner of the realm."

I flash an appreciative—albeit, nervous—smile and nod, readying myself mentally for the trip.

But my heart pounds a second later when I realize what he's just said. "I never said I was going to the Coast of Dreams... How did you—"

Leumas tuts, waving a thin hand, his robes falling to his bony elbow. "You didn't have to. The Councilspirits receive the visions of the natural deaths, remember? We assign them accordingly, and this one was given to you by yours truly."

With understanding, the pinch in my chest eases. I can't spend the rest of my life doubting this Councilspirit, or any of them for that matter. So what that he sent Nerul to the Wraiths? The man begged for it. Leumas didn't even seem like it was the outcome he wanted. Maybe he's not so terrifying after all, as long as I follow my orders.

Before I can thank him for entrusting me with the collection of this soul, he continues.

"Now, you better go. I believe that soul is about to pass, and you should be there when it does. Enjoy your stay in Kalápana. May it be everything you dreamed of."

The town of Kalápana, located just along the southern tip of the Coast of Dreams, is nothing like the places I'm accustomed to.

The streets are far thinner, for one, with no need to accommodate the hundreds of people that typically flood the streets of Azarrac City. Instead, I see only a few citizens out carrying baskets of seared smelt and pollock, freshly plucked lavender, and baked horsebread and oatcakes. I see no signs of beggars, and where I would normally see trash scattered throughout the streets of my city, instead all I find are windblown sands.

This town is quiet.

Aside from the occasional clopping of hooves or heels on the pebble road, all I can hear are the waves somewhere in the distance.

The people here even seem to be less afraid of Reapers. Each person I pass, though they shy away, they still nod in greeting or flash a quick smile before hurrying by.

I haven't felt this welcome anywhere since my initiation, and it's no wonder Leumas suggested I take some time to relish in my being here once I've completed my contract.

Which, I remind myself, is the reason I'm here. Although I'd love nothing more than to follow these streets down to the beach so that I can actually glimpse the infamous Starry Reef, I have a job to do first.

Pulled by instinct—and with Sidian guiding me in the sky above—I wind through the narrow roads until I reach a door that I recognize, even though I've never visited it before.

My hand falters on the doorknob. It feels wrong to barge into someone's home, at least through the front door, even as a Reaper. When Nerul and I had fazed into the orphanage, that had been different. The people there had specifically requested us and we hadn't needed to come in through the front door.

But this? Although the man I'm here for is on death's bed, and although I'm sure he's been expecting me any day now, I can't bring myself just to enter.

Despite every Reaper instinct yelling at me to do the opposite, I knock. Once, twice, three gentle taps.

It takes a long while for someone to answer, but I hear her slow shuffle inside and so I wait.

"Hello?" her voice rasps, before she has the door open all the way. Once she does, once she finally glimpses me, her tired eyes pool with tears. Without a word, she presses her lips together and steps aside for me to enter.

I stand in the entryway, ignoring the modest kitchen to my left, and the even more modest seating area to my right, staring straight ahead to the doorway covered with beads. A furry neko prances out of the bedroom, full of purrs that are louder than even the beads that chatter in its wake. It struts toward me, whiskers aimed at my ankles, and I almost lean down to caress its soft back, until I remember what destruction a gentle touch from me could bring.

The hunched woman closes the door, startling my attention away from the neko. She hobbles to my side. "Do I have time to say goodbye?"

I heave a deep sigh, but before I answer, Sidian does so for me with an obnoxious and unforgiving squawk. The woman startles a few steps away until I wave the bird away.

"I don't think you do," I answer her softly. "But you can be there with me, if you'd like?"

A tear breaks away when she nods before leading me into the room where I know her husband awaits my services.

Lavender is hung from every corner of his room, but the flickering flames of candles outnumber them tenfold. The only window is cracked to let in the fresh ocean air to help cycle out the old, but nothing has succeeded in getting rid of the stench of vomit and diarrhea.

Even from the doorway I notice the rose spots covering his wrinkled skin, and the jagged teal rune on his cheek that notes his terminal status.

He exhales a ragged, wheezing breath when the old woman grabs his hand.

"I love you, Engeram," she tells her husband, her voice strained but holding strong. "May the Altúyur guide you into the next life, and may I find you there again when my time comes."

She kisses her husband's hand before prying herself away from him.

A shallow, shaking breath hisses from his lips, and I know it is time.

I take a step toward the bed, Sidian leaping from my shoulder to perch on the man's knee. It watches me intently, as if it fears I will fail in this simple task. Behind me, the woman's silent tears become audible sobs. Every step that brings me closer to the dying man makes her weeping grow louder.

My hand stops outstretched, frozen between my body and his cheek. It feels wrong to do this with her watching. He's lived a long life, he's earned the peace I can provide him, and yet, it still feels wrong to make her watch.

But before I can turn around and ask her to give us some privacy, a final, croaking breath whispers out of him. I snap my attention back to him, watching his gaunt face become placid. It's too late. He's already passing. Before I have time to react, a teal swirl of color appears on the man's throat. His final rune. The rune of death.

Caw! Caw! Caw!

Sidian goes wild. Flapping its wings like it's shooing us out of the room, it hops along the man's body, stopping on his chest. Instinctively, I back away, slamming into the wall as I watch what happens next with morbid fascination. An opaque haze spills from the man's lips like he's exhaling a tuft of smoke. It coalesces above him, an amorphous blob without anywhere to go.

But as Sidian cracks his beak wide, the shape is drawn inside him. It goes slowly at first, like it's fighting to break free. But with each swallow, the task becomes easier, and the crow drinks the cloud like a glass of water on a hot day.

When Sidian is done, we leave the woman to care for her husband's corpse.

"Did we do it?" I ask the bird who seems to be staring at me with disapproval from my shoulder. "Did we collect the soul?"

A single screech is all I get in response. Despite its obvious annoyance with me, I still smile.

Out past the cottages and shops, the waves crash against the shore. I know I have the Festival of Wings to return to and that the people of Oakfall need their king, but I can't quite pull myself away from this place just yet.

Sidian squawks in my ear again.

"Yeah, I know. We will. But first, I want to see the Starry Reef."

If crows could cross their arms, I'm sure mine would. But since it can't, it simply launches into the air, and I resume my stroll through the streets of Kalápana, with nothing but the ocean's breaths to guide me.

13

HORSEBREAD

SINISA

Rory swings her arms around me, squeezing me so tightly that I'm afraid she might break my bones.

"It's been a pleasure," she says into my hair.

To my horror, Hayliel throws herself into us, as well. "The pleasure has been ours. Good luck in locating the Prophet on Nadina Isle."

When they peel away from me, I start to wonder if I will *ever* get used to human touch again. Maybe I'm just not built for it, Reaper or not.

Then Rhet extends his hand and I realize I don't despise all types of contact. I take his palm into mine, shaking it like it is an honor to do so. To me, I guess it is. I haven't had the opportunity to thank him yet for saving me from Veltuur, or at least for the role he played. He could've left me and Acari in the woods that night, he could've left me at the barrier of their encampment, and I could've spent the rest of my days as a Reaper, stuck alongside my crow.

But he didn't.

Instead, he took a chance on me.

I don't know if he is able to read my eyes, but I use the moment to silently thank him for everything. Maybe when our paths cross again, I'll give him a proper thank you.

"This is where we leave you," he says, releasing my grip. "The people of Kalápana know this coast, and they know their islands. If there is a cave here, they will know where you will find it."

"I know," I say, and then when Hayliel elbows my ribs, I add, "Thank you. I'm sure we'll find it."

I settle for waving goodbye to the rest of them as they veer down a different road from us.

Hayliel's eyes bore into me. "Is it difficult to be back here? You know, home?"

"I...don't know," I say, surveying the quaint buildings. "I hadn't really thought about it. This place doesn't really feel like home. I've been gone so long, and I was so young when I lived here, I'm not even sure I'll remember anything."

A sad smile draws the edges of her lips up. "Still, even that sounds like it would be difficult. I'm sure some things will come back though."

Without any set destination, we start down one of the cobblestone roads, hoping to find someone with any information about the legend of the neko in the cave.

An hour in, and we are nowhere near closer to our answer. Although the people of Kalápana are far friendlier than those from the other cities we've visited or gone through, their hospitality disappears the moment we utter any word of the neko or a cave. Not only are we strangers amidst this small town, but we're poking at wounds that are still too fresh for anyone to want to open. Uncertainty clamps their mouths closed, fear locks their window shutters and doors.

"I don't understand it," Hayliel says, exasperated. "You said you knew of the legend growing up. Isn't that right?"

Between bites of glazed mackerel, I manage a noncommittal jerk of my head. "Uh-huh."

"Then it's common knowledge, not something that they should be guarding like a secret. It doesn't make any sense."

"A lot can change in a few years." I shrug, picking my teeth with a fishbone.

She frowns at me, unconvinced, but falls into silence. This spot on the beach can do that to a person. From where we sit on the bench, we have a magnificent view of the indigo and navy waves that sway like liquid night along the black shoreline. Even as a child I remember gazing out at sea for hours, wondering where the starry water ended, and where the crystal clear waters began, wondering why, exactly, our coast was so different than everyone else's.

"Who told you about the legend of the neko?" Hayliel asks at last, pulling us both out of the ocean's trance.

"What do you mean? Everyone talked about it."

"Yes, but who was the first person?"

I snort a laugh. "I can't answer that. The other kids and I used to talk about it all the time. It was like a spooky bedtime story, or a myth that we all thought we'd be the ones to crack, even though no one else had for generations before us."

Mentioning the kids I grew up with sends me through a cascade of memories. Just me and countless other children running through the fields, lounging by trees, and relaxing at the coast, talking about whatever came to mind. It's so strange how detailed these recollections are, considering up until a few days ago I didn't have them. They almost feel more like someone else's memories than mine, but I guess that might just be part of growing up.

Hayliel sighs. "You don't remember a single person who told you about it?"

Though I have my memories back, some of them feel like they're locked away. It's like a dam has been constructed between me and the majority of them, just waiting for someone to release them one at a time because the rest of my mind couldn't handle an entire flood.

And that's exactly what Hayliel's question does. It wasn't until she asked it that I remember that there *was* someone. Someone I confided in about everything. Someone who treated me like an adult even though I was only ten. Someone who would tell me stories over a baked loaf of pumpkin bread until the sun rose.

I bite my lip. "There was someone, I guess."

Hayliel perches so eagerly at the edge of her seat that she nearly falls off. "Who?"

"My aunt Theffania."

"That's great! That's good news!" Blinking, Hayliel slides back against the bench. About a half dozen thoughts race through her mind, and I can tell because she opens her mouth for every one of them, but it's a long while before one makes it past her lips. "Would you still remember where she lives?"

I twist around in the bench to look up the boardwalk, bringing Hayliel's gaze with me. When she looks, all she probably sees are the different oceanside vendors and inns, people lounging on the black sand. But my eyes are trained on one building among the dozens, to the large open window and the flaming brick oven inside, to the mounds of dough waiting for their turn in the oven, to the woman with a beige hat tied over her head working inside.

If we had walked that way already, I might've already remembered the place, but looking at it now, even at a distance, I'm flooded by my past.

"Is it close?" Hayliel asks.

I actually laugh before standing from the bench and dashing for the place that feels so much like home. Each step feels like hope, like excitement, like love.

Until we're so close that fear starts to eat away at me.

My strides slow, the hopeful smile I was wearing fading like smoke.

It has been a long time since I've seen my Aunt Theffania. A lot has changed since then—*I* have changed. Who's to say she will even want to see me? After all, not once did I hear from her after I was relocated to Azarrac City, not to mention the fact that she was the only family I had left and yet she did not take me in.

By the time we reach her bakery, I've already decided to keep walking by. It's better this way. We can both just fade from each other's memory, if I haven't already faded from hers. We've gone this long without each other, so I'm sure we'll both get on just fine.

"Sinisa?" a warm voice calls from the window.

My joints and muscles become stiff. I can't will my legs to keep moving, nor can I bring myself to turn toward the voice that's so familiar and yet so strange.

"Wings, give me strength—Sinisa? Is that really you?"

Out of the corner of my eye I watch my aunt wipe the flour from her hands on her apron while she charges for the door. Though weighted down by a baker's love of bread, she still manages to break into a run and haul toward me.

"Aunt Theffania," I utter, voice cracking, my breaths ragged.

The large woman crashes into me, burying my face into her bosom. She feels and smells just as I remember, like she's made from dough herself. And perhaps it's the incoming memories, or how much has happened in these few short days, but as she rocks me in her arms in the middle of the street, sobbing into my hair, I, too, feel tears sting my eyes.

14

FALSE HOPE
SINISA

"Sorry, sir. We're closed," Theffania says, reaching across the counter that extends out from the window and into the street.

"But it's not even—"

"We're closed." Her words are a little sharper this time, edged even further by the thud the counter makes as she closes it over the window, effectively slamming it in the man's face. Any irritation she may have felt though is gone by the time she turns around to address us. "Would either of you like some freshly made oatcakes? Or, I just pulled a loaf of horsebread out from the oven."

Hayliel glows. "We'd love—"

"We're fine for now," I say, interrupting her.

I don't mean to sound so harsh; there are just too many things running through my mind right now to want to waste any time on the frivolity of being waited on. All this time, I thought I was alone, that my parents' death had left me without a single soul to call family, but I'd forgotten about my aunt.

She scowls at me now, the backs of her wrists planted on her wide hips. "Sinisa, dear. You have never once turned down my baked goods, and I will not have you starting today. Offering you something to eat is the least I can do to celebrate your return. I haven't seen you in six years."

Before she can see the pain lancing through my eyes, I bow of my head. Six years I've been away. Three of those I spent in the darkest, most miserable prison I've ever known, and then I went to Veltuur. Where was she? Why didn't she come for me? We were supposed to be family.

Hayliel flashes her a warm smile. "Oatcakes and horsebread will be lovely."

As my Aunt Theffania retreats to grab the delicacies, Hayliel scoots closer, eyeing me with that knowing look about her. "I'm sure she has her reasons."

She grabs my hand, giving it a gentle squeeze, and I squeeze hers in return, thankful to have something to hold onto.

My aunt returns a few moments later with a modest tray of sliced breads, herbs, oils, and the oatcakes.

"I've waited so long for this moment," Theffania says, setting the plate on the table and taking a seat opposite us.

Perhaps it's the pleasantries, or maybe it's the fake smile on her face that's souring my stomach, but I can't stand the act any longer.

Nails digging into my palms, my fists drive down as I spring to my feet. "You've waited for this? Don't lie! You left me. After my parents died, I could've come here. I could've lived with you, and instead, you let me rot in an overcrowded orphanage halfway across the country. You haven't looked forward to this reunion. You were happy to let me disappear from this family."

As I speak, Theffania's eyes grow wider and wider, her skin paling before pink tinges her cheeks. She lets me finish my tirade, but when I'm done, heaving and ignoring Hayliel's tugging hand at my own, my aunt straightens, sets her oatcake back on the table, then holds my gaze.

"I did not abandon you," she explains, cool eyes fixed on mine. "For months, I searched for you, all throughout the town, all throughout the rest of the Coast of Dreams, but you were nowhere to be found. Eventually, I had to stop looking. My children needed me here, and I...I know it's not fair, but I tried. When I finally had to stop, the only solace I had was knowing you'd return when you could, that you'd come looking for your parents."

Hope rushes over me. Suddenly, the past six years don't even matter. "My parents? Are they...are they here? They're alive?"

Seeing my hopeful eyes light up, my aunt covers her mouth with a soft gasp. "Oh, dear. I am truly sorry. That's not what I meant."

And just like that, I am sinking. Into myself, into the chair I drop down on, and back into the darkness that, I realize, has been my comfort long before I ever became a Reaper. My parents are dead, and they always will be. And, even if they weren't, even if I found out that all of this time they had actually been alive, that would almost be worse. Better to have lost them to death than to have lost them because I was abandoned or forgotten.

Theffania retrieves the oatcake from the table and takes a small bite, giving me time to process before she continues. "I didn't mean that you'd find them here. If they were alive and well, you bet the brightest feather that they would've been to retrieve you by now, Sinisa. Your parents loved you so very much."

Heartbroken and embarrassed, I channel those unwanted feelings into building up my frustration instead. "Then what did you mean?"

"Well, they *are* why you've returned, aren't they? To uncover the truth about their deaths?"

Hayliel's gasp is subtle and soft, kept more to herself than anything, but sitting beside her, I hear it clear as day. She stares at me expectantly, waiting for me to take the bait. But I've been given false hope before. Dozens—if not hundreds—of times. No answer she could possibly give me could be worth it again.

Better to remember them fondly, as they were, and to remember their deaths as I choose to, where neither killed the other but where they are both victims.

"We came to ask you about the legend of the neko," I say

sharply.

My aunt blanches. "Altúyur forbid...you shouldn't talk about such things."

"Why not? We used to talk about them all the time."

She scoffs. "Yes, well, that was before all those poor children died."

"What do you mean?" There's a pang in my chest. I can't help but wonder if I knew any of them, if some of the ones who died were the same blurry faces present in almost all of my childhood memories.

"That's awful," Hayliel says, breathless. "What happened?"

"There was a group of them who spent their days daring one another to go have a look, to see if they would be the one to prove the legend's truth and save the neko. Thirteen deaths in two weeks. It became so bad that a Reaper started living at the cave's entrance, just waiting for more reckless, foolish souls to try their luck." She pauses, bringing a shaking cup of cider to her lips and sips on it. "Why in all of Tayaraan would you come all this way to ask about the legend of the neko?"

There is no time for subtlety. Even if there was, I'm too annoyed now to care for it.

"Because after I was sent to Azarrac City, I killed a man. I became a Reaper." Her gasp makes me pause, but only for a moment. "A few days ago, I... I guess you could say I escaped. I became a Guardian to a little girl—the last soul I was meant to take to Veltuur—but she is not just any person. She is a Prophet, and she foretold a series of events that begins with me saving the neko."

Slowly, my aunt blinks, her head swaying a little. Every one of the things I told her about would be shocking enough for anyone. Mortals don't seem to have any knowledge of the Guardians, nor of Prophets, nor that a Reaper can "escape," not to mention that my aunt likely didn't even know I ever was one.

She sets her cider down, freeing her hands to rub at her temples. "I'm not sure I'm following all of this... You were a Reaper?"

I scowl at Hayliel, a silent plea for help.

She lays a calming hand on my knee, licks her lips. "She was a Reaper, but that's not what's important right now. We know it's a lot to take in. I'm still trying to figure it out myself. But we are trying to save someone else from the same fate, another Reaper trapped in Veltuur. According to the prophecy, we need the neko to save him."

"So," I start. "Do you, or do you not, know where we can find it?"

My aunt just shakes her head. I don't think she's stopped shaking it since I told her I had been a Reaper. "You cannot just skip over all of the details like that. I have questions."

Without further warning. she launches into a litany of them, and I should've known better than to give anyone so insistent and chatty, let alone my aunt, so many details. We spend the next hour addressing each one of her confusions, but my answers often lead her to more questions. *How did you become a Reaper? How did you escape? Who's your Prophet? The prince has a sister? What's a Guardian?*

A heavy sigh precludes her next question. "So the prince is in Veltuur now?"

"I'm afraid so," Hayliel murmurs, her head falling. "But you see, that's why we need to find the neko. We believe that Gem's vision was showing us how to save him."

My aunt grabs another oatcake from the table, silently biting into it as she thinks. "You really think you can save him?"

"They helped me, didn't they?" I say with a shrug. "I don't see why I couldn't return the favor."

"I suppose they did. But this is Veltuur, dear. The underrealm. I'm not sure anyone living has ever gone there, and if they have, I don't think they've come back."

It's not something I've allowed myself to consider yet, but she makes a fair point. The vision Gem shared with me ended once we reached the gate to Veltuur. Nothing came after it. Perhaps that's because nothing does. Perhaps that's where things end for me.

But I can't let that deter me.

"You don't understand, Aunt Theffania. It's my fault he's there." She and Hayliel both try launching into reassuring me it isn't, but I barrel through them. "It is. I fled the Guardians when they told me about my crow. I abandoned him, giving him no other choice but to do the one thing he knew would save his sister. If I had been less selfish, if I had been more willing to see that he and his sister were far more important to me than some stupid crow, he wouldn't be a Reaper now.

"I owe it to him to try to save him. Without Acari, I would still be in Veltuur myself."

My aunt worries at her lip, silence stretching over the room as the weight of our predicament sets over us.

Finally, after what feels like eons, Theffania claps her hands on her knees. "All right. It goes against my better judgment, but if you say this little princess saw your victory in a vision, then I suppose I have nothing to fear."

I don't dare correct her to say that I saw no apparent *victory*, but I'll make sure to spare Hayliel from any potential demise that might be awaiting us on the other side of that gate in Kallinei.

"I will tell you what you need to know about the neko. As you might recall, the cave is off Nadina Isle, along the Starry Reef. At high tide, it is completely engulfed, but when the waves pull back out to sea, the cave's entrance can be spotted from Lover's Wharf. I know you already know this, but I wouldn't be a good aunt if I didn't warn you about getting caught anywhere near the cave at high tide. You'd be trapped inside. Drowned."

"I know, Aunt Theffania. We'll be careful."

"We have prophecy on our side," Hayliel adds with a reassuring smile.

Despite it, my aunt still has her doubts, but to her credit, she says nothing more of them. Instead, she ushers Hayliel into the back room to try on a pair of trousers left behind by her late husband. When they return, I have to stifle a laugh.

"You said you wouldn't laugh," Hayliel protests.

"When did I say that? And I'm not laughing, I just...it's

different."

"I feel so ridiculous in this. I look like a man."

I'm about to tell her that she, of all people, could *never* look like a man, when my aunt walks in behind her and guffaws. "Better to look like a man and survive, than to dress in skirts and drown because you're sodden, dear." Theffania taps the tip of Hayliel's nose once for emphasis, before rounding the seating area and gesturing back to the table. "Are you sure you two don't need anything else? You could bring some oatcakes with you for the road?"

"I think we're okay," I tell her at first, but then my stomach grumbles. "Okay, maybe a few."

She beams a satisfied smile and gathers what's left of the oatcakes in a cloth napkin. I stuff it into my bag and walk to the door. We step outside, the air remarkably cooler compared to the warmth from her hearth.

"And will I be seeing you again, niece?" I open my mouth to answer her, but she buries me into her bosom before I can say a word. "It's all right. Your face already says it all. If you do ever find yourself back in Kalápana though, know that you always have a place here, dear."

Hayliel and I walk along the pier, headed back to where we first departed from Rhet and the others. There's a part of me that actually hopes we will run into them again. This task of ours would feel a lot more achievable if we had more help. Then again, what we're about to do will be dangerous, and I for one do not want to rope anyone else in.

When we reach the bridge that connects Kalápana and Nadina Isle, Hayliel slows. I just assume she's nervous about crossing a bridge that's so precariously suspended over the high drop, or worried it won't be stable enough for us to cross safely, so I charge forward to show her that everything is all right.

"It's nothing to fear. Dozens cross this bridge every day—"

But when I spin around after a few steps in, I find she's not looking at the bridge. She's not looking at me at all.

Lips parted, her gaze has drifted to the pier ahead of her, past the bridge. I follow her wide eyes to a young man in a red tunic leaning against the railing, black hair rippling over his head with the gentle ocean breeze.

Hayliel looks at me. "Acari?"

The name pulls his attention back from the starry depths below. He follows it to Hayliel, confused on sight. He doesn't recognize her. He can't. Memories of her is just one of the many casualties of his initiation to the underrealm.

It's easy to see the pain it gives her, to know that he does not know her at all anymore, but if I thought she was in agony before, it only becomes worse when he notices me on the bridge.

"Sinisa?"

Heat floods through me until I am certain my face is on fire. I tell myself it's just because it's awkward for him to recognize me and not Hayliel, but as I watch him push himself off the railing, I find myself drawn to the determination with which he moves. There's a confidence to him that wasn't there before. Even when he trips over his own feet, he corrects his fall in stride, unabashed by the quirk that has somehow always made him endearing. He's more self-assured than I think he's ever been, and it's difficult not to see that being a Reaper somehow actually suits him.

A crooked smile inches up his face and I burn hotter.

As he draws near, he speaks over the crashing of the waves, his voice bubbling with wonderment. "What are you—How are you—Why do I keep running into you? Why do I even remember you when I can remember nothing else?"

Hayliel follows close behind him, head bowed but not enough to hide the disappointment in her face. She fidgets with the brown trousers the entire way across the bridge, as if pulling on them will make them feel more natural to her.

"I could ask you the same thing," I say to Acari, coolly, naturally, like nothing has changed between us these last few days, even though *everything* has. "Taking one of those infamous Reaper strolls?"

He snorts a laugh. I didn't expect him to be able to do that still, to laugh, to find enjoyment in anything other than killing. The entire time I was a Reaper I'm not sure I ever laughed, not a true one anyway. Not until I met him.

For a moment, I start to doubt whether he will even want to be saved. If he's happy, if he's able to smile, then perhaps this life is better for him? After all, if he became mortal again, he'd have the throne waiting for him, and he never wanted to be king anyway.

But when his smile fades at the sight of his crow—his *father*— soaring overhead like the watchful eyes of the Councilspirits, I remind myself that no one would choose the torture of spending eternity with the person they murdered hovering over them.

Caw, the crow cries, landing on the rail beside us. Out of spite, I almost squawk back, but I stop myself when I remember that he is not the vile abuser that my crow was.

Acari sighs, long and forlorn. "I guess I *should* be getting back. We just came to see the reef. Well, that and to take the soul of a dying man, but I mean, we came *here* to see the reef. Back at the palace, they're probably wondering where we've been all day."

"What did you just say?" Hayliel nearly chokes out the words, and I can't tell if she's appalled by his reasons for being here, or if she's as surprised as I am to hear him talking about the palace. She looks from him to me. "You never mentioned a palace in the underrealm."

Shaking my head, I give her the only answer I can. "That's because there is no palace."

As he reaches for the back of his neck, head buried in the crook of his arm, Hayliel and I stare wide-eyed at the sigil pinned on his shoulder.

"You were crowned king," I breathe.

"King?" Hayliel gasps. "How is that possible?"

Caw-caw, the bird beside us protests. I don't have to be able to understand it to know that the king—the *former* king, I should say —is still not pleased with how his son came to claim the throne.

"I was just as surprised about it as you are," Acari says, bashfully. "The Councilspirits decided it would be too much for the kingdom to lose both their king and their heir in the same day."

"So they let you stay in Oakfall?" I ask, bewildered and maybe slightly envious. I've never known the Councilspirits to allow a Reaper to stay in Tayaraan longer than was necessary. Then again, I guess I've never known a Reaper who was also King.

Frowning, he nods. "Yeah. I return to Veltuur every morning for my orders, and then I spend the rest of the day at the palace. Although, today when we finished here, I wasn't ready to go back yet." His eyes flit up to mine. "Can I ask you something? Did I want to be king when I was still, you know, mortal?"

The change in subject is so human, so innocent, it's hard to believe he's even a Reaper. It makes me wonder just how much the underrealm changes a person. Maybe my initiation isn't what made me so cold and heartless. Maybe I have always just been that way. Or maybe that's just the way the cruel world molded me to be.

But Acari, he was a butterfly on a spring day. His heart was so full of compassion that maybe Veltuur's darkness couldn't quite snuff *all* of it out.

"No," I answer him with an emphatic laugh. "As far as I could tell, being king was the last thing you wanted."

Out of the corner of my eye, I see Hayliel nodding. She's put on the same pitiful expression Acari always wore when speaking of his former life at the palace.

The new king assesses me for a moment, the blacks of his eyes as dark as any night in Veltuur. But even though Acari has taken to his role so seamlessly—the sudden confidence with which he carries himself, the ease with which he talks about claiming the souls of the dying—it still doesn't feel like Veltuur quite has its claws in him. In some ways, he's still the Acari I met, the goofy, kind young man who wanted nothing to do with the throne waiting for him.

"What *did* I want then?" he asks, shifting his eyes to the wooden rungs below our feet. "I mean, if we were friends—which I'm not even sure I understand since you were a Reaper, and I was a prince, and now you're *not* a Reaper but I am, but now I'm also a king, so... it's all rather complicated."

Another dry laugh escapes me. "You don't even know the half of it."

"Yeah, that's kind of the problem," he says with a sigh.

Watching him, I bite my lip. Aulow had said it would be difficult to break the news to him, that he might not be ready. Our quest has always been to get to Veltuur, to free him once we were there, but looking at Acari now, he seems ready to me. Maybe we don't need to go all the way to the underrealm to save him.

But Aulow had also said that too much information could scare him away. It could make him flee deeper into himself or to the underrealm.

I have to believe in Gem's prophecy. I have to believe that all of these tasks are leading us to the point in time when Acari will be most likely to let go, and not a moment sooner, no matter how badly I want to strangle his crow and rip him free from the Councilspirits, forever.

Still, it doesn't mean I can't plant the seeds now though. Every interaction we have, every bit of information I can give him, might help us down the road.

My hand grazes the dangling pouch at my hip, and an idea strikes.

"What's that?" Acari asks as I untie the small bag from my belt.

Hayliel gasps. "That's a wonderful idea! With the memory leaves he can—"

I silence her with a glare. My conversation with Aulow at the camp had been brief, but she'd made one thing clear: we needed to take care when approaching any of this with Acari. I know first-hand how jarring new memories can be.

"It used to be yours," I tell him softly. Reaching inside of the pouch, I pluck out a single leaf, yellowed and drying. "You asked me what you wanted before you became a Reaper. I can't give you that, but this might help you with something else. It'll give you some of the answers you've been seeking."

"A leaf?"

I smile wanly. "Not just any leaf. It's from the last memory tree, the one in the Forbidden Garden at the palace."

Caw!

Acari glares at the crow, losing his patience. "Just a minute."

But the bird has no more patience to give either.

It leaps from the railing and flies straight toward me. I flail backward, the leaf slipping from my hand and drifting over the railing and into the ocean below. Tripping over a raised board, I stumble farther, falling to my rear and knocking the remaining contents of the bag onto the bridge. Most of them sift between the boards to disappear into the crashing waves.

If I had any purpose for them, I might start scrambling to salvage what's left. All I care about is helping Acari, and before I can crawl to my hands and knees to retrieve the remnants of the memory leaves, blackness begins to build around the boy in red, the king, my friend, Acari.

"No!" he yells. "Not yet!"

"Acari!" Hayliel and I shout in unison.

But the smoke continues to coalesce and darken, Acari's crow croaking at him furiously.

They're trying to stop us, I realize. Whether it's his crow, or the Council, or the Wraiths, or whoever, they don't want Acari to know anything else about who he was before he was a Reaper. They're terrified that I just might help him leave Veltuur.

And that, in and of itself, is enough to make me all the more determined to do so.

Before he can vanish completely, I yell across the bridge. "The memory tree is in the Forbidden Garden! Make a tea! Focus on a memory!"

Then, just like that, he's gone.

15

BLESSINGS
ACARI

"**T**here you are," are the first words I hear as a new scene materializes around me.

I expect to arrive in the dark confines of the under-realm, to fill my lungs with the dense fog that's always present in the forest there, but instead I find myself blinded by the dazzling gold gilding, the pristine marble floors, and the peach curtains of the Halaud Palace.

Captain Borgravid crosses the ornately decorated hallway, green cape billowing behind him like it's a force all its own. But none compared to the captain himself. "The palace has been looking all over for you. First, you were absent for the Face of Pecolock, and now you're—"

I wave him off, mind still reeling from Sinisa's last words. I can have the answers I've been seeking with just a single memory leaf. The only problem is Sidian whisked us away before it was mine. But I haven't lost all hope. Sinisa already told me where I could find more, and if I can just get my bearings and figure out where I am in the palace, I can figure out how to make it to the Forbidden Garden.

The statues lining every wall are a dead giveaway.

No hall is more devoted to inspiration than Peacock Court.

"Why did you take us here?" I growl at Sidian. "The garden is halfway across the palace."

Pushing past the both of them, I head for the door. Not the closest one, but the one that will lead me to the Forbidden Garden first. Sinisa's instructions still echo through me, but I'm afraid if I wait, I'll forget part of them. Or worse, lose my brazen curiosity.

It's time I find out what really happened that night. It's time I learn if this was the life I truly wanted.

"Acari, stop," Borgravid commands.

Despite being king, it's as effective on me as it would be if I were one of his soldiers. I halt in the doorway, though my feet itch to keep moving.

"It's the Festival of Wings. A king can't just disappear all morning like that."

"I'm a Reaper. My duty lies with Veltuur first."

"That's not what you told the people during your coronation. You made a vow to serve them, to protect them, to honor their celebrations." Unwavering, he crosses the room, his steps echoing up the decorated walls. "I am no advisor, but if I were, I'd remind you that your people are still unsettled by having a Reaper on the throne."

"You think I don't already know that?"

He holds a hand up. "No, I'm sure you do. But you haven't been acting like it."

"How should I act like it?" I ask, exasperated and wanting him to get to the point. "Please, tell me how I should act like I'm an outsider leading a kingdom that doesn't want me? Because I thought that was exactly how I was acting."

Borgravid glares at my outburst, daring me to go on. I don't.

He straightens, as if he already wasn't large and intimidating enough. "Your actions are separating you even further from your people. Would your job not be easier with their devotion and respect?"

It feels like the obvious answer, but I give it to him anyway. "Yes?"

"And have your actions—disappearing during festivities where a king's presence is expected—have those garnered any trust or respect from your citizens?"

Hesitantly, I answer, "No?"

Satisfied, Borgravid stands there, crossing his arms as if to say he's made his point. Which he has. I've done little to prove myself to an already weary kingdom. Every chance I've had to flee from my responsibilities here, I've taken. And though I could argue that it's partially not my fault since Veltuur summons me as I am needed, I did linger at the Coast of Dreams far longer than was necessary today.

"I don't know how to be both," I admit at last. And I know I'm ridiculous for saying it, but it's the truth. To avoid eye contact, I watch my boot as I toe a crack in the marble floor. "I know it's only been a few days, but this is already too much. Every day I jump back and forth from one role to the other, from Reaper to king, and it's exhausting. I'm not doing either job well."

He claps a hand on my back. The force of it makes me stumble forward, and I chuckle. "There you go again with your displays of affection. Aren't you afraid I'll kill you?"

His smile is mischievous and challenging, but his tone remains as warm as a hearth. "Only your skin can harm me, not this dingy cut of fabric you Reapers call a robe."

"Hey," I stammer, my jaw popping in false offense. "It's called a tunic."

After a moment, we both burst into laughter. I haven't laughed like this in...well, I can't remember when since I don't remember much, but I get the feeling that it's been a long, *long* while. Borgravid, too, sounds as if joy is foreign to his throat. But I can tell by the way he lets himself get carried away with it that he's been craving the release just as much as I was.

Giving my back another hearty pat, Borgravid turns away, beckoning me in the opposite direction. "Come. There's still time to get you ready for the Ceremony of Blessings."

My first instinct is to groan. My second, to duck out the door and vanish down the corridor before he can say anything else, is equally as enticing.

But, before I can succumb to the second—already having groaned loud enough to wake half the kingdom—I remember the advice he'd given me just moments prior.

It's true that I don't know how to be a Reaper King, but I'm also stuck doing it, at least for the time being. So, the real question I have to ask myself is whether I want to make things more difficult, on myself and everyone else, and suffer through the years or not. Do I want to continue falling short on my responsibilities and spend all of my extra time repairing the damage I've done to my reputation with the Council and to my people?

The answer to that is a resounding no.

If I am to be stuck straddling both realms, I'd prefer everything to run smoothly.

If this is to be my life now, I need to make this work. If the Festival of Wings is the most important celebration to my citizens, then the Forbidden Garden will have to wait. After all, the people need their Blesser of Compassion—a title which I will refrain from informing them is quite ironic to bestow upon a Reaper.

If anything, it is them who I hope to gain blessings from.

With Sidian already gliding ahead, I too follow Borgravid to the temple.

16

SACRIFICES

SINISA

"Sinisa, did you hear him? Did you hear what he said about being king?"

Crouched over the boards, I nod before gathering what's left of the memory tree leaves.

"How is that possible though?" Hayliel demands, her voice as tumultuous as the ocean itself. "How can he be king?"

"I don't know," I admit, just as confused by the discovery as she is.

I shove the leaves back into their pouch and stand to tie it at my waist. When I finally look to her, wetness trickles down her cheeks.

"He didn't recognize me. We've known each other almost all of our lives, and he didn't recognize me. Maybe if I had stayed at the palace—"

"He still wouldn't have recognized you, and you'd be stuck there, helplessly watching him live a life that you thought you could save him from."

She sniffles, pats her cheeks with her fingers. "Thank you. You're right. Being his handmaiden now when he doesn't even remember me would be unbearable." She's silent as we finish crossing the bridge, all the way until we take our first steps onto

Nadina Isle. "He recognized you," she says, a whisper of jealousy tinging the edges of her words. "He knew you last night too, didn't he?"

"He only remembers me because I was there during his final moments as a mortal."

Hayliel catches my hand into hers, spinning me around to face her. "I'm so sorry. I have no right to be upset at you for who he does or doesn't remember."

"It's fine," I say, shrugging my hand from hers. "Let's just get to Lover's Wharf and find the cave. That's the best way to help him get his memories back."

Night falls swiftly over the crashing waves. Soon it'll be nearly impossible to discern the horizon from the swirling, shimmering shades of the sea. But neither Hayliel nor I marvel at the magnificent sunset. Our eyes are trained instead along the craggy cliffside of Nadina Isle.

Leaning over the pier on Lover's Wharf, Hayliel cranes to get a better view of the coastline below us. "Is it high tide now? Maybe we can't find the cave's entrance because the ocean's already covering it."

I shake my head. "The sailor said it won't be high tide until the moon reaches the center of the sky."

"And when will that be?"

Averting my gaze skyward, I squint at the pale moon that shines against the dark blue sky. It's in the same position it was when we first reached the pier, still climbing its way through the clouds, and still devouring the last shades of the sun's pink rays.

But I am no sailor. I have no idea how long it takes for the moon to complete its nightly conquest of the sky.

"We'll be fine," I say to her, hoping to curb any doubts she's having since I can't curb my own. "We still have a few hours, at least."

I hope.

We return to our respective examinations of the sparkling black beaches that contour the coastline, but all I see are rocks, seafoam, and strings of seaweed.

"Wait. Over there! I think I see it! Look, Sinisa!"

Leaving my half of the ledge and the nothingness I was finding, I join Hayliel to peer down at the beach. Just below a field of wildflowers, there's a cove on this side of Lover's Wharf, one that has created its own little sheltered pool with a large boulder in the center that's shaped like a heart. Even now, a few of the locals hike down the path through the tall grass to reach the beach where they'll join the others climbing up the boulder's jagged edges and leaping into the waters that glisten like they are full of stars.

Hayliel points past the cove that gives Lover's Wharf its name, past the rocks that give it its privacy from the ocean, to a jagged cliff of rocks.

"There. You see it?"

Squinting, I stick out my neck farther. "No. I don't see any—" But then, leaning so far out that I'm afraid I might fall, I catch sight of the dark hollow at the base of the cliffs. Joyous laughter brightens my voice. "You're right. That's got to be it."

"We really did it," she breathes.

My eyebrows knit together, and I tilt my head, ready to remind Hayliel that finding the cave was only the first of many tasks in fulfilling Gem's prophecy, but when I see her triumphant smile and the glow in her cheeks, I close my mouth and let her relish the moment. It might be the last one we have for a while.

"Now all we need to do is get down there," she says when she steps away from the pier's edge.

"Well, well, well," a silvery, feminine tone calls from behind us. "Look who missed us so much that they couldn't bear being away from us."

Already recognizing the voice, I turn around to greet our friends.

"Bels!" Hayliel cries, racing toward the woman with her arms outstretched. She repeats the gesture with each and every one of them, down the line until she reaches a new face. "Oh! You must be the new Prophet."

Rhet growls, eyeing the people passing us by. "Mind what you say. There are ears all around us."

"M-my apologies." Shuffling backward, Hayliel retreats until she is cowering beside me like a scolded pup.

There's something about seeing him reprimand her that grates against me. I step forward until I am square with Rhet, my nose barely coming to his chest.

"Why?" I ask, and once I do, the questions continue rolling, ones I didn't even realize I had. "Why does it matter who knows about the Prophets? Or the Guardians for that matter. Why is it such a secret? Why does no one seem to know about us or how to save Reapers from themselves?"

Rhet's glare deepens as I roar, but when I finish, I can tell by the way he's looking at me that he's trying to determine whether he needs to give me an answer or not, whether I'll leave it alone.

Mimicking him and his intimidating posture, I cross my arms and hope it conveys just how determined I am to stand my ground on this matter.

Before he can either walk away or answer me, a hand rests upon my shoulder. When I turn, I expect to find Hayliel, so I'm surprised when instead I come face-to-face with another man's chest.

"Most of those who dwell in the realm of Tayaraan are unable to remember the Guardians, for reasons unknown." Dethoc continues like he's reciting a legend of old. "Even once they are told of one, they soon forget of their existence again."

Suddenly, I remember what it was like traveling with Acari, how sometimes he would seem so focused on his quest, and then other times like he had forgotten what it was he was searching for. I'd always just assumed it was part of who he was, or perhaps that he'd been so distraught about his sister that it made him distracted.

"What about Hayliel? Why does she remember then?"

"Actually," Hayliel grimaces. "There have been a few times I've forgotten. I still knew who you were, and I always remembered that you were once a Reaper, but it's like…sometimes the Guardian stuff just drifts away. Like a cloud. Only, it takes someone else saying something to remind me that the cloud is still here and didn't actually drift away with the wind."

Dethoc nods. "People who spend enough time around us are better able to retain their knowledge of the Guardians for longer, but we think that's mostly because they are confronted by our existence so frequently that they don't have an opportunity to forget."

"Okay? None of this explains why we keep ourselves a secret though. If anything, it's all the more reason to tell people we exist. We could even live among them instead of in some secluded village in the woods, that way they couldn't forget."

I don't know where the argument is coming from or why I suddenly feel so strongly about it, but I'm more startled by my use of the word *we*, so I decide not to hold anything back. I'm tired of not knowing about the things that impact me anyway. I'm tired of all of the secrets and half-truths. For once, I'd just like to feel like things around me made sense, like I'm not following people who don't have my best interests at heart.

"They would though," Rhet insists, curt and foreboding. "Eventually, one way or another, most of them would forget about us and we would have to start from the very beginning again. There aren't enough of us to be in constant presence of every person in Tayaraan.

"But that's neither here nor there. None of us care if the realm knows of our existence. But Tayaraan still abides by the Law of Mother's Love, a decree that permits the infanticide of those born with abnormalities. It was a law created out of fear for the power that the Prophets held, and yet, even though most don't know about their power any longer, they still uphold the law. Fortunately, there are some who take pity on the newborns, who keep their hearing loss and clubbed feet a secret as long as they can, but the number is small, and it would be even smaller if they knew the power they would one day grow into.

"We stay hidden to fulfill our greatest duty of all: protecting the

Prophets, and all the others we save. Even if we told all of the realm who we were and who the Prophets were, they would still hunt us down until every last Prophet was killed."

I'm about to ask how the people would send Reapers after Prophets who had already earned the protection of a Guardian, when I notice Rhet and Dethoc exchange a look. Dark shadows cross over the two of them, and it becomes painstakingly obvious that the scenario that I thought was hypothetical isn't at all. I remember what Rory had said, about the two of them being on their own until they finally found Aulow and her people. I wonder what they did until then. Would they have tried to live among the people? Would they have traveled from one town to the next whenever their neighbors had grown too anxious about living in such close proximity to a boy whose existence was forbidden?

"It's best that they think we are bandits stealing their young," Rhet growls at last, ending the conversation.

Something bitter bites into me. What a shame it is that the world will never really know what types of sacrifices these Guardians have made for people who otherwise would've been unjustly slain. They don't even do it for the glory. They do it for duty, something I understand all too well.

"So," Rory sings awkwardly, trying to redirect the conversation. "I don't see a cute, furry, little neko in your hands. You two still searching for the cave?"

Without missing a beat, Hayliel brightens. "Actually, we found it just before you walked up. It's down there, just past the cove below us."

"Speaking of, we should get going," I say, and start walking toward the path that I know leads down to the enclosed waters.

But Hayliel's voice rings over mine. "Since you've found the Prophet, maybe now you could help us."

When they don't instantly deny her, I turn back around to find them glancing among themselves, silently trying to determine which one of them is going to volunteer for the task.

But no one does. I can't say I blame them. They just saved yet another Prophet, one whom I don't see a Reaper attached to, which means that he too will only be safe back at the village. They've only completed part of their task. The rest is to see him home safely. Anything else is a distraction.

"Well, if none of you will do it, I will," Belsante says, flipping her dark hair out of her face with a huff. "But then someone will have to figure out a way to explain to Aulow why I went down to Lover's Wharf with two other beautiful women."

His arms already crossed, Rhet rolls his eyes. "I'll go."

"But what about Gilliame?" Hayliel asks, a hand to her mouth.

"He will be fine." Bending to one knee, Rhet faces the boy beside him and pats his shoulder for reassurance.

Dethoc breathes a reluctant sigh. "No, I'll go."

Abruptly, Rhet stands to face the man. Though he tries to whisper, his voice is still too resonant to be stifled. "What about your son?"

"He has you to protect him."

"I'm not talking about protection. A boy needs his father—"

"And a Prophet needs his Guardian," Dethoc counters. "Maybe even more so."

Gilliame protests, throwing himself against his father's waist and wrapping his arm around him. Since Dethoc's mind is already made up, there's little comfort to be given by the rest of us, and so the others walk toward us to give the father and son some space.

"I guess that means I'm coming too," Rory adds cheerfully, warranting a pout from Belsante who seems to honestly wish she could've come. Were Aulow here with us, I think she would. But she's already spent a night away from her, already risked her life to save not one, but two Prophets, and I don't blame her for wanting to return home to the woman she loves rather than risking her life yet again. Once is enough for a day.

"You don't have to," I tell Rory.

But she waves a hand at me and blows through her lips. "Nonsense. Dethoc is right. A Prophet needs his Guardian."

She winks at me, and I realize she's just using Dethoc as an excuse. If he hadn't volunteered, she would've come with us anyway.

Hand-in-hand, Dethoc and Gilliame return to us, and the boy gives us his blessing to have his father's aid. For the second time that day, we say our farewells before departing on separate paths, one group headed back to the encampment and safety, the other to a dark cave that could mean the death of us all.

17

CAVE OF DEATH

SINISA

We follow the winding path, through fields of yarrow, fireweed, and salal, until we reach the secluded cove below Lover's Wharf. Those who had been diving from the rocks to swim in the dark waters have cleared for the day as it has settled into night, so no one watches us approaching the cliffs, and no one warns us about the danger of going into the cave just beyond.

The gentle onyx sands become more rugged as we walk, until we are staggering through a hill of rocks and boulders. What little conversation was being shared between Hayliel, Dethoc, and Rory ends as the four of us shift our focus to ensuring our balance. They become so quiet in fact that all I hear is the lulling breaths of the waves, and on more than one occasion, I pause to look behind me to see if my travel companions are still there.

With only the moon to light our way, we have to rely on other senses. I crouch as I climb, my hands acting as my guides. They land first on the rocks ahead of me, scoping out the craggy terrain before I decide where to scale next. Still, it proves more challenging than I expected. My feet slip often on the wet, sometimes slimy rocks, and I am not the only one to slam my knees into their jagged edges.

I reach the top of the rocky crest first. Hayliel, Rory, and Dethoc are not too far behind. As I gaze triumphantly at the cave just on the other side of the cliff, we set our packs down. Once we're inside, if we encounter deep waters, the packs could weigh us down.

It's so dark now that the only reason the cave is still visible is because of the hundreds of glowing creatures that have collected along the coastline, and even in the cave itself. Glow stars, one of the main sources of this reef's name. They illuminated the dark waters like stars burning in the sky.

"Almost there." Even winded, Hayliel still sounds more spirited than I am when I'm not exerting myself.

We turn our backs to the cave and descend the other side for the final stretch of this trek.

At the bottom, our feet dip into the cool, purple waters up to our ankles. I don't have to be a sailor to know that the tide is already coming in and that our time is dwindling. But after running into Acari yesterday on the wharf, I say nothing of my concerns. Seeing the way his crow fazed him away the moment before I could give him the memory leaves, there's no doubt in my mind that the Councilspirits will do whatever it takes to keep us apart. By now, they surely know we're on our way. They probably already sent him to the Wraiths just for conversing with me, a known fugitive of the underrealm.

In Gem's vision, there was no explicit mention of time, but I feel the urgency regardless, and so, we wade across the bay and into the cave, the ocean foaming at our heels.

"Now what?" Rory asks as we enter, plucking one of the bioluminescent glow stars from the cave wall with a loud suctioning pop.

"Now," I say, doing the same. "We find the neko."

With a glow star in my hand, I hold it overhead to get a better look inside the dimly lit grotto.

The cavern walls ripple with reflection and texture, like they've been molded from the waves for centuries, each crash adding a new layer to the deepening cave. We wander in, the water tapering off at our feet once we've passed the entrance. I know better than to think we're safe here. The tide isn't too far behind, and soon the ocean will seep farther and farther into the cave.

I stop at a ledge to kick off a strip of seaweed that's collected at my boot. It's a short jump down that will surely lead us deeper. Once the tide comes, the most dangerous place to be will be deeper down. As the waters come in, they'll fill the deepest places first, so we should try to stay on high ground. But this is the only way to go. And we've already come this far. We can't turn back now. Not without the neko.

With a glow star overhead, I turn to face my party, casting their faces in a dull blue shine. "We have to go down, so let's be quick."

Rory takes the leap first, followed by Dethoc. While the two of them help Hayliel descend next, my gaze catches on a figure in black at the cave's mouth. The Shade raises his head, hood falling back to reveal a pale, familiar face that gleams in the luminescent light like seafoam.

Nerul's grin is malicious, and it takes everything in me not to scream at him, to tell him to leave us alone and go rot in the pits of Veltuur where he belongs. But then his presence and its meaning hits me. Most soul-collection is left to the Reapers. However it's not unheard of for a Shade to collect on contracts, especially those that others have already failed.

My eyes fall below to my companions waiting for me to join them, to Rory who never completed her collection of Dethoc's soul, to Hayliel who fled the palace after the king's murder. He could be here for either one of them. He could be here for me.

Or, maybe he's just come to try and deter us. After all, the Council has already made it abundantly clear that they don't want me helping Acari. Nerul might just be a ruse to distract me from my path.

I have to believe that's why he's here, as a taunt, as a scare tactic.

"Are you coming?" Rory calls up, a quirk to her smile.

My companions didn't see him, and if I don't want them to

know, then they won't. They won't have to worry about what his presence means and which one of them could die.

"Yeah," I say quickly, turning my back to Nerul and hopping below.

My feet are immersed once more in cold water, my knees aching from the impact.

Rory smacks the glow star against her palm. "Flightless bird. I can barely see anything with this thing."

As I straighten, I see she's not wrong. Down here there are fewer of the invertebrates to light our way and the path is too wide to contain what little luminescence is coming from the glow stars we hold in our hands.

"I could go back up. Get some more glow stars?" Dethoc offers. "It wouldn't be hard to climb—"

"No!" I blurt, thinking of what any of them will do when they see Nerul. They look to me, startled and confused. "We should keep moving. The tide is coming in, and when it does, the bottom level of the cave will fill up before the top. We don't want to be down here longer than we have to. We can manage with what we have."

"Okay," Rory sings. "But if I bump my head on any of those sharp pointy rocks hanging from the ceiling and I become unconscious, you better carry me back out."

"Of course," Dethoc answers her loyally. I hear the love in his voice and wonder if Gem and I will ever reach that level of closeness.

Rory leads us through the cave's channels, the water deepening and lowering and deepening again as we traverse the innerworkings of the cave that are as everchanging as the sea itself. We enter expansive caverns, slide between jagged rocks that have almost entirely blocked parts of the cave from others, all the while following the mewling call of the legend that I grew up so familiar with.

I wonder what the neko looks like. If it's just like the pets I've seen, the ones I've helped cross over to the underrealm, or if it's somehow mutated. Living for years in the darkest depths of a sea cave has to have side effects, right? Maybe it's gone blind? Maybe it's grown a set of gills? Or maybe, it's nothing like I'm imagining at all...

The damp air becomes thicker, staler like it's been trapped down here for decades. The deeper we go, the less I can hear the crashing waves outside, which is both calming and unsettling. It means we have no way of knowing if and when the cave will start filling, no way of knowing how much time we have left.

But without the constant howling of the ocean, a new sound becomes audible.

A gust coming from deeper still carries with it a quiet whine.

"Do you hear that?" Hayliel asks, bubbling with excitement. "We're getting close."

I nod, charging forward to take the lead.

Around the corner, the path rises and the ceiling narrows, until the two of them very nearly touch.

Rory curses. "Now what? It's a dead end."

Shaking my head, I race across the chamber to the steep slope. Another draft of stale air wafts across my face. "No, it isn't. There's an opening up there. Someone push me up," I yell over my shoulder, already scrambling against the bumpy surface.

Rory's behind me first. "By the dove, she's right. I can see it. There's a hole. It's small though. Are you sure you can fit through?"

"Yes, I'm sure." Despite expecting the cave's floor to be just as rocky as the entrance, inside the stones have been grinded away, formed by the ocean's hands until the floor and walls are smooth— if not a little lumpy. It makes for terrible footing, so I lay on my stomach. "Just give me a push. I can't reach it."

The others do as I ask and shove against my feet. I slide forward, fingers barely falling short from the opening.

"It's so close."

My voice echoes around me until I feel them pushing me again. There's not enough room to look behind me, but I hear someone grunting as they lay on the slanted wall and position my feet beneath their shoulders. With a heave, my heels press into them as I catapult forward.

My fingers grasp the edge of the hole and I pull myself forward. I can't see anything inside but darkness, but I feel the wind on my face, and I hear the whining that grows louder still. Looking forward, I nod and toss my glow star inside. To my relief it doesn't fall far, and when it does, it hits only dry ground.

"I'm going in," I tell the others.

"You can't go alone," Hayliel protests.

"She'll be fine," Rory grunts behind me. "Just make it quick. Yell if you need anything. If you can fit, so can I, and they can hoist me through if you need me."

Clutching the smooth ledge, I drag myself through the small space and plop onto the other side with an ungraceful thud.

"You all right in there?" Rory's voice echoes from the narrow channel.

"Yeah," I say, standing, clapping my hands on my thighs.

When I get to my feet, the first thing I do is retrieve my glow star. No matter how high I hold it though, this room is so massive that I can't see more than a few feet in front of me. I lower it instead so that I can see the floor, making sure I don't accidentally step through some unseen hole or shallow.

The low whine is intermittent, but frequent enough that it's easy to follow. It guides me forward, into the expansive cavern, growing louder with every step, like it wants me to find it.

I wonder how long the neko has been trapped in here, how it has survived all this time without food, with the coming and going of the tide. It's only then that I realize the floor isn't just not flooded, it's almost entirely dry. Perhaps that's how it's survived down here. Perhaps this chamber doesn't fill.

It might be useful information to hold on to, in case we need a backup plan.

But before I can file it away completely, up ahead something glints in the darkness.

It flickers in and out of existence and I stop dead in my tracks.

My skin turns cold. Whatever it is, it's much too high off the ground to be a cute, little neko.

The thing twinkles again, like an eye in the night.

I am not alone.

My heart thunders inside my chest. I tighten my grip on the glow star, the only weapon I have available, as if it will help me at all. Judging from the height of the thing that could be a blinking eye, whatever beast is in here with me is at least as tall as I am, probably far larger though given the expansive room.

"Neko?" I ask into the darkness.

As if in response, the thing glistens again, and this time I can tell that the shine is not coming from an eye at all. It's something metal, something swaying.

Caution softening my every step, I inch forward slowly until I can reach the dangling item.

When I grasp it in my hand, the whining stops.

I raise the glow star high enough to find that I'm holding a thick, rusty, iron key. I glance around the room once more, like I'll suddenly find the neko I was told all my childhood was down here, but of course, I find nothing. Staring at the key, I run my finger across the bow of it, where two feline ears perk up.

"It can't be," I utter, trailing my finger down the stem to two neko paws.

I blow through the top of the key to test a theory. I'm proven right when it whines, the same strained wail that led us all the way here.

All these years the people of Kalápana have believed that a living neko was trapped down in these caves. They were haunted by its constant mewling, confounded by its survival. Countless lives were risked coming to try save it, but all this time, all that was down here was this key.

"You've got to be kidding me…"

"Uh, I hate to rush you," Rory hollers from the hole. Her voice is far more unsteady than I want it to be. "But you might want to hurry up. It's getting pretty wet out here."

If Gem's vision hadn't sent us down here, looking at the key now I might've just ignored it, lazily regarded it as a lost treasure of the sea. But I know better. There's only one reason Gem's vision brought us here, and it's for this key. There's no doubt in my mind now that it will open the gate to Veltuur.

And so, I use the leather the neko key is hanging from to tie it around my neck and dash back toward the hole. Rory clears out of the way as I clamber back through, sliding down the bumpy slope until I reach the bottom. No one warns me to keep my mouth closed so I swallow a mouthful of seawater as I land, the room already having filled up to their shins. Rory mentioned the water starting to reach them back here, but I hadn't realized how badly it had become. We are running out of time.

Still coughing the saltwater from my lungs, Dethoc pulls me to my feet. "We should go."

Rory glares at him. "We didn't come all this way for nothing. I'll go back in. I can keep looking."

Confused, it takes me a moment to realize they don't know I found it. The key around my neck isn't obvious enough because they had been expecting me to return with a furry creature, claws digging into my arms.

"There's no need," I sputter, reaching for the key. "I found it already."

Rory shines her glow star on it. "*That's* it? That can't be right."

"Are you sure?" Hayliel adds, though she continues eyeing the cave's exit while her hands fidget with themselves at her chest. "You said Gem's vision was about a neko. Shouldn't it have...whiskers?"

"A tail," Rory adds, snappishly.

I shake my head. "This is what we were sent for, I'm sure. It has a neko on the top of it. It'll get us into Veltuur."

Rory scoffs, crossing her arms. "Well, someone sure got their legends wrong then."

When I notice the modest waterfall that's already pouring through our exit, panic beats through me. We're about to be trapped. Even now, if we turned around and fought our way back to the entrance, I'm not sure we'd make it.

I glance up the slope that led into the secret chamber where the key was kept. From what I can recall, the floors had been almost entirely dry in there.

"I don't think the water can reach inside," I say abruptly.

"You don't *think*?" Dethoc asks.

He's skeptical and rightly so. If we were to scramble inside, only to find out once this room fills that the water actually *does* pour inside, I will have backed us against a wall. We'd have no chance of escaping.

He leans past me to examine the slope, a thoughtful twist to his brow. When he pulls back, he's shaking his head. "Besides, it's too far up and the slope is too smooth. We'd have to help each other up just like we did with you, but then there'd be no one to help the last person climb. Someone would get left behind."

"That ain't happening," Rory scoffs. "Let's get going then. This room is about to become our aquatic grave if we don't move now."

She charges back the way we came, reaching one of the ledges we had to climb down. Water cascades from it, pummeling her in the face, but she scales the wall just as easily as she did the orphanage. She helps Hayliel up next, then me.

I hug the wall, burying my face into the frigid, pouring water as I reach up for her hand. Her fingers are slick, and it takes us a moment to get a good hold on each other, but when we do, she wastes no time in hoisting me up. Dethoc follows, tall enough that he doesn't need Rory's help, but being his Guardian, she still gives it. Once he's almost all the way up, she grabs his belt and hoists him the rest of the way.

Water crashes into the cave walls. It bounces from side to side, knocking each of us off-balance in turn while the cave guzzles down drink after drink. We run as best as we can while wading, slipping and sliding our way back out through the narrow channels and vast caverns.

We turn a corner just as another wave pours in. It barrels into me. My legs slide out from under me and I'm swallowed by the current. It slams me into the rock wall before knocking me into the next.

My head spins as disorientation takes hold. I can't tell up from down or left from right; rocks surround me on every side it seems. Everything is darkness.

But even if I could figure out which way was up, where I could find the air my lungs so desperately need, it's only now that I'm remembering I never learned to swim.

This is it.

This is why Nerul was here, to return to Veltuur with me so he can mock me for eternity.

Someone grips my shoulders. They yank me above water and my lungs nearly burst.

"I gotcha," Rory says, grunting from the effort.

Before I can slip again, I grab for her arms.

"You okay?" she yells over the roaring of the ocean.

I nod, still sputtering. She takes my hand, our fingers becoming a formidable knot, and starts pulling me forward. Now that I'm upright again, I notice that Dethoc and Hayliel are nowhere in sight. I can only hope it's because they're closer to the exit and not drowning somewhere behind us.

Rory shields her eyes as another wave crashes into us, the water chest-deep now. "The cave dips up ahead. We'll have to swim."

"I—I can't," I yell back.

She stops charging forward long enough to smack her forehead. "Flightless bird... you've got to be kidding. You grew up by the beach for crying out loud." Before I can explain myself, she continues. "All right. It's fine. We can do this. Just hold on to me. I can get us out."

She utters another curse, wading forward through the tumultuous waters.

"Take a deep breath," she yells, and it's all the warning I get before she bobs below, dragging me down with her.

Weightless, the current pulling against us, we move slower than

I expect. Slower than bodes well for either of us. Although I'm not sure if it helps, I kick my feet and scoop my free arm, the one that isn't locked in a death grip with hers. I blink against the sting of the saltwater, trying to discern anything around us, but everything is black, aside from a few glow stars speckled throughout the cavern she's swimming us through.

My lungs start to burn, but I clench my jaw. Nerul can't have the satisfaction. He just can't. I didn't come all this way—I didn't become a Guardian—just to die here like this.

I feel Rory tug me upward, the weight of the water flushing past me, and a second later, I surface with a rasping breath of air beside her.

My feet brush lightly against the floor beneath me, not enough to find stability, but enough to make me feel like I'm not about to be sucked back into the dark abyss we narrowly escaped.

"Easy," she croaks, swallowing some water. She spits it out and points. "There. Up ahead. We have to make our way to the entrance."

Blinking, I strain my eyes to see where she's pointing her glow star, and I can just barely make out a sliver of an opening. The cave is almost entirely flooded. We nearly didn't make it.

Rory flashes me a triumphant smile, one I return. Neither one of us are watching the cave's entrance, so we don't see the next wave that surges in. It smacks into us both, shoving us back into the wall behind us.

This time, I'm able to grab on to one of the jagged surfaces. My fingers peel against the rocks as they strain with all they've got to hold on.

Rory, however, is not so lucky. She doesn't have a rock wall behind her. All that's there is the cave's throat.

She hits the back of it with a gush of air from her lungs. Her grip on my wrist loosens, her body going limp in the swirling pool beside me.

"Rory!" I yell at the wilted form slipping from my grasp. With all my might, I squeeze, but the weight of her makes my grip loosen on the rocks that are anchoring us both. "Rory, wake up!"

She doesn't blink. Another wave rolls over her and I can feel my grasp on her wet skin lose the battle it's working so hard to fight. My fingers sting to stay closed. I dig my nails into her skin, but they only claw her as she slowly slips away and is swallowed into the black abyss.

"Rory!"

Sobbing, I stare helplessly into the dark waters. I want to let go. I want to swim after her and save her like she saved me. But I can't do it. To dive after her would be nothing more than committing suicide. And somehow, making the conscious choice not to recklessly throw everything to the wind and go after her makes me feel even worse.

There's a splash at the cave's opening. With the help of the current, Dethoc reaches me in no time.

"Rory," I sputter, pointing down the cave's throat.

He takes my hand, using me as an anchor when he ducks under the raging waters. I grip onto him like my life depends on it, and watch, terrified from above, hoping he'll resurface. Through the darkness, I can see the glow star he was holding. I watch him let it go, see the current that takes it swiftly.

When Dethoc pops back up, his eyes are heavy with sorrow. "I can't hear her thoughts anymore." He looks to me. "Is she still alive?"

"I don't know."

"Can you still sense her?" he yells louder.

"I—I can't..."

Trembling in the dark, icy waters, I realize what he's suggesting. Aulow had explained that Guardians had a certain calling to life, that they could sense souls if they focused hard enough, but that the brightest ones were always their fellow Guardians. My power is so new to me that I hadn't even thought to use it. I try focusing inward on it now, to the power that I still don't quite understand. I

search for anything, any sign that she might still be alive: a heartbeat, breaths, the warmth of a living body.

But no matter where I search, all I find is darkness.

"I don't know," I yell again, battling the echo of the crashing
waves.

Dethoc curses, smacking the water around him. He reaches for
my hand.

"No," I whimper. "No! We have to go back for her!"

But he ignores me. His mouth is clamped shut as he pries my
pruned fingers from the rocks and drags me, kicking and screaming
the rest of the way out of the tunnel.

Hayliel is waiting for us on the rocks, shivering.

Dethoc throws me beside her, and I crash onto the sharp rocks,
barely able to support my weight.

"We can't just leave her." My voice is ragged, my entire body
weak and waterlogged.

But Dethoc ignores me. He leaves me where I landed and
storms away to an isolated spot across the rocks. He sinks down
into them, hunched over his knees and buries his head.

I finally stop yelling when Hayliel wraps her arms around me.
This time, I wrap my arms around her as well, grateful to find that
at least she is still alive.

We sit there, cradled in each other's embrace as she sobs into
my shoulder. My tears, however, have dried. There's no use in
crying. Everyone dies eventually, I remind myself. It is the way of
things, the counterbalance to life. So I don't understand why losing
her hurts so much, someone I barely even knew.

The longer I stare at Dethoc and his buried face, the more I
realize just how much I've failed. All of this is my fault. If I had just
reached Acari in time, we wouldn't be on this dangerous quest. If
we hadn't accepted Rory's and Dethoc's help, or if she had just left
me when I'd slipped, Rory would still be alive, and Dethoc wouldn't
have to grieve her.

The crashing waves inch their way up the cliff, but it's not until they are splashing us with their mist that I gently push Hayliel away from me.

"We should go," I tell her. "Before the water is too high for us to get back."

She wipes her cheeks. "I'll get Dethoc."

I shake my head. "No, I'll talk to him. Will you grab the bags though? Maybe put Rory's in one of ours, so he doesn't have to see it."

Nodding, Hayliel makes her way back up the cliff to where we discarded our bags. I watch her as she goes, afraid to let her out of my sight for fear that a fate worse than drowning will befall her.

The thought reminds me of Nerul, and for the first time since entering the cave, I'm worried about where he is. Perhaps he took a dive to claim Rory's soul before she was able to die. Or maybe he's already gone, maybe he only came to scare me.

"Dethoc," I say over my shoulder. "We should get going—"

But the words die on my tongue when I turn and find a shadow looming over the mourning Prophet.

Nerul throws back his black hood. His grin is vicious and menacing when he sees me watching him, like he's just won a game that I didn't even know we were playing.

But I know now.

Dethoc is a Prophet. He has been protected by his Guardian for I don't know how long. The one thing I do know, is now that she's gone, his life is fair game. Any Reaper could come and claim his soul; any Reaper could fulfill the contract that had once had his life written on it. But they didn't send just any Reaper.

Nerul wanted to be the one.

He reaches out a hand, his pale skin sickly beneath the moonlight.

"No!" I scream, reaching out for them.

Dethoc looks up at me, and it's then that I realize he's not afraid. He knew this was coming. He knew before I did that Rory's death would mean his own too, and he didn't say anything.

Nerul wastes not a second more. As I clamber toward them,

desperate to stop what is already in motion, he reaches out his hand and caresses Dethoc's cheek with his slender finger.

Dethoc's body falls limp. His shoulder smacks against the sharp rocks first, but the jolt sends his head into another jagged boulder. The crack that rings in the air is louder than the churning ocean. From atop the rocks, Hayliel shrieks. Limb after limb Dethoc tumbles, breaking bones and gushing blood until he makes his way down the cliffside and into the ocean below.

"Oops," Nerul snickers.

I tear my horrified gaze away from Dethoc's body just as another wave comes to carry him to his watery grave. I glare into Nerul's wicked eyes as if the malice oozing inside me is a projectile I can wield with my gaze alone.

He will pay for what he's done. I don't care if it makes me a Reaper again; I don't care if it makes him my crow; I will kill him for what he's done.

Nostrils flaring, nails digging into my palms, I sprint for Nerul. When the rocks shift, I don't lose momentum. The rugged terrain has become second nature in my determined dash, his smug face fueling my rage and adrenaline.

But as I lunge, my fists cocked and ready to crack into his cheekbone, smoke engulfs him. My fist collides with air, and I stumble forward as Nerul disappears into the underrealm.

On my knees, I throw my head back and unleash the shriek clawing its way up my throat.

18

TRUTH WILL SET YOU FREE

ACARI

As consciousness greets me where I lay in my warm bed, I sink into the throbbing ache of my muscles. For hours I blessed the people last night. Hundreds of them. The temple was packed with the citizens of Azarrac City all the way up until midnight, and I got to meet every one of them. My constituents. My people.

When I try to swallow, it feels like someone has poured sand down my throat. How many times did I recite the words to bless my people with compassion for the year? How many times did I assure them they would remain on the right path and value life above all else?

How many times did I realize how much of a hypocrite I am and how these people, this kingdom, deserves better?

Blearily, I toss the covers aside and sit up to rub my eyes. In all the night, only a few times did it feel like my presence was actually appreciated at the ceremony, despite Borgravid's insistence that it would be. As we were leaving, although he reassured me my presence mattered, I got the distinct feeling like it only prevented the people from having an additional excuse to hate me, but it didn't actually ensure anyone's love or devotion. In fact, they might've been happier if I had done whatever I wanted last night, that way they *would* have one more excuse to hate me.

The thought puts a smile on my face, but only momentarily. That is, until it reminds me of the thing I had planned on doing upon my return to the palace.

With a burst of newfound energy, I spring from my bed and rush to the wardrobe. I tug the tunic over my head and place the king's sigil on my shoulder before rushing for the door.

Sidian squawks, a reminder that I need to report to Veltuur.

But I have other plans first, ones that require me to lie to my crow and hope that he can't see through me.

"Can I at least bathe first?" I protest, running a hand through my dark hair. "We spent all day at the coast, and I'm covered in sea —*sand*, whatever. Probably the sea too."

Though we never actually made it down to the beach, the winds were harsh enough that any time I ruffled my locks last night, black sand would fall to the floor. By the time we were done, the cream robes I was wearing looked like they had been sprinkled with pepper.

"I think when I was leaning over the wharf, I even put my hand in"—I lower my voice—"bird f-fecal matter."

Sidian raises its head indignantly, denying my request.

Exasperated, I throw my hands in the air. I could just leave the room and force the bird to follow, but even in our limited time together so far, I've tried doing things without Sidian's consent before and they never end the way I'd like them to. Despite being a king, I actually have no power over the bird, not like it has over me, anyway. If it wants us to go to Veltuur, if it is truly dead-set on the idea, then that's where we go. If it's tired of being at the coast, then we leave. I never have a say in any of it.

To leave without Sidian's approval would be an instant loss. I have to convince it to allow me to go, and to do that, I have to let it know it has all the power on the matter.

"I'll be quick," I plead, trying to appeal to its ego. Then, to sweeten the deal, I add, "You can even get some more sleep while you wait."

Caw! it cries, swooping across the room from its perch on the desk and nearly pecking me in the eye as it flies past me to land on the tea table by the door, like it's blocking my exit. Wait no, not like it's blocking me, but like it's insisting it comes along with.

"Come on," I groan. "Do you have to come? It's kind of…embarrassing to be naked around you. Will you please just stay here? Or go fly outside or something. I won't take long. It's just a bath."

The crow eyes me for a moment, blinking in time with the twitching of its head. Finally, it flies back across the room and through the open window, disappearing outside. I have no way of knowing how long it'll be gone, how much time a bird deems necessary for a bath, and so, without wasting another moment, I yank my door open and dash into the hallway.

My feet echo down the hall, but thankfully no one is near to hear them. This section of the palace was reserved for the royal family, and since my mother, father, and brother are all dead now, and none of the servants want to risk interacting with me unless it's absolutely necessary, not many of them spend time here anymore. I'm grateful not to have their curious eyes on me as I slide down the corner in my slippers, nearly slamming into the wall before correcting myself and racing down the next corridor.

Fortunately, the Forbidden Garden isn't far from my chamber. If it had been across the palace grounds, I might not have enough time to go there and come back before Sidian returns to faze us to Veltuur. But as it is, if I can be quick, I just might be able to get back without it knowing I've done anything I shouldn't have.

If it knew what I was up to, I'm sure it wouldn't hesitate to take me before the Council, and I have even less doubt that they'd send me to the Wraiths for something like this. I'm not even sure it is a violation of anything specific, but I know they don't want me to know about my past for some reason.

When I see Captain Borgravid standing guard, I curse under my breath. I hadn't had time to consider him being there, even though I should've since he's there almost every morning.

My running slows until I'm standing before him, sheepishly.

"I already told you," he begins, his back rigid and parallel to the wall. His gaze remains fixed ahead. "The garden is forbidden to all. Even to you."

I prop my hand on the wall and lean into it, trying to appear casual. "That's not completely true. It's not forbidden to the groundskeeper." When he scowls at me, my cheesy grin meets him. It stays there when I plead. "Nor forbidden to me, at least today. This once. Please?"

He barks out a laugh when he folds his arms.

Sighing, I pull myself away from the wall, all hunched shoulders and deflated posture. "Look, I know we used to be close. I mean, I don't personally remember it, but I can tell. You care about me—"

He shifts uncomfortably. "You are my king."

I roll my eyes. "Yeah, sure. Whatever. What I'm trying to say is —" I pause, realizing I'm skipping too far ahead. "Let me start over. I forgot to tell you that I ran into the Reaper girl again yesterday. Sinisa."

"Forgot?" he grumbles. "So that's where you were all afternoon."

"Not *all* afternoon. I only saw her toward the end, just before Sidian..."

A single eyebrow raises, and I can tell he's amused that I'm defending myself.

I shake my head. "Nevermind that. The point is, I saw Sinisa and she told me about the memory tree. She had some of the leaves with her, and she was going to give them to me until Sidian decided it was time to go, but before we fazed away, she told me what the leaves could do. She said I could get my memories back."

I wait for him to respond, but his scowl is unreadable.

"The strangest part was how Sidian reacted to her telling me about them. It was like it didn't want me to take them. Or maybe it's the Council—those are the people in charge of Veltuur—maybe they don't want me to regain my memories."

Captain Borgravid strokes his dark beard. "Why wouldn't they want you to remember your life from before?"

"I don't know. It's strange, right?"

When he grunts, his scowl is so deep that it's difficult to tell whether he finds it as bizarre as I do, or if he doesn't believe me.

I don't have time to worry if it's the latter though, so I give him have a few moments to think before I ask, "Doesn't it kind of make you want to let me into the garden?"

He glowers.

I hold out my hands to placate him. "Sorry. Sorry. I just don't know how much time I have. Since I didn't think the Council wanted me to have anything to do with the memory tree leaves, I told Sidian I was going to take a bath so that he'd leave me alone for a few, but he could be back any moment. I know this place is forbidden, but...wouldn't it be nice if I had my memories back? Don't you want the old Acari back?"

He stands his ground, glaring at me for longer than I'd expected. It might have something to do with not liking being manipulated, but I can't say I regret using my missing memories against him.

"Please? I won't touch anything but the memory tree."

Finally, begrudgingly, he steps aside, freeing the path to the Forbidden Garden's door.

"Don't tell the king I let you in," he says.

If the man is sparse with his smiles, he seems to be stingier still with his jests, so the joke catches me off guard at first, but then I glimpse the crooked smirk curving the edge of his lips.

"Okay," I agree with a breathy laugh. "Don't worry. I won't tell him." Grabbing the double doors, I swing them wide. "Thank you, Captain Borgravid."

Inside, the place is magical. Truly, no other word comes to mind to describe it. It's like stepping into a dream of an enchanted forest. Walking the pebble paths between the large fan leaves, smelling the aromas of each exotic flower, marveling at the stunning colors of all of the flora, it makes me feel as if I've crossed into a magical world in a storybook.

Seeing the beauty and magnificence of it all makes me regret my promise to leave everything alone but the tree. I could spend hours here—if they'd let me. Then again, I doubt my kingly or Reaperly duties would ever allow it.

Thinking of the people—or rather, the Councilspirits—who run my life is all the prompting I need to remember that I don't have much time. If Sidian returns and finds me in here, it will never let me out of its sight again.

I head for the only tree in the room, magnificent in the center of the domed space. A wide canopy of leaves showers down from its branches, all the way from the ceiling.

When I'm finally close enough, I reach up for a leaf. It's soft against my fingertips, like a rose petal.

"Wait!" Captain Borgravid hollers from just inside the doorway.

I jerk away and spin around. "What?"

"Don't touch it! You'll kill it if you do!"

I snap my arm back so fast that my hand smacks into my chest. Dread roils inside me. How could I have forgotten? My touch is death to anything living, and I just touched the last living memory tree. I am going to go down in history as the Reaper and king who killed the last species of its kind...

My eyes are closed as I turn back around to examine my handi-work, terrified to see a tree of such beauty wither away. But I bring myself to open them and face the damage I've done.

To my surprise, the tree is exactly as it was. Its leaves are still green; its branches have not withered. It still glows like it is life itself.

"Th-thank you," I say to Borgravid when he jogs to my side.

He nods, slamming his fist into his shoulder. I shuffle backward, confused and dazed. I don't understand. My touch should've killed this tree. How is it still standing?

With a raise of his eyebrows, Borgravid indicates to the tree, asking if he can help.

Maybe I didn't actually touch it. Maybe I just thought I did.

Or maybe not.

Either way, I'm not willing to risk it again, at least not on the last living tree of its kind.

"By all means," I tell him, gesturing him forward.

Borgravid reaches up, plucking a leaf from the tree and holding it like he's afraid he'll break it.

"Now what?" he asks.

I shake my head, too preoccupied with trying to understand what just happened and how this memory tree is still standing. But my nervous gaze catches a black shadow beneath the mayapples, and for a scary moment I fear Sidian has returned. Relief overcomes me when I confirm that the shadow is in fact just that, however it is a solid reminder that Sidian could come back at any moment and that I can't afford to waste any more time.

"Where can we make a tea?" I say at last.

Instead of running all the way across the palace to Macaw Wing where the kitchen and servants reside, Borgravid guides me to the guests' apartments. Their rooms have hearths for comfort and warmth, and cups for entertaining. While he's working to start a fire, he sends me back out to Sungema Court with one of the cups. I dip it into the fountain, fairly certain that the water spewing from the top is not meant to be consumed, but I let the cup fill anyway. Even if the water is undrinkable, I'm sure a quick faze to Veltuur would cure me of whatever damage it wreaked.

When I return to the guests' apartments, the fire is already burning. Borgravid grabs that cup of water from me and crumples the leaf into it. He stirs the concoction with his finger before gently, precariously setting it beside the fire.

Then we wait.

I could down it immediately, but I'm worried what will happen to the potency if I drink it too quickly. If the leaves aren't cooked, will they still be alive? Will they die on my tongue and the memory leaves will lose their herbal qualities, or will the leaves withstand my Reaper touch regardless?

With every second that passes, I risk Sidian finding us and fazing me back to Veltuur.

Or worse, to the Council.

"That's probably good enough," I say, biting my lip and reaching for the cup.

I tap the handle, expecting it to be hot, but the pottery is only a little warm. When I look into the liquid, I don't see steam either. But I don't have time for worry or doubt. This will work; it just has to.

With the cup to my lips, I look across the brim to Borgravid. "Wish me luck."

Before I take a drink, I remember the last thing Sinisa said to me, about recalling a memory. There's only one I have from before, so it's not difficult to choose. I recall standing in the bathing house, my feet wet from the splashing waters beside me, as I raise my gaze to meet the girl in red.

Then I take a gulp.

The memory comes to life around me, a curtain dropping from the darkest depths of my mind.

No longer am I standing in the guests' apartments with Borgravid hunched over the hearth in front of me. I am inside the bathing house, or at least, I feel like I am. The muggy air is damp with steam. My skin beads with sweat.

I glance down into my hands to the glass box I'm holding. Inside, it's filled with nothing but wood chips and sticks, and a rock nestled in the corner. But one of my steps forward jostles the container, and the rock inside moves, reminding me that it is no rock at all, but an aacsi, the very creature that killed my brother and mother.

Looking just over the lid of the box, I can see a head of thick, dark hair resting against the edge of the bath in the floor in front of me.

Frantic desperation pulses through me. It tells me to run from the room in one breath, but in another it's urging me to open the lid of the container. But I know that every second I waste agonizing over my decision is one less second that Gem has left at life. The Reapers could take her at any moment. I have to act fast. No regrets.

The only solace I find is in knowing that my father brought this upon himself.

I crack open the lid and tilt the box forward.

The aacsi needs no coaxing. It's ravenous tentacles twitch in response to the close proximity to living skin and it bounds from its cage. It lands silently on my father's shoulder, but the deafening quiet of the room is quickly consumed by my father's frantic flails. He'd scream if it weren't for the rocking waters he swallows.

He kicks and splashes, gargles and sputters.

When his thrashing finally slows, I'm surprised to find that, although I feel sad that he's gone, mostly I just feel relief.

Gem is safe now.

No matter what happens to me, Gem is safe.

And that's all that has ever mattered.

At least, until I hear my name called.

I raise my head and spot Sinisa standing across the room.

"No...you didn't. Please tell me, you did not just kill him?"

I'm speechless, surprised by her presence but even more so by her concern. The last I saw her, she was running away from me, running away from the truth that had been unveiled to her. I was sure she'd gone back to Veltuur and that I'd never see her again.

But here she is, staring at me like I've just shattered everything she ever knew.

It's only then—while gazing into her beautiful, tragic eyes— that I notice the runes on her forehead that shouldn't be possible. My gaze drifts down to her delicate hands to find that they, too, are covered in swirling, lavender designs that dance around her fingers.

"You... your hands are... What did you do? How did you—"

I can't even form words, not that that's ever been my strongest asset anyway. But I know what those markings mean, I know the sacrifice she had to make to get them. I know that she had to forgive the man who had violated her all those years ago, that she did it to save Gem, to save me.

And I suddenly know the mistake I've just made.

I didn't just save Gem.

I only condemned myself.

19

THE SEABIRD'S HOWL

SINISA

No matter what I did all night, I couldn't sleep. I just lay there, staring up at the wooden rafters, wondering what would've happened in the cave if Dethoc and Rory hadn't come with us. Would I have drowned instead? Would Hayliel have? If we hadn't even run into them at Lover's Wharf, might we have made it to the cave quicker and without incident?

But I rationalize their involvement. If they hadn't been with us, and if Hayliel, or I, or both of us had died, Gem's prophecy would've died with us, surrendering Acari to Veltuur for years; sentencing Gem to a life without a Guardian.

And every time I reach the conclusion that this was the best possible outcome, the one that is most likely to ensure Acari's return and that my Prophet remains alive, the guilt sinks its fangs into me all over again.

After all of the people I've killed with my own bare hands, it's frustratingly ironic that it's the two deaths that I didn't physically cause that are keeping me up at night.

In the bed beside mine, Hayliel sits up with a yawn. If I'd had my way, we would've slept on the docks last night so that we would be ready when the captains and crews had awoken. But with our sodden clothes and the miserable states of our spirits, Hayliel had insisted that we needed a good night's rest.

"Did you sleep okay?" she asks groggily.

I rise as well, giving her a noncommittal nod before throwing my legs over the side of the bed to where my boots await me. "Will you be ready to leave soon?"

"I was hoping we could have a warm meal, but I guess if you think we should go—"

"We've wasted time this morning just by being here. The boat we need will set sail soon."

She winces at the bite in my tone.

I could apologize. I could explain to her that I'm not mad at her, I'm mad at myself. I could tell her that I'm worried that the Pyrethi Tower or the Kallinei Swamp will be just as dangerous as the neko's cave.

But I don't say any of it.

"You know there was nothing you could do to save Dethoc. Nerul was too close. If you had reached him, he would've killed you too."

"I could've though," I snap. "I saw Nerul before we went inside. I knew he was there. I should've known he was waiting for us when we escaped the cave and I should've stopped him. I could've used my power and created a barrier like Miengha did for that infant. Instead, I just let him die."

Hayliel bites her lip. "It's not your fault that you don't know how to be a Guardian yet—"

"Please, just stop. I appreciate what you're trying to do, but I've thought about this all night, and there's no point in talking about it now. We need to go. If we miss this ship, it will put us even further behind and I'm not even sure if there will be another ship until tomorrow morning."

Gathering what's left of our scattered belongings, which is mostly just the damp clothes we hung around the room to dry, we leave the room above my aunt's bakery and are greeted by the warm aroma of baking dough. I don't know why I'm surprised that she's already awake and baking. The woman has always only ever been dedicated to her work.

When Theffania sees us descending the stairs and catches my worrying glances to the steaming plates of biscuits that await us, she holds up her dusted hands. "Now, before you say you don't have time to eat, growing lasses need sustenance, especially after the kind of evening you two had." She sneaks a worried peek at me. "But I knew you'd be in a hurry to catch the ferry, so I made sure that it was something you could take with you."

Hayliel practically skips to the counter. "Blessed by the Divine Aracari himself, you are. Thank you, Theffania."

A step behind her, I grab my biscuit as well, and though I'm not feeling especially hungry, I nibble the outer edge and utter my thanks.

"It was no bother at all. I only wish you were able to stay longer so I could make you a proper meal. I make a mean pigeon crostata and clove apple pie, as I'm sure Sinisa here has told you all about."

"She has," Hayliel says politely, even though we've had no such conversation. "I hear they're delightful. Another time though. We have a ship to catch."

"Ah, that's right. It's to Pyrethi Tower next, eh? Does that mean you're seeking out your father's old friend then, to see if he'll let you on his ship?"

Hayliel practically chokes on her biscuit. "Father's...friend. You know the captain of the ship we'll be boarding?"

Out of the corner of my eye, I glare at them both.

My aunt holds up her hands. "Oh fine. I get it. You two are in a hurry and there's no time for chitchat. Give Brükmir my regards. And promise me, if you're ever in Kalápana again, you'll come by for supper."

After agreeing to her terms, Hayliel and I leave, headed for the docks.

According to my aunt, every captain in all of the Coast of Dreams will give free board to anyone who has braved the neko's cave and lived to tell the tale. Fortunately for us, that's not a bargaining chip we have to rely on.

My father came to this harbor often. As a tradesman, he was frequently traveling between countries, by whatever means necessary, even by ship when the occasion called for it. Though he had long since departed from his life at sea, everyone knew the best way to get to the Pyrethi Desert was by boat, and he was friends with one of the best sailors who made the journey.

I only know this because my mother and I would come here to wave goodbye as he set sail.

"You never said it was your father's friend's ship we'd be sailing on," Hayliel huffs beside me.

"It didn't seem relevant." I shrug, not wanting to break our pace. "I don't even know the man; I can hardly even remember him."

As we approach the docks, the sight of masts rocking above the waters is a relief. Dozens of ships are still docked here, which means the odds of Brükmir's vessel being among them are good.

The memory of sending my father off on his voyages is just as foggy as the morning coastline, but when I see the dark oak hull and the red masts that make one ship stand apart from all of the others, I allow myself to be drawn toward it. We walk closer, this time ignoring all of the other ships until we reach the front where a lorikeet figurehead, the blue and orange and green paint faded from years of sea weather and travel, makes even my murkiest memories clearer. This is it. This is the ship I remember from my childhood.

"Aye, we sail for Port Talas," a seaman tells us on the docks, grunting as he lifts a barrel of something stringent and sloshing onto his shoulder. His black hair is already slicked to his forehead with sweat, despite the cool morning breeze. "But this here ship is for seadogs and grog blossoms, and I'm afraid ye lasses are neither. Piss off."

Hayliel gasps, clutching the chemise at her breast before tugging on my arm.

I shrug her off. I will not be cowed by this man. "I'm looking for Captain Brükmir."

The sailor stops to assess us, his arms bulging from the weight of the barrel.

I stand straighter when I add, "Tell him Arik's daughter has come to see him."

With that, the man grows even wearier. His scrutiny becomes harsher, eyes roving over the details of my face like he can't decide if I'm telling the truth, like if he thinks he should recognize me. Maybe he's been one of the crewmen for a while. Not that I would know. Every time we came here to say our farewells, I was almost solely focused on my father. The only reason I even remember Brükmir is because of the friendly, albeit boisterous greetings he'd give my father upon arrival, like they were thicker than thieves.

It would be entirely possible for the sailor before me now to have met me back then, even if I don't remember him. Still, I'd be surprised if he recognized me. I was half a decade younger, face still plump like a babe. And none of that even accounts for the fact that my whole life, I've been told I look almost exactly like my mother, except for the one feature I got from my dad: my eyes.

After a long, uncomfortable inspection, the man before me steps back, unconvinced. Before he can turn around and leave us for good, I blurt out the only backup plan Hayliel and I have.

"Every ship in all of the Coast of Dreams has promised voyage for anyone skillful enough to brave the neko cave and survive." My voice shakes but I try to steady it to sound as convincing as possible. It's not like it's a lie. However, there have been too many before us who have tried and failed for anyone to readily believe the two of us could've accomplished such a thing. "Well, I survived the neko cave, and I demand voyage."

The brute turns back around, one eyebrow raised. "Aye, I'm sure ye did, lass."

When he starts to walk away again, I realize I have nothing to back up my proclamation. Everyone in the Coast of Dreams has heard the legend of the neko, the mewling creature trapped in a cave so brutal that no one may enter and leave. Every single citizen believes it is an actual creature, not a key trapped inside, and therefore the one dangling from my neck is no proof at all to anyone. He wouldn't believe me even if I insisted.

But...perhaps he'd believe something else, something that, to him, could have no other explanation.

I tear off one of my leather gloves and shove my runed hand into the air. "I earned these for saving it."

Half smiling to himself, the sailor faces us one last time, and when his eyes fall to my fingers, his smirk fades. Frowning, he sets the barrel back down with a thud that shakes the planks below our feet, and in three swift strides that continue to rock us, he's standing before me.

He jerks my arm closer to him.

"Hey! Let her go."

But the man snarls when Hayliel gets too close. She slinks backward, eyeing me apologetically for her helplessness. But I hold no ill will toward her for trying to stick up for me, nor for retreating. He is exactly where we need him and so I act like I don't care about his calloused hold on my arm. Instead, I worry more about his close examination of my runes, the way his breathing keeps hastening the longer he stares at the dots around my nails and the swirls dancing along the back of my hand.

"I...got these from saving the neko," I say again. The lie comes to me quickly, and when it does, I'm relieved to find that it actually could make sense. After all, the people don't know about the Guardians, and no one has ever returned from the cave alive to say otherwise.

The man jerks his head up. He pins me down with his sage eyes, scrutinizing and doubtful. As he dives into my gaze, searching for something like a sunken treasure hidden there, I lean into the lie.

"Have you ever seen runes like these? Where else would I have earned them?"

He's so close to my face that when he snorts, I feel the gust of it breeze over my skin. Nodding, he releases my arm before turning his back to us and walking up the gangplank.

Defeated, Hayliel and I watch him go without a word. If they won't let us board, it's possible there's another ship that will, but I don't know it. Of the dozens of ships here, they will all have their own destinations. It would take us all morning just to inquire with all of them to find out if any of them are going to Port Talas.

"Why did you show him your runes?" Hayliel whispers finally.

I shake my head. "I don't know. He was going to leave if I didn't say something. I just said the first thing that came to mind."

"Do you think it worked?" she asks, the hope in her voice doing nothing to keep her growing concern at bay. Beside me, she glances nervously at the other sailors and seamen who have arisen and begun readying their ships.

While she becomes distracted by them though, I find myself diverted by something else. A trickle. A tingle. It starts in my chest but the more awareness I bring to it, the more it floods throughout me entirely. Thanks to Aulow and the brief conversation we shared over dinner, I recognize the sensation instantly.

There's another Guardian nearby.

I press onto the tips of my toes to get a better look over the hull. The dock is so low by comparison that it hardly does much. I can just barely make out the sailor we were talking to. He's stopped just over the plank, talking to someone with a worn, three-pointed hat.

"What are you doing now?" Hayliel asks, leaning with me.

Just then, the sailor we'd been talking to shifts on his feet, leaving a direct line of sight between me and the stranger.

But when our gazes catch, familiar and knowing, I realize he is *no* stranger. Even after all of these years, I recognize his fire-like beard like it was just yesterday that I saw him.

"It's him," I say, winded and astonished. "That's Captain Brükmir."

Reuniting with Aunt Theffania is one thing. I spent many a day and night with her, we shared many a conversation, but this is a man whom I barely know. Although I visited the docks with my mother and father frequently, I can only recall meeting Brükmir a handful of times, sharing words together even fewer.

And yet, I feel drawn to him. Even though my father is gone, it's like Brükmir is a part of him, a piece of the life he left behind, the life that my father didn't live long enough to tell me about.

The two sailors finish their exchange and descend the gang-plank. Despite the rocking of the boat, despite the reverberation of every thundering step down the gangplank, despite the swaying of the dock, Captain Brükmir's bright eyes never leave mine. The closer he comes, the more my skin pricks with anticipation. I want to simultaneously scramble away from him and the past that I can never have back, and run to him.

It's not until I notice the runes like seafoam etched across his knuckles and lacing up to his wrist that I realize it's more than just history that connects us.

The two men stop before us, boots thumping on the floating deck. The first sailor retrieves the barrel of grog he'd been carrying with another grunt and excuses himself, leaving us with the captain. My father's friend.

A Guardian.

"Tell me, lass," Brükmir says, bobbing his beard toward my ungloved hand. He holds his own out arm, the familiar markings glistening in the light as he twists and showcases it. "I've never set foot in the neko cave, so how do ye explain my runes?"

Hayliel bows her head, but it doesn't hide her widening, fearful eyes. "We are so sorry for lying. Please forgive us. We just needed—"

The hearty bark of his laughter ripples all the way through him and the open ocean air. We shake with it, Hayliel and I, our legs unsteady and not yet trained by the sea. They will be soon though, if he'll let us board.

"The Divine Quetzi skipped over the two of ye this year, did she? Not an honest bone in the likes of ye. And to think, I thought Arik had raised ye better."

A blaze of heat sparks inside me. My thoughts aren't my own as a litany of replies fire through me, each more enraged than the last.

Don't talk about my father that way.

He raised me as best he could with what little time he had.

Like you're any better? You think I don't know the lies that lead people to a life at sea?

Maybe it's Hayliel's soft touch on my arm, or maybe it's the sting of the cold air, but my temper cools just enough for me to remember that we need this man, as disrespectful as he may be. Without him, Acari will be stuck that much longer in Veltuur.

"You're a Guardian," I blurt finally, and though there's still an ounce of annoyance in my tone, I'm mostly able to conceal it in confusion. "I don't remember you being one... I don't remember your runes."

"Aye, that be because ye weren't one yourself then, but I can see now ye are. So, what brings ye to the Seabird's Howl?"

Blinking away my remaining questions about what led him to the life of a Guardian and whether or not my father knew, I answer him first. Fortunately, I don't have to explain all of the backstory, since he already knows about Guardians. "I remember my father talking about your daily trip to Port Talas. It's just south of the Pyrethi Desert."

"Aye, it is."

"My Prophet had a vision, one that involved my friend and I retrieving the Mirror of Truth from Pyrethi Tower."

"The Tower o' the Lost? Are ye lasses that determined to reach Veltuur so soon? Especially someone who's already come and went," he adds, nodding to me and the runes on my hand that mark me as a former Reaper.

Down the dock a few ships, a different crew draws their gang-plank back aboard, their sails up and ready for the sea. A few others look like they're getting ready to leave as well, and I have no way of knowing where each one is headed, but any one of them could be headed for Pyrethi Desert, and if Brükmir won't let us board, then we need to find someone else who will before they're all gone.

"Will you let us come with you or not?"

He combs his fingers through his bushy beard, nails black with dirt, and sighs. "If it's Pyrethi Tower ye need to go, then this ship'll take ye as far as she can. A Guardian's honor. But mention nothing to me crew of your runes again, and tell no more tales about the neko cave, or ye'll be fed to the sharks." He spins back to his ship, the heels of his boots clomping across the wooden plank before he adds, "But ye better climb aboard now, for we set sail when the sea swallows the moon, and the blighted sun rises haggard from its slumber."

Hayliel and I don't need much more convincing. We scramble up the gangplank after him, and watch as the busy crew readies for their departure.

Aboard the Seabird's Howl, even while we're still docked, it feels as if we're floating in darkness, so I keep my gaze set near the rising sun as a marker. It is the only distinction between the night sky and the dark waters. The Starry Reef only sparkles because it is so shallow that you can see the glow stars lining the sandy floor. But the ocean itself—the Midnight, as the sailors call it—is dark as pitch once outside of the reef.

I've never been at sea before, let alone on the Midnight. Sure, growing up in Kalápana, I've seen the ocean more days than not, and I've waded through the shallow beaches, but I've never been aboard a ship before.

As we set sail, with no distinction between the water's surface and the sky ahead except for the rays of sunlight that start to bleed into the sky's horizon, it looks like we're floating in a black abyss. It reminds me all too much of the way I fazed between the realms when I was a Reaper. I never had any sense of direction in that in between place. I could never tell which way was up or down, forward or backward.

I'm grateful when the bright blue sky becomes stark against the black depths of the Midnight. Just like that, the swaying of the ship is no longer disorienting, but soothing. The waters are so calm and dark, it's so quiet that it reminds me a little of Veltuur, and for the first time since becoming a Reaper, I find comfort in knowing that I can still have *my* "Veltuur" even if I'm no longer a Reaper.

Perhaps I could become a sailor. Perhaps I could join Brükmir and his crew when this is all said and done, travel across the oceans, trading goods. Just like my father had done. I think it's a life I could enjoy.

"*Cari?*" a voice whispers on the wind.

I snap my neck in search of the source, but the gust at my back blows my dark hair wildly around me and I can't see much of anything.

"*Cari okay?*" the voice says again when I wipe my locks aside and pin them down to my neck. But with nothing blocking my view, I'm finally able to see that the only people on this ship are the crew, and this small, timid voice certainly doesn't belong to any of them.

It's only then that I realize what the girl was saying.

"Gem? Is that you?" I ask aloud, drawing Hayliel's worried gaze.

"Are you talking to Gem? How is she? Is she okay?"

I settle her with a harsh hush, then I try reaching out to the small child again. I'd almost forgotten Aulow said we could do this, otherwise I might've tried reaching out to her already.

This time when I speak, it's not verbally, but instead I focus the words in my thoughts.

"*Are you there, Gem?*"

Coy silence follows, but I feel the distinct jostling of a nod somewhere in the empty void between our thoughts.

I can't help but smile at this minor accomplishment. I know I haven't been a Guardian long, and I'm sure the longer I am, the stronger I'll become, but being a Reaper was never so difficult. Everything came so naturally to me. One of the Councilspirits had even thought I had so much potential that he helped me speed up my trajectory of becoming a Shade, and likely would've helped me go farther too, if I had stayed there longer.

But being a Guardian has not come to me so innately. For all the powers in protection that I'm meant to have, I have not been successful in summoning any of them. I've spent these last few days feeling utterly useless and human that at times I've even forgotten I have any powers, let alone the bond I'm said to have with my Prophet.

Speaking to her now is the only practice I've had.

Hayliel nods at me, eager to know everything about the conversation that has still only barely happened.

"*How are you?*" I ask Gem on Hayliel's behalf.

"*Save Cari?*" she repeats.

Sighing heavily, I slump to the damp floorboards. "*Not yet, no.*" Remembering her limited ability to talk, and worried that she might also not be able to understand me if I complicated things too much, I add simply, "Mirror of Truth next."

She's quiet for a moment before answering, "*Okay. Save Cari. Bye!*"

A smile sneaks its way up my cheeks again, and I shake my head.

"Tell her I said hi," Hayliel whispers.

"She's already gone. She just wanted to know if we had saved Acari yet."

"Oh," Hayliel says, dimming. But her eyes pop wide again. "You didn't tell her about—"

I shake my head before she can say their names.

"Good. Good. Gem doesn't need to hold all of that..." Even though Hayliel is still wearing a pair of trousers, her hands seem to think otherwise because she tucks her invisible skirts beneath her when she sits beside me. "You know, when we first left, I thought it would be quicker. I don't know why. Foolish hope, I guess. But we're not even halfway finished and we've already lost so much..."

The pause that follows is heavy. It anchors us both into a sorrow we've been unsuccessfully trying to avoid.

"When do you think the others will find out about them?"

I know who she's talking about, *what* she's talking about. "I don't know."

"I wish you could tell Gem, that way they would know, but I don't think—she shouldn't have to tell them. I'm not even sure she could."

Nodding, I agree. The thought had, of course, crossed my mind too. Communicating with Gem is the only way that we can deliver information to the camp, but telling her that Dethoc and Rory have died, forcing her to be the deliverer of that news to the others, is a burden I cannot place on her.

Hayliel heaves a sigh. "This journey is daunting. All we've done is obtain the neko key. We still have to climb the tower, find and take the mirror, travel through the Pyrethi Desert to the Kallinei Swamp, and then face the serpent, all without dying." She pauses before busting into a hysteric laugh. "What were we thinking?"

Maybe it's because I didn't sleep at all last night, or maybe it's because I've never seen her laugh at something so grim before, but I can't help but join her in a chuckle or two.

"In my defense, I'm used to being able to travel across the kingdoms in a blink of an eye. I'm not sure what your excuse is."

"Hey," she says, nudging me.

As the laughter fades, we finish the rest of the biscuits my aunt gave us and spend the remainder of the boat ride trying to stay out of the crew's way.

When I wake up hours later on the sea-soaked floorboards, it's to someone hollering, "Land ho!" from atop one of the masts.

Hayliel stirs beside me too, picking her head from my shoulder like it's as heavy as a sack of flour. I don't know where the blanket that's laid out on top of us came from, and judging from her surprised expression, I don't think she does either.

As I wipe the sleep from my eyes, something kicks the bottom of my heel. I peek through my fingers to find Captain Brükmir standing over us.

"You, lass, look like ye could use a clap of thunder," he says, extending his stein down to me.

I might've taken it, if the fumes didn't burn my nostrils. "No thanks."

When he offers it to Hayliel, she declines as well with a scrunch of her nose.

He shrugs, knocking the mug back and taking a great swig. "I know not what ye have been through, but I sense the darkness follows ye closely. Ye can't hornswaggle death forever, not even as a Guardian. The Tower o' the Lost be a dangerous place. Ye who enter, never escape, and no one knows for certain what's inside. Are ye sure it's something ye'd like to discover for yerself?"

"We have no other choice," Hayliel pleads. "We need the mirror if we're going to survive Kallinei Swamp."

With a whistle, he brushes his free hand through his beard. "Blow me down... Not many venture there and live to tell the tale either. This Prophet of yers, ye sure they aren't feeding ye to the fish?"

"We're trying to save her brother," I say sharply.

The captain squints at me before finally holding out his hand, still clutching his stein in the other. "I mean no offense, lass. I've lost some mateys to these very places. Yer father's wife among them. Deceived by the serpent, she was, and forgot her life, her husband. Arik went to the tower for the mirror, and I never saw him again."

My stomach twists into knots as he speaks. I've heard the story of their deaths a dozen times, but his retelling is different. And yet, no other rendition has ever sounded so true.

"My...my father didn't die in the swamp?" Scowling, I kick off the blanket and stand. "And my mother. How do you know what happened to them?"

The ship bumps into the docks as it glides into the harbor. As the sailors guide it in and race to their stations, I sway alongside

Hayliel who jumps to her feet as well. She eyes me sideways, a cautionary warning in her gaze, but I heed it none. These are answers I've wanted ever since my parents died. I deserve to know what happened, why my life became what it was.

"Aye. Arik was a good man. To the bitter end. But prophecy drove him mad."

"My father wasn't mad," I snap without thinking. Hearing the rest of his words though, I blink. "What prophecy?"

"The one he spoke of often. The one that weighed on his wife and marriage. The one that led him to the swamp to save his little girl."

"To save me? From what?"

My mind is reeling. There is so much that I don't remember from my life before. I was so young when my parents died. I hardly knew anything, let alone what secrets were rotting through our family, but I remember the feeling. The skittish glances, the late nights, the occasional hushed argument I'd walk into before being shuffled back to bed and kissed goodnight.

My parents loved each other, I know that without a doubt, but all marriages have their strains. What could've possibly driven my parents to the fate I've been forced to live with?

"Long ago," Brükmir begins. "A Prophet foretold of a young Guardian who would destroy Veltuur if she entered the gate between realms. This Prophet warned yer father, told him that the Guardian would be his own child, and so we braved Kallinei to destroy the gate before any could enter.

"But a serpent lurks in the swamp, one no one knew of before. And yer mother wasn't supposed to be there, but she'd followed Arik, afraid of what he might do. The serpent trapped yer mother's mind, filled her head with another life and shattered yer father. He couldn't live without her, and he made it his life's quest to return her to her true self.

"He went to Azarrac City first, to plead with the king for a single memory leaf. I'm sure ye remember."

But I don't. None of this story is familiar to me. I have no memory of him bringing me to Azarrac City. Further alarming is the fact that I'm just now realizing I don't even know how I arrived at the orphanage. One day, I was at home; the next, I'm waking up in a strange bed with the matron standing over me.

I feel like I'm inside the neko cave again, tumbling backward as wave after wave of new information crashes over me. Everything he says unravels the story I thought I knew, or at least, the one I'd always been told to believe.

Testing my voice, I ask him the first question that I need answered. "He...he didn't die? My father, he's still alive?"

"I didn't say that, lass, but he didn't die in the swamp. Neither did yer mother."

"So, what happened?"

"The king denied him the leaf and he knew he only had one option. So he left ye in Azarrac to go to the Tower o' the Lost for the mirror. And no one saw him after."

My head is swimming, the rocking of the boat only adding to my disorientation.

All this time, I thought I'd been sent to Azarrac City as an orphan already, but it turns out, my father left me there, planning to return for me later. Since my father's death, I've never once blamed him for anything. Even when people told me he had murdered my mother—one speculation among the many—I knew it wasn't true and so I was never angry toward him.

But I'm angry now.

He could've just left me in Kalápana with my aunt. He could've returned me to her when he failed at the Halaud Palace, or sent me south when his journey needed to continue east. He could've put me on a boat with Brükmir for all I care, but instead, he sent me to an orphanage, to the darkest, vilest existence I've ever known, the very place that led me to my Reaper life.

If he had just left me in Kalápana, I never would've become a Reaper, and consequently never would've become a Guardian. It would've ended the stupid prophecy he was so afraid of. Instead, he helped manifest the very chain of events that he was trying to stop.

My life would've been completely different. I would've grown up in my aunt's loving home, learning to bake pastries and loaves of bread and pies. I would've had friends. Maybe I would've even fallen in love.

But if I had never been made a Reaper, I never would've met Acari. The Councilspirits would've sent a different Reaper after Gem, one who might've succeeded in her execution of the prince's sister. If that had happened, Acari might've killed his father anyway, and there wouldn't be a Guardian in Tayaraan trying to help bring him back.

As furious as I am with my father, with Brükmir, with the Prophet that made it sound like a Guardian ending Veltuur was a bad thing, I realize, for Acari's sake, I'm glad I am where I am.

Once the sailors drop the gangplank, Brükmir walks us over to it. "If ye survive this mad quest yer on, know that the Seabird's Howl is always available to Arik's daughter."

Numbly, I nod. As much as I appreciate all the gaps he's been able to fill and the idea of having people to rely upon, I'm increasingly doubtful that I'll see him or any of these people ever again. Kallinei Swamp took my mother. The Pyrethi Tower, my father. The neko caves, so many others.

It's only a matter of time before I'm no longer able to defy the odds.

20

THE TOWER

SINISA

Haaliel waves down a vendor on the outskirts of the market. "Hi, yes, we'd like to hire a magrok, please."

A thick piece of fabric is tied around his nose and mouth to protect him from the frequent sandstorms that occur in this area. We, on the other hand, just have the crooks of our arms, which do an abysmal job of keeping the harsh sands from our lungs.

The man stops collecting the saddles he's putting away for the day and waves us over to meet him near the corral. "Come, come. We have the best magroks. They do not tire beneath the blistering sun. They know the desert better than even the camels. They will get you where you need to go. Only sixteen puhrr for two."

Grimacing, Haaliel digs into her coin purse. "We don't have puhrr. We're from Oakfall."

"Ah, okay. I can do eight hundred rupees."

"Eight hundred!" Haaliel exclaims.

Beside her, I eye the sturdy magroks. With skin like dried clay and wide, stout bodies, they are animals built for transporting goods, and I imagine they can carry loads twice their weight.

"Two hundred for one," I counter. "And that includes a saddle."

"Two fifty," he counters.

I glance at Hayliel, making sure we have enough before agreeing. She nods and I seal the deal.

"The saddle only seats one person," he warns.

"Then I guess someone is going to have to hold on tight."

The vendor holds his hands up, frowning as he walks back to his stall to retrieve one of the saddles hanging from the post. He lugs it into the corral to one of his largest beasts and flings it atop the creature. The magrok doesn't even flinch, like its skin is so tough it doesn't even notice the weight of it. The vendor finishes securing the leather belt around the magrok's waist before fitting it with a bridle made specially for these creatures, one that takes into account the tusks that jut from its mouth and bypasses the two horns on top of its head.

He waves us over to him, takes payment from Hayliel, and then helps us both up. We climb atop the giant magrok, Hayliel situating herself into the saddle while I take a seat behind her. Wrapping one arm around her waist, I trail my other hand along the magrok's gray, wrinkled skin. The only other time I've ever touched one is when I had to take its life. A creature of this size doesn't die forgettably. I remember the way its body shook the earth when it crashed, remember how my foot became trapped underneath it until Crow fazed us away, remember the nasally grunt it made as the last breath of air escaped its lungs.

Back then, I wasn't able to truly appreciate just how magnificent and tough such a creature was, so I take what time I can to do so now.

The vendor walks the magrok with us on top of it to the gate on the other side of the corral. There's nothing but open desert after it, a prophecy beckoning us.

"The magrok will take you where you need to go. When you're done with him, tell him to go home and he will return to me. Don't try to leave Marágros with him. He won't go. He is a creature of the desert and will stay that way."

As we utter our understanding, the man yells, "*Hiyah!*" and smacks the magrok's rear. It bolts into a lumbering stride, and I almost fall off the back of him. But I manage to wrap my other arm around Hayliel just in time.

We leave a plume of dust in our wake, the small oasis disappearing behind it.

"I don't know how to steer this thing!" Hayliel yells, her body tense as she, too, tries holding on.

"Magroks are one of the smartest living animals," I yell back over the thundering of the creature's powerful feet. "People train them to learn trade routes and other destinations. The man said he knew the desert, which means we can probably just tell it where to go."

Nodding, Hayliel tries steeling her voice, but instead swallows a mouthful of the sand blowing in her face. "Pyrethi Tower, please."

The magrok grunts a roar and our speed increases.

I hide my face against Hayliel's backside, feeling slightly bad that she doesn't have the same option. Still coughing, eventually she folds forward, using the bulk of the magrok's thick neck to shield herself in what little ways she can. It leaves me wide open, even though I lean forward with her. I spend the rest of our trek with my head down, wincing at the shards of sand that pelt me in the top of my head, but thankful they're not slicing into my eyes or lungs.

We ride like that for an hour or more, until the sun has long since set.

Though my back burns from the awkward angle, I don't dare sit up until the magrok slows. Even when it comes to a full stop, and Hayliel and I ease our way upright, sand is still swirling around us from the unrelenting winds. It's almost impossible to see the tower that's just a few paces ahead.

I climb down first, burying my head in my arm when my feet reach land. Blindly, I feel along the magrok until I find its reins, taking them from Hayliel to help her down next. With her hand grasping my belt, I guide the three of us closer to the tower, fling open the door, and dive inside, my arm still stretched outside with the reins.

"There's nowhere to tie him off," I say to Hayliel, spitting out a mouthful of sand.

She too, is hunched and coughing, smacking grit from her face, hair, and clothes. When she can finally see again, she looks around the room. Frowning, she shakes her head.

I curse, leaning back out of the tower.

"Don't go far! We'll be right back."

I'm not sure if the creature will listen as I release the reins and it goes clomping away. For all I know, it's already running back to its keeper, trained to transport customers one-way before abandoning them high and dry. But despite having a renowned temper, magroks are also known for their intelligence, so I have to hope that the beast will stay close instead of leaving us stranded in this desolate, cursed place.

I close the door behind me, shutting us into darkness, and turning my attention to Pyrethi Tower, the Tower of the Lost.

The moment the door slams shut, flames ignite the torches hung around the circular room.

Hayliel and I turn, watching each one burst with fire, until they reach a staircase and start lighting the path upward as well, like they're designed to guide us to the place we need to go. But as I start to follow them, Hayliel gasps, stumbling backward into the stone wall. I turn to face her, but before I do, I see what's alarmed her.

The floor is scattered with bones. Human, judging from the size of them. Most are just piles upon piles of femurs and hands and ribcages, but some are laid out in the perfect shape of a human body, undisturbed and leaving no room for uncertainty.

Hayliel slides along the wall to grip my arm. "Do you think a Reaper lives here? Waiting to collect the souls of anyone who enters?"

"No," I say confidently. I've seen the bodies left behind by Reapers; I've even left behind a few thousand of my own. "That's not how these people died. Look at the way they're placed. They were comfortable—until their bones were swept aside into piles—like they just sat or laid down one day and it was over."

Hayliel swallows. I start to ascend the steps again, not wanting to look too long at the bones and risk recognizing something of my father's among them, when she tugs on my arm again.

"How did they die then?"

"I don't know," I admit. Reflecting back on the prophecy that Gem shared with me, I turn to face Hayliel. "Aulow said the Mirror of Truth shows the onlooker what they've been hiding from."

"But why would that kill anyone? Why did your father come and then never leave?"

"Maybe he did," I utter, recalling the story that Brükmir told us about my mother. Perhaps my father discovered that she couldn't be saved, that I couldn't be stopped from achieving my fate, and perhaps he fled. As Hayliel casts a sympathetic glance upon me, I add, "Some truths are too unpleasant to learn. Most people prefer to live in denial about certain things. Maybe these people didn't die because the Mirror of Truth killed them, maybe they died because they no longer wanted to live."

Worrying at her lip, Hayliel finally releases my sleeve.

I take it as my cue to start up the stairs again, but she calls out in a hushed voice.

"Don't you think we should try to prepare for what truths might be thrown at us?"

With a half laugh, I shrug. "I don't think I have any more secrets from myself. Becoming a Guardian revealed everything I'd ever forgotten, or wanted to forget. And the rest of the blank spots were filled in by Brükmir. I have no more secrets to unearth."

"Right."

"What about you?" I ask her. "Is there anything you're hiding from?"

She's quiet for a long, painful moment. I finally turn back around, already a few steps up, to find her head bowed into her hands.

"What is it?"

Her sob finally breaks free. "I don't think we can save Acari."

"Of course we will. Gem's vision—"

She rips her hands away from her face, tears streaming down her cheeks. "We don't know that though. We don't know anything. You said yourself that the prophecy only showed us entering Veltuur. It didn't show us what lay on the other side."

I've argued this point before, only this time I have new information, a dueling prophecy I hadn't yet considered.

It seems to cross Hayliel's mind at the same time. "And what about the prophecy your father was told? Perhaps the only reason we're being sent to Veltuur is because you're supposed to destroy it. What happens to Acari then? Will he be trapped there forever? Will he be gone?"

"No," I growl, seething at the thought. "I'd only ever destroy that place once he was free of it. I'd never abandon him there."

"What if you don't have a choice? What if we're walking right into the mouth of your destiny and the moment we cross over, the deed will be complete?"

Not convincing either of us, I shake my head. "Would you rather we stop?"

"What?" She blinks up at me, droplets sticking to her long lashes like dew.

"What you said, about playing into my fate's hands. Would you rather we stopped and found another way?"

It's not fair of me to put this on her, to make it seem like it's her burden to bear and hers alone, but it's not a decision I can make without her. Both options terrify me. If we weren't out here doing what needed to be done to return Acari to the mortal realm, then I'm not sure what I'd do with myself. I suppose I could wait for our paths to cross again, or hope that he's taken the memory leaves and will become a Guardian on his own, but waiting means doing nothing.

"No," she says at last, her voice but a whisper. "I think we should continue. At least until we reach the gate. We can decide there." Wiping her eyes, she adds with a sniffle, "We can do this. Let's go."

"Are you sure? I can do it alone if you want to wait."

"No, I'm okay. I think I just needed to confront that now rather than later. I'm ready now."

The torches continue lighting our way up the winding staircase. As we climb the stone steps, some impeded by piles of bones and decay, I'm surprised that the smell isn't worse. But I don't have to wonder for long when the higher we climb, the more rancid the stench of death becomes. Bodies accumulate with every step, half-rotten and mice-eaten.

I use the rickety railing for what little support it provides, and I hike over the ever-growing mounds of flesh and bone.

When I slip, my hands splaying across the squishy flesh of a man's bared chest, Hayliel shrieks behind me.

"It's fine. I'm fine. It's just a dead body. They don't bother me. Former Reaper, remember?"

I can hear her gagging, falling behind me as she ensures her every careful step. As true as it is that the dead are not new or disturbing to me, I have far less experience with the decay. Shielding my disgust from her, I wipe my hand on the thigh of my trousers and continue climbing, much more careful this time to not accidentally fall into another pile of rot.

I quickly lose interest in taking my time though. The longer we're here, the more likely I am to find my father or what's left of him, and I think I'd rather just pretend he's still alive, out there searching for my mother somewhere. I've lost them both already, after all, and to be able to hold out hope that they might both still be alive is something I can't let go of.

As the stairs end, the room they lead to ignites as well, torches beckoning me inside.

"Wait for me," Hayliel calls from below, a cautious warning in her breath.

But I heed her none.

Crawling across the final pile of deceased, bones clattering, flesh squelching, I clamber into the room at the top of the tower and follow the trail of torches that guide my gaze to my destination at the other end. I stare wide-eyed into the massive, glistening mirror that takes up the entire wall across from me. My skin turns ice-cold when I notice I don't actually see my own reflection in it, only the dusty room around me. I start to pull my gaze away, to take notice of the details of the room reflected back at me—like whether there truly is a sheet-covered chest behind me, or a portrait hanging on the wall at my left—but no matter how much I pull, my eyes won't leave the frightful mirror.

Despite standing still, despite my feet being planted on the dusty floorboards, I feel myself being pulled toward the mirror, until it is all that I can see, until I feel like I *am* the mirror itself.

The room flips. I'm staring at the staircase now, listening to the grunts that echo up the winding chamber of a man making his ascent. I see his shadow first, crawling across the stone wall like a ravenous hyena crouched over the corpses. But when he finally makes it into the room, stumbling over the last body before standing tall to face me, I recognize his long braided hair, the constant squint of his blue eyes.

"Father." The word lumps its way into my throat, and I'm not sure it finds its way out.

But when he halts in the center of the room and stares at me, I think he just might've heard me.

He takes a few cautious, dragging steps across the dusty, wooden floor, one arm extended. But when he starts speaking, I realize he's not looking at me at all, but into the mirror.

"No... She does not know who she is." His voice is calm, quiet, like a peaceful stream trickling through the forest. But it becomes harsher, a course of raging rapids over the rocks. "She cannot be happy, if she does not know who she is!"

It takes me a moment to realize he's talking about my mother, the whole reason he came to the Tower of the Lost to begin with.

He dips his head, like he means to avert his gaze elsewhere, but his eyes remain on the mirror, on the horrors being reflected back at him, of the woman he loves being content without him. My mother and I have that in common, I realize. Without any memory of our pasts, we were able to enjoy the lives we found. He was never a Reaper, so he can never truly understand just how blissful ignorance can be.

He falls to his knees, arms limp at his sides. Before my eyes, he becomes emaciated, like the days are coming and going with every blink he takes. When he is nothing more than skin, bones, and the loose fabric hanging over him, he shuffles to the corner of the room, slides down to the floorboards, and closes his eyes one final time. He doesn't move again.

"No!" I run toward him, screaming, only deftly aware of my unmoving body.

I grab his vest of bear hide and shake him, violently.

"Father, no! Get up! I'm here for you. I've come. We can be a family again. We can find Mother."

His skin rots away in seconds, leaving only the rattling of bones inside. I release him and fall to my knees, sobbing.

"We can help her. Father, please."

When I peel my wet face away from my hands, I'm standing across from the stairs once more. His agile physique makes quick work of the mountain of bodies again and he crashes into the room.

"Father!" I yell, racing toward him.

My arms smack into him when they wrap around his waist, as if I'm ten years old again, barely as tall as his chest.

But his arms do not cradle my back like I expect them to, like he used to do.

"No... She does not know who she is. She cannot be happy, if she does not know who she is!"

His words are familiar, but every time I think I understand them, the thought slips through my fingers like a slimy eel. Everything squirms like that. I can no longer remember where I am, how we got here, or what it is I feel like I'm supposed to be doing. All I know is I'm with my father again, and it feels like it has been so long since the last time I held him in my arms.

Around his waist, I see the bodies on the floor and instinct tells me we have to leave.

"Father, let's go. We can't stay here any longer."

But when I push away from him, his cheeks are hollowed. The eyes that are usually as bright as the sky are dull. He crumples to his knees, and I stagger backward, averting my frightened eyes to the floor. It strikes me as odd though, how my feet don't leave scuff marks in the thick coat of dust that's settled on the wood.

It's then that I allow my attention to be pulled beside us, to two new sets of footprints. It's difficult to tell from the size alone whether they belong to a man or woman, but something in the back of my mind tells me that they belong to a woman, one who I think I know.

I look toward my father again, just in time to see him crawling to the corner to die.

On my next blink, I'm staring at the stairs.

My father staggers into the room, and I throw myself at him, elated to be reunited after so much time. But he acts as if I am not here. He becomes skin and bones before my eyes, dying only a mere few minutes after our reunification.

"*Not real*," someone whispers.

My eyes dart across the room, scanning every nook and shadow they can find. But all they see is darkness, all they roam over is nothingness.

"*Not real*," the child's voice says again. It is a gentle caress on my cheek, a kiss to my forehead that makes all of my woes disappear. "*Save Cari*," it reminds me.

Just as my father stumbles into the turret again, that one, simple word—no, name—brings with it a rush of understanding.

I am in the Pyrethi Desert. I climbed the Tower of the Lost. I have faced the Mirror of Truth, and I am trapped by my own lies.

Before me, my father collides to his knees on the floor and I watch for the dozenth or hundredth time, I don't know, as hunger emaciates him, as the truth that he couldn't live with devours him.

"You are dead," I say slowly, voice harsh and chest aching. "And no matter how long I stay here to be with you, I can never bring you back. I... have to let you go."

Suddenly, I feel like I'm falling. The mirror spits my awareness back into my body like I'm a rotten peach that it no longer wanted to taste. I stagger at the feel of being in my own limbs once more, at the weight of air and the strength of my muscles.

As clarity returns to me, I'm unsteady enough to tell that it's been at least a day since I've eaten, at least a day since I've moved. I don't dare raise my gaze forward to see the mirror again, even though I'm fairly certain I've already passed its test.

Instead, I show the mirror the top of my head as I keep my eyes pinned to the back of the room. I mean to search for my father, but instead, before my gaze can wander that far, I find Hayliel kneeling beside me.

I give her a feeble shake, my voice tired. "Hayliel, you have to stop looking at it."

Her neck and limbs are loose as I shake her, but her gaze doesn't break away from the mirror.

I cover her eyes with my hand.

A high-pitched screech escapes from her lungs, shattering my eardrums. Yanking my hand away, she only stops shrieking once she's able to see the mirror again.

I curse under my breath, glancing around the half of the room that I dare to look at. Mostly, all that's up here are bones and cobwebs, a few mice droppings, and a busted chair and desk. I'm not sure who it belonged to, but I consider for a moment what this place was like before the mirror claimed this tower as its own.

But I don't think about it long.

Without wasting another second, I grab the chair, and keeping my eyes sheltered, I fling it across the room. Glass shatters everywhere. Hayliel shrieks again, but this time it's different. It's not a constant cry like it was before, just a single wail before she collapses to the floor.

"Hayliel!" I shout, racing to her side and skidding to my knees.

She trembles when I flip her to her back, but I'm relieved to find her blinking. She's alive. It worked.

For the first time, I let my gaze flit to the side of the room where the mirror had been mounted. Where its gleaming glass had been, all that's left is the russet, gilded frame. A few pieces of the mirror are stubbornly hanging on to the edges of the frame, but the rest of it is littered about the floor.

Deciding Hayliel could use some time and space to collect herself, I stand and cross the room. My boots crunch on glass as I search the shards for anything useful. When I finally find a fragment that's as wide as my hand, I tear a piece of fabric from my sand-colored undershirt and crouch down to pick it up.

Hovering over the glass, the magic inside it tries once more to take its hold. My life as a Reaper flashes in the reflection below me, a murderer with no remorse, a brutal killer who ruined so many lives. But I already know the monster inside me. I've already accepted the things that I've done in the name of duty, and so the mirror loses its hold on me once more.

I drop the strip of fabric and let it fall over the mirror before wrapping it up and sliding it into my belt. Then I go to Hayliel and help her to her feet, only glancing at my father's bones once as we leave the room, and I abandon him to the Tower of the Lost.

21

FATHER CROW

ACARI

A man wheezes at my feet, blood staining his teeth and sputtering from his throat. I eye his mangled body, splayed out across the snowy rocks, and wonder why anyone would ever risk climbing these icy slopes and dying in such a horrific way.

The Ghayaman Mountains moan, snowflakes blizzarding in the air. I spy the ledge he fell from above us, a distance not so far to kill instantly, but enough that if I leave him here, eventually he will fade on his own. Slowly and painfully.

And the commands I received from my tree were clear: this is meant to be a natural death, like the one I took care of in Kalápana. I'm supposed to stand over this man's broken body and wait for him to take his last, ragged breath before I let my *crow* engorge itself on his soul.

But, it isn't *just* a crow, now is it?

The bird that wasn't always a bird circles overhead, grinding at my nerves. I don't understand why my father became my crow. I don't understand why I'm being punished for killing a man who sent a Reaper after his own daughter. And I don't understand what the harm is in ending the man in the snow's suffering now.

The bird glides in, low to the ground, as I approach the man's dying body. Black and harsh against the white landscape, Sidian squawks once in warning—only, it's not Sidian at all, I have to keep reminding myself. The crow who has been by my side night and day, fazing me to and from place to place, the crow who glared up at me when I was crowned king, the crow who took me away from Sinisa moments before she could deliver me the memory leaves, is the very king I killed, my very own father.

Not wanting to let him know I know though, I have tried to pretend he is still just a bird, I try to hide my distrust and confusion.

I ignore his warning, taking to a knee at the dying man's side. He's so bundled in leathers and furs, his face guarded by goggles, that I have to untie the furs wrapped around his shoulders just to pull his camicia down to be able to find bare skin.

When I do, I make sure I do my job quickly.

Any further protesting that Sidian—*my father* might've done, stops. His eyes turn wild and hungry when the mountain man finally croaks, and the crow launches himself toward the new corpse to guzzle down his soul.

I avert my gaze, uninterested in watching my father cannibalize the soul of a man.

Rubbing my hands over my biceps, instead I stare out over the peaks and try thinking of more pleasant things, like how warm it'll be to sit by a fire once we get to go back to the palace, how comfortable I'll be once I'm done with my duties for the day and I'm back in bed.

But even that thought is soured by the presence of my crow. Everywhere I go, he is there, watching me, judging me. I will live the rest of my days with that damned bird—my father—at my side, unless I can do what Sinisa did, unless I, too, can learn to forgive.

Glancing over my shoulder, I watch the bird pluck the last tendrils of the gray soul from the climber with the snap of his beak. His eyes glow red, satiated, before glowering at me next.

Caw! my father calls, as if to ask me what I'm looking at, and that simple, single noise is enough to send me over the edge. For two days, I've held it together. For two days, I've pretended that everything is the same as it was, but I can't do it any longer.

"Why couldn't you just let her live!" I shout, arms clutching my body tighter, nails digging into my shoulders. "If you would've just accepted her for who she was, none of this would've happened! You'd still be alive—you'd still be king! I wouldn't be trapped inside my worst nightmare, reigning over a kingdom that I never wanted with you lurking over my step every shoulder of the way!"

Caw-caw-caw, he responds, as if mocking my inability to speak, like always.

"You know what I meant! This is all your fault! You're dead now and I'm a Reaper and it's all your fault but you'll never admit it. You'll just sit there blaming me for everything for the rest of our lives when you could've stopped all of it!"

Chest heaving, my breaths billow out in tufts of clouds from my lips as I pause to catch my breath. This isn't helping. Without him to be able to say anything in return, I might as well be arguing with the mountains themselves. I can't get what I truly want from him, what I need: an apology, any sense of accountability.

But I'll never get that from him.

And maybe, that's okay.

Maybe an apology isn't what I need at all—it's not like he can *actually* apologize for something like sending a Reaper after his own daughter and forcing his son to become one instead anyway. Whatever apologetic words he might've been able to utter as a human would've been false, disingenuous, and certainly unable to make up for the enormous disaster he's made of everything.

No, I don't need his apology.

I need to prove him wrong. I need to change the very laws that he refused to change, the archaic ones that would've made Gem's survival legal.

My mind racing now, I turn my back to him. "Just take us back to the palace."

When the snowfall turns gray, and the peaks start to disappear behind clouds of smoke, I realize I do feel a little better. Perhaps the wound was too fresh, but now that I've said what I needed to say, now that I have an idea of what it is I can do to make it all right, maybe all I need is time to be able to forgive him.

Maybe. But something tells me we are still a long ways from that, no matter how much I want it.

Once my chamber manifests around me, I notice my father is nowhere to be found. He's probably gone to Veltuur to tell them that I know about him being my crow. Any minute now, I'll likely be summoned before them to explain myself.

Seizing what will likely be the last moment I'll ever have alone again, I fling myself onto the bed. My chest rises and falls, but I can't clear my head. Before the mattress can even finish contouring to my weight, I roll back off it and storm out of my room. I don't know where I'm heading, but when I have the choice to turn left toward the front of the palace, to where the throne room and expectations of me lay, or to keep to the back of the palace and to walk toward the courtyard, I choose the path of fewer expectations.

The hallway leads me outside to Sungem Courtyard. Back here, nestled in the farthest corner of the palace, things are always quieter than they are elsewhere, and I welcome the silence. The only real issue I find is that I have limited options of where to go next. I could take another trip into the bathing house, possibly take a soak and melt away the ice left in my bones by the Ghamayan Mountains. But ever since I watched myself kill my father with an aacsi there, I haven't cared much to reenter the place. I could walk in circles along the white gravel path around the tower in the center of the courtyard, but just the thought makes me dizzy.

My eyes wander up the length of the stone tower at the center of the square. I've been everywhere throughout this palace since my return. I've been summoned to banquets, meandered the hallways and corridors aimlessly, wandered the servants' quarters, the stables, my mother's old chambers, but I have not yet made it past the first floor of the tower.

I leave my shoes on the veranda, and the door creaks when I

push it open. Although the windows are small, and no candles are lit, inside the temples seem to glow from all of the gold accents and paint.

I'm relieved to find the place empty aside from the carved, golden statues of the Divine Sungema that surround the altar of offerings. In two days, this is where everyone who is anyone will gather, all the lords and ladies of Oakfall, all the barons and baronesses, even the servants who live here, they'll come to celebrate the day of Sungema, as the bishop reads to us the histories that the Altúyur holds for us.

Cowering beneath her powerful, lifelike presence, I hug the side of the room until I reach a door. The staircase inside is narrow and humid, baking, but it leads up to a single door. Walking into the room is like waking up from a dream that you can't quite remember. I have the vague sense that I should recognize this small space, the tattered cot, the single crack of a window, but no matter where I stare, nothing holds concretely in my mind.

As I cross the room, my foot kicks the homemade doll and sends it sliding across the floor. I follow it, intent on inspecting it more closely, to see if I can glean anything from it that might jar my memory of this place, but before I can retrieve it, a bookcase catches my eye instead. It's sparse with tomes, but there's something about them that's familiar as well.

Dust clouds in my face when I blow on them, but instead of reading the titles that become visible, the cloud forces me to step back, coughing and swatting the air.

When I turn my head to keep it away from the plumes, I find another text on the simple bed, one that has clearly been dusted recently.

Picking I up, I read, "*Scriptures of the Divine Altúyur: Stories of Reapers, Guardians, and Other Beings.*"

I sit down on the edge of the bed and start reading.

22

DECEPTION

SINISA

Hayliel's silence as we ride across the Pyrethi Desert is heavier than it was the first time we were on the magrok. Though she leans forward to shield her face from the sand, I can tell she is trying to hide from more than just the harsh winds.

By the time we finally reach the outskirts of the swamp, where the land starts to sink beneath our feet, the magrok roars, a snotty, guttural sound, and stomps its feet. I decide against trying to force it to continue, remembering instead what its owner had said about it being a desert creature. Once the magrok calms, I swing my leg over the side and hop down, helping Hayliel to do the same. I check my belt to make sure everything is still where I left it—Acari's pouch, the mirror shard, most of all—and I check my neck for the key before swatting the magrok's rear and telling it to return home.

At the edge of the swamp, where the trees don't yet shield us from the blistering sun, we watch, quiet and unmoving, as the magrok stampedes back across the desert like a living sandstorm. When I glance over my shoulder at the soaked earth behind me, I can't help but wish I had forced the creature to stay. It's not the first time I've realized just how completely underprepared we are for exploring Kallinei Swamp, nor will it likely be the last.

With one hand resting on the shard of the Mirror of Truth, I tap Hayliel with the other and lead us both into the swamp. I'm so thoroughly drenched in sweat and caked in sand that I don't even mind the water seeping into my boots. In fact, I'm tempted to dip my hands in it for a nice, quick bird bath.

I keep my gait slow, sneaking a concerned glance or two at Hayliel every few steps.

She catches me and smiles weakly. "I'm okay. I just… I thought I was ready to face it, but I guess I wasn't."

"Face what?" I ask cautiously, not wanting to send her back into silence.

She sighs, closing her eyes before answering, "Acari as a Reaper, as the person he's become."

"Is that what the mirror showed you?" I ask, balking enough that I have to explain myself. "I thought since you confronted your denial about that before we reached the mirror that maybe it was something else that the mirror preyed upon."

Trying unsuccessfully to tuck a loose strand of steamed hair back into her headband, in frustration Hayliel rips the tied strip of fabric off her head. She stops, ankle-deep now in murky, tepid water, and stares at the hairpiece in her hand.

Her nervous fingers work over the knot. "It was something else, something other than us not saving him. It showed me the other thing I've been afraid to admit, so afraid that I didn't even know I was avoiding it."

"What's that?"

Her eyes meet mine, heavy and tired. "That the Acari I knew, the one I—I fell in love with, is gone."

The confession hits me unexpectedly. I don't know why, but it feels like taking a knife to the heart. Fortunately, I'm too stunned and confused by my reaction for words, so she continues walking me through what the mirror showed her.

"He's been a Reaper for days now. He's already had to kill

people and take their souls back to Veltuur. He... No matter what we do, he will be changed by this. We can't save the Acari he *was*. I keep telling myself that when this is all done, if and when we're successful, that he and I will return to the palace and everything will be normal again... But it won't be, will it?"

Slowly, I take a few steps toward her. Without much prompting, she leans into me, her tears ready for a shoulder to fall on. I wrap my arms around her, even though I know this isn't what she wants. She *wants* me to tell her she's wrong, to tell her without a doubt that I know we can save *that* Acari.

But I can't tell her that.

I know from experience that being a Reaper changes you, even one who's only been a Reaper for a few days. Reapers have power over life and death; they have the ability to faze in between the realms; they are the loyal servants to Veltuur. No matter how long Acari is a Reaper, the experiences he's had—even just the knowledge that he knowingly decided to take his own father's life—those moments will change him.

But unlike Hayliel, I am not so sure change is a bad thing.

I didn't like the girl I used to be. She was fragile, a target, someone who let others dictate her life. Granted, she was also only a thirteen-year-old child with little power over her circumstances, but I have no doubt that had I not killed my abuser, had I continued to live the life I was living, I would be more or less the same person I was today.

Do I regret wasting years of servitude to Veltuur with my abuser by my side? Absolutely. It enrages me just to think about it. But do I think I'm a better person now because of it? Well, that question is too complicated to answer, but I know I am stronger; I know am more confident; and I know I am more fearless than I ever was before, or ever would've been.

"Yes, Acari will be changed by being a Reaper," I say to her. "But change is part of life. We all change. And I have no doubt that he will come out of this stronger than he ever was, especially if we can be there by his side when he finds his way through."

Nodding, Hayliel finally pushes away. "No, I know. You're right. I'm sorry. I'm being selfish. I'm okay, or at least I will be. You don't have to worry about me."

"Are you sure? We can wait—"

"No," she says, a soft smile forming. "We can't. We have a job to do, and we've come this far."

With a renewed sense of vigor, Hayliel storms forward, and I stride right beside her farther into the swamp.

Once the ground starts to disappear, once every step sinks us deeper into the murky waters, my gratitude for being wet diminishes. Being immersed—even just up to my knees—feels too much like being in the cave we were nearly trapped in the other night. Although I can take comfort in knowing that no wave will gush in and knock one of us under, there are perhaps far more dangerous things that lurk in the swamp.

"Why didn't we bring a boat?" Hayliel groans when the water gets so deep that she has to raise her arms to keep them dry.

I don't blame her. There's a small comfort in having my hands where I can see them and not submerged into the muddy waters, available to whatever danger lurks below the surface, beyond what my eyes can glean.

"I really don't know..."

"You...you don't think the Deceptive Serpent is *in* the water, do you?"

I almost laugh. Of course that's what I think. What better way for a serpent to earn the title *Deceptive* than by lurking beneath the water's surface, where it is so muddy and green that it's impossible to see anything below. It could be coiling around us right this moment, ready to squeeze our bodies together and crush our bones, and neither one of us would be any wiser.

"No," I say finally, gesturing to the canopy hanging over us. "I'm sure it's in a tree or something. Most snakes don't like water."

Hayliel finds little comfort in the thought. She flinches, ducking away from the low-hanging branches that droop with moss as if one of them is actually the serpent.

The conversation retreats again, only this time, instead of retreating to our thoughts and griefs, our attention is sharply focused on the outside world. Every leaf that the wind blows, every plop a fish makes, Hayliel and I focus on it like we are hawks spying prey. Though I know we are far from it. If anything, we are most certainly not the predators in this scenario.

It feels as though something is watching us.

The depth of the swamp continues to ebb. Sometimes we're walking in water so deep that it reaches our shoulders, while other times we find a shallow stretch that is barely ankle-deep. All I know is once we're done here, once we complete Gem's prophecy, I don't ever want to be wet again.

For a moment, I think about my parents, and what it might've been like for them to come here. My father was a traveler. He visited many towns and traversed many terrains to trade his wares. I imagine he was used to journeys that left him waterlogged, covered in salt and sand. My mother, on the other hand, was not so well-traveled. Wading through the murky swamp seems like the last thing she would've wanted to do, which just makes me realize how desperate they must've been to stop the prophecy my father had heard.

I wish I knew more about it, wish I understood how anyone— even a Guardian—could do something like destroy Veltuur, and what that would mean for our way of life. I, of course, have my qualms with the Councilspirits, but despite Aulow's insistence that souls don't need to be collected, I'm not so sure that the services Reapers provide are useless.

What would happen to Tayaraan if we didn't have Veltuur? If the two realms truly do balance each other, would it be like tipping a scale to destroy one of them? I can't say I want to find out, and even knowing the possibility exists, it doesn't make me hesitant to continue our mission to save Acari.

With the water rising back up to our waists, we wade past a collection of tree stumps that have splintered like sharp teeth reaching out from the swamp. Even covered in ferns, we're both too skeptical of them to dare to veer too closely.

We give the stumps a wide birth, hugging a particularly thick tree trunk that almost looks like its bark is made from a collection of twisting vines.

Hayliel gasps, shuddering when she whispers, "Something just swam past my leg."

I search around us, looking for movement or any signs that there's something in the water with us. But after a moment, I find none. The green algae on the surface is undisturbed except for the path we've taken. There are no ripples, no bubbles to indicate something breathing below.

With my heart racing, I slide my hands into the waters to feel around. When I feel Hayliel's leg, we both jump, but then I extend my reach, into the open waters that feel like I'm reaching my hand out into a beast's open maw. But still, I touch nothing but the grimy sediment floating around us.

"Maybe it was just a fish," I say, trying to sound reassuring, but I don't even convince myself.

Suddenly, the idea of being near those broken tree stumps sounds a lot better than being in the open. If anything lunged at us, at least we could've climbed atop them for safety. But the tree beside us offers no such option. The trunk is too thick for either of us to wrap around, the base too skyward to be able to step onto its roots.

"How are we going to find this thing? How are we going to outsmart something we can't even see?" Hayliel asks, coming unhinged. She pulls herself back though. "Oh! What if it's not a serpent? What if, just like the neko, it's something else that just *looks* like a serpent. Like that vine over there! That could be a snake?"

Still staring into the water around us, continuing to look for any rippling, I tell her, "It's definitely a serpent. I only misunderstood Gem's vision regarding the key because I knew of the neko legend and I let my interpretation of the vision be clouded by it. But the part about the Deceptive Serpent, that was different. I had never heard of such a thing, so I was paying attention to *all* of the details in that part of the prophecy.

"It is most definitely a serpent. According to Aulow and Brükmir, it's one that preys on travelers' intelligences."

Hayliel sinks back into herself. "Well, I can't say I'm not disappointed. I was hoping it could be something else. Something less terrifying."

I snort. "It's guarding the only physical way into Veltuur. It's probably something horrific."

"You know, just once I wish you could say the reassuring thing, instead of the honest thing."

"I'll work on it."

We keep walking, searching despite our growing realization that we might not be able to outsmart such a creature after all.

We find another part of the swamp where the ground is barely submerged. Neither of us hide our sighs of relief at being able to see around us once more. Still, I don't think either of us for one second believes we're truly safe though. The deeper we go into the swamplands, the more it feels like eyes are following us, even when we're on land. Wherever Hayliel looks, I fix my attention in the opposite direction, trying to ensure that nothing sneaks up on us.

As I glance behind us to make sure a crocodile—or something worse—isn't charging toward us from the rear, I see a thick, scaly mass as tall as a magrok slither around the perimeter.

"There!" we both shout.

I spin around to see that Hayliel is also pointing at the slick skin of a snake as it coils around the clearing, cutting off all of our exits.

My hand drops to the mirror at my waist. I wiggle it left and right, trying to pull it free but it snags on my belt with each jerk. Before I can get it free, the serpent's high in the trees, watching us. Calling to us.

Its red eyes pin me in place. My hands stop working at the shard of the mirror wrapped in my belt. Hayliel stills too.

A forked tongue flicks from a sliver along the serpent's jaw. As its massive body trails behind it, slithering out from the murky waters, the rhythm of its hissing lulls me. I start to sway, mesmerized by the dancing of its tongue, the red of its eyes that glistens like pools of decadent wine.

Hayliel squeals beside me, and though the sound is almost strange enough to rouse my interest, nothing can pry my gaze away from the serpent's ruby eyes. Still, I'm deftly aware of Hayliel out of the corner of my eye, running across the clearing toward the serpent's towering head. She stops in the clearing surrounded by its coiling body, and hugs nothing that I can see but air.

I hear her words about as well as I can see through a fog.

"Oh, Acari! You're all right! You're safe. I knew you would be."

When the serpent leaves my gaze, I watch it fondly, like a child does a mother. It is the most beautiful creature I have ever laid eyes on. It's magnificent, and glorious, and I want nothing but for it to be happy.

As it drops its head closer to Hayliel, jaw cracking wide over her, contentment floods through me to see the creature smile.

23

WHAT'S BEEN FORGOTTEN

ACARI

I flip to the next page, hungry for the story unfolding at my fingertips. In all seven of the days that have passed since my becoming a Reaper, never once has anyone mentioned why we *really* celebrate the Festival of Wings. Though I never thought it odd before, as I read the real story now, I do.

The Festival of Wings, the ten days on which we celebrate the Divine Altúyur and the gifts they bestow upon us, represent the final ten days of the War of Divinity and, apparently, what happened to the beloved beings.

"*Every day for a week and two days, one of the Divine Altúyur vanished.*" I pause, scowling away from the sienna pages and then say to no one but myself, "That can't be right."

I do the math again in my head and unsurprisingly, but baffled nonetheless, I come to the same solution: a week and two days is nine.

"But there are only eight Divine Altúyur though..."

Further confusing is the fact that the festival lasts for ten days, not nine, let alone eight.

I read on, trailing my finger over the words to locate each of the days and the Divine Altúyur that were lost on them, but I skim too far ahead and have to backtrack. Day nine: we lost Sungema, the Altúyur of memory. Days four and three: Iracara and Pecolock.

"Days one and two, the Divine Veltuur declared for himself as days to honor and respect the balance he bequeaths upon the realm."

My eyes widen, gaze drifting once again from the pages, and I suddenly remember the empty throne in the Pit of Judgment.

"Veltuur isn't just a place... he's a Divine Altúyur, one the people have forgotten—"

A burst of cheers outside draws my attention to the window. I slam the book closed, the histories already fading into the backdrop of my mind, and tuck the tome under my arm as I stand from the cot. The window is hardly wide enough to see through, but considering there's not much behind the palace anyway, I'm not sure I'd find anything.

A chorus of applause rains again, and for some reason, this time it's enough to remind me of what I'm missing.

"Lorik's Kabaddi Tournament!" I exclaim, peeling out of the room.

My feet practically slide down the stairs; I'm running so fast. I can't afford to be absent from another of the festivities, especially not one that I've already had to change. Typically, the king himself participates in the tournament, so that the men may prove their courage to their monarch, as well as the Divine Lorik. But for a Reaper to participate would almost certainly mean death for all of the others.

I tear out of the tower and start to head toward Lorikeet Wing when I remember the book buried under my arm. Already, I'm starting to forget what made it seem so important earlier, but not enough to think showing up to Court with it in hand would be a good idea. I veer east instead, dash to my room, and cram the book between my headboard and the wall.

The palace is mostly empty as I fly through the halls, save for one or two servants wrapping up their tasks, which makes it easier to maneuver through the corridors.

By the time I arrive to Dove Plaza, the courtyard is packed and stifling. On the outskirts, people stand pressed against each other, shoulder-to-shoulder, like sweltering hogs inside a pen. But when they see me, they squeeze tighter together, finding the space they need to let me cross without fear that I might accidentally touch them. I nod my thanks as I walk by, though I don't fool myself into thinking it's received well.

At the center of the courtyard, the roaring and applause continues, the spectators consumed by the adrenaline of the match. I make my way to the stands that have been erected for the evening, to the throne that is empty, except for the crow perched atop it.

Glaring at him the entire time, I climb to the throne and take my seat.

"I was starting to worry," Borgravid says, standing guard behind me.

"I'm sorry," I say over my shoulder, not wanting to tear my gaze away from the court for fear of insulting anyone more than my tardiness already has. "I forgot about the tournament. I was reading."

Even before the excuse leaves my tongue, I sense his disapproval. Getting swept up in a story is no excuse to miss a royal responsibility. At the time, it had felt important, though now I can't remember why. Just more boring histories and it's not like we don't have an abundance of them.

Below us, a single Ghamayan raider steps onto the court. Oakfall's team of defenders await him, all donning forest-green dhotis, their chests bared. The raider is quick on his feet, bouncing on his toes until he decides to strike. He jabs forward, eyes on the bonus line, but Oakfall's team coils up. Before they can close in, he bounces backward again, failing to claim his point.

He tries the other side, but again our team is too quick. They close in on him like a scorpion about to strike, and so, the Ghamayan raider changes tactics. He reaches out for one of the defenders, fingers dragging over their chest.

The crowd boos and jeers, disappointed to lose one of their players so early in the game.

"Now where are you going?" Borgravid growls just as the Ghamayan raider dives for the midline, somehow managing to avoid getting tackled by all seven of the opposing players.

"What do you mean? I'm not going anywhere." I lean forward to the edge of the throne. "Clearly, I've come to watch the tournament."

He gestures to my feet. "Your smoke says otherwise."

Even more surprised than him, I blink down at the clouds of gray spilling around me. It's like every time I'm finally settling into my role as king, every time I almost get to prove to my people that I can do this, something from the underrealm intervenes.

"I—I thought I was done for the day. Father—I mean *Sidian*, is this you?"

But the bird doesn't make a sound. He hasn't since the mountain. Instead, he just dives into the smoke with me and the two of us are swept away to Veltuur.

It's finally happening then. He's told them I know who he is, and they are finally ready to discuss the matter with me. Perhaps they'll erase that knowledge from my mind again. The thought *should* scare me, but I can't deny that *not* knowing made it immensely easier to continue working with him.

Leumas bows his hooded head when we arrive. "Wretched day, Reaper Acari."

I snort. "You're telling me."

His smile deepens, coiling around his cheeks. "Hopefully this assignment will help ease your woes."

I have to shake my head to clear it. "You summoned me here because I have another contract?"

Leumas cocks his head. "Should I be summoning you for another reason?"

"No! No, I just... I thought I was done for the day."

"Yes, well, my apologies, but this is a special assignment, one garnered from the Councilspirits and meant only for you."

I scan the surrounding trees, still unsure that the Wraiths who prowl there aren't about to jump out and drag me under. Bringing my gaze back to his, I ask cautiously, "W-what is it?"

His smile dims. "There's a girl in Kallinei Swamp. Her life is about to end, and she awaits your assistance."

"Okay?" I say skeptically. I know Leumas is a member of the Council, and therefore I'm not supposed to question any order he gives me, but I've never received a direct order from a Councilspirit before, so I don't know how to respond. When his pale forehead crinkles, absent of any eyebrows and looking all the more malicious for it, I correct my tone. "At least it's not back in Ghamaya."

My forced, awkward laughter is met only by silence.

I clear my throat. "Kallinei Swamp. A girl. I can do that. Is there anything else I need to know about this one? Like is this a natural death or did another mortal request it?"

"Neither."

With my jaw still quirked wide, ready to ask him to elaborate, the Councilspirit waves a hand at my bird, and we are fazed away.

When my feet land on the soft, moist earth, I search for my father-crow first and realize he's nowhere to be found. There are so many trees around, he's likely to have taken roost in one of them, but there's too many branches and dangling threads of moss and other mucky foliage to be able to tell which tree he's in. It's not like him to be too far away from a meal, but I have greater things to worry about, like ending this life so I can hopefully make it back to the palace before I've disappointed too many of my citizens...again.

As I trek forward, the underbrush is so thick I'm left with no choice but to push branches aside to pass. I do my best not to touch them with my bare hands, but it's difficult when leaves are everywhere, smacking me in the face or brushing against me as I tread through. They die on contact, and as I walk past their blackening branches, I wonder what set the memory tree apart from them.

Off in the distance, a chilling, low roar rumbles the earth every time something dies that wasn't supposed to, and I cringe, wondering if I've upset the Council, or if the deaths of the fauna around me were part of this mission too.

Up ahead, I catch a glimpse of movement. Something slow but powerful slides along the ground, pulling the long length of its thick body in and around the obstacles that cross its path. Its scales shimmer like it's covered in ten thousand golden puhrr.

Crouching, I slink toward it. I know I'm the Reaper in this scenario and therefore the giant serpent on the other side of these bushes should fear *me* and not the other way around, but there's something about the way it moves, like it knows it has full command over this place, that makes me hesitant to draw its attention.

I push aside the blade of a fern, the leaves dying as I halt in the dead underbrush. The serpent stands in the clearing on the other side, circling something like it's found a meal.

I inch closer, stepping onto the root of a tree to gain higher ground. And that's when I see her, the girl with gray eyes like a storm. Sinisa.

My mouth dries. She *can't* be why I'm here. This can't be how our entangled stories end.

She tried helping me. Before I became a Reaper, she tried stopping me, she even forgave the crow who'd been leashed to her since her initiation, just to ensure that I wouldn't have to make the decision I still wound up making.

Even after I became a Reaper, she's continued to help me. She tried giving me her memory leaves—which I guess she said were technically mine, but whatever. When that didn't work, she told me where I could find some for myself.

I can't kill her.

I won't.

The serpent's giant head weaves from side to side. I recognize the killer intent behind its terrifying, red eyes, but just when I think it's about to lunge for Sinisa, it veers. I notice her friend then, running with her arms wide. She wraps her arms around the air in joyous glee, like danger isn't hovering over her and watching her like a snack.

Meanwhile, Sinisa just stares, watching, smiling.

Something isn't right here. I don't know what it is, but I know something is wrong. Neither of them seem to know they're about to be eaten, like they can't even see the serpent that's ensnared them.

In my grasp, the tree bark gnarls and crumples. I curse under my breath and use a low-hanging, already-dying branch to swing myself over the serpent's rotund body. But I don't make it over. I land on its scaly backside on unsteady feet. The creature hisses, its skin twitching and roiling beneath me, but it remains focused on the target before it.

Careful not to touch it, I leap from the serpent's body into the circle, far more coordinated than I'm used to being.

"Acari?" Sinisa says hazily.

I start to veer off course, to rush to her instead to see if she's all right, but the serpent's rageful hiss draws my attention back to Sinisa's friend. Bolting once more, my feet slick against the wet earth, I spring for the young woman. Our bodies collide, but I am careful to grab the hooks of her elbows, to where her long sleeves cover her skin, as we fall. My head smacks into her shoulder when we thud to the sodden floor. I release my grip, slightly dazed, slightly worried that we're both about to be devoured.

But I hear Sinisa start to yell something, feel the rumble in the ground as the serpent shifts its attention to her instead of us.

I plant my arms wide, taking extra precaution not to chance touching the young woman's pinned hands, and I push myself off her.

But once I've created enough distance between us, once I can see her face, I realize the girl beneath me is beaming, a radiant smile that gives me pause. I don't know her, at least, I don't remember knowing her, but her gaze, her warmth is familiar. And I can tell by the look in her eyes that she knows it too.

Since becoming a Reaper, no one has looked at me like this. Everyone stares at me with fear and contempt, everyone except maybe Borgravid and Sinisa, but neither of them are the warm and fuzzy type anyway.

Clearing my throat, I avert my gaze, just in time to see her hand a moment too late.

"Acari, it really is you," she says in a dreamy daze.

But when her fingers catch the stubble on my chin to bring my eyes back to hers, my power surges into her. Black smoke seeps into her skin like liquid death. No matter how loud I scream at myself to stop, it won't listen.

Her hand drops, her warm skin paling.

With a regretful sigh, I peer up at the woman who knew my name to find that the light has faded from every inch of her. I'm surprised by the guilt and grief that weighs down on me. I didn't know her. I've only ever met her once on the bridge between Kalápana and Nadina Isle. And yet... her familiarity with me says otherwise.

Since my touch isn't a danger to the dead, I reach across her, grab the back of her neck, and hold her up. A sinking feeling takes hold of my gut.

"Who did they send me to kill?"

24

THE MIRROR OF TRUTH

SINISA

Seemingly out of nowhere, a young man leaps from atop the serpent's scaly back, landing on the saturated earth floor with a squelching thud. At first, I'm too enthralled by the serpent's magnificence to pay the man any attention, but the color of his red garments is too contrasting against the rest of the green scenery to be ignored.

Pulling my gaze to him is a slog, but when my eyes settle on him, something clicks.

"Acari?"

Once I see him, I start to wonder if he's even really there. He's staring at me like something's wrong, but I don't think I'm the one who's supposed to be being saved. My mind is foggy, but when I look at his Reaper tunic again, and see him tearing across the clearing toward Hayliel, I'm sure that we are supposed to be saving *him*, not the other way around.

Squinting my eyes, I give my head a thorough shake, trying to clear the fog that seems to have settled around me. I only make myself dizzy though. My head throbs. I rub my eyes, but my vision remains blurry, like I'm staring through water or unpolished glass.

Glass.

That word stirs something inside me.

My hands trail from my face, down my bust and to my waist. I search myself, certain that the answer I'm looking for is somewhere on my person. Then my fingers freeze on an angular slab tied in my belt. I yank it free, still unsure of what I'll find inside, but certain that it will have the answers I need. Letting the cloth drift to the mossy ground below, I reveal a jagged piece of glass.

A mirror.

It demands every part of me, and I obey. I stare into the shining glass and let myself fall into it.

Through the mirror's reflection, the fog in my thoughts clears. I watch myself and Hayliel walk into the serpent's trap, watch it weave around us until it is ready to strike. The Mirror of Truth shows me Hayliel and the way the serpent preys on her desire to be reunited with Acari, how it gets her alone so that it can strike.

My head snaps up.

"Hey!" I yell across the clearing to the serpent. My eyes flit to Acari, if only for a moment, and my heart catches in my throat. He's holding Hayliel's head, and I, of all people, know that only one outcome can come of that. But I shove that thought aside. "Deceptive Serpent! I've come to outwit you! Come to me!"

The serpent hisses, recoiling from Acari and Hayliel before lunging toward me.

My palm bleeds against the shard from the Mirror of Truth in my hand, unsure of what to do next. I don't know if the mirror was just meant to allow us to see past the serpent's false perceptions, or if it can be used directly on it, but I thrust out my arm and the mirror hoping that the creature doesn't swallow me whole.

The rumbling in the earth stops. Everything is black, and it's then I realize I'm squeezing my eyes shut. Cautiously, optimistically, I open one eye at a time, to find the serpent is staring straight into the mirror, lulled like we had been at the Tower of the Lost.

I did it.

I, Sinisa Strigidae, an exiled Reaper who still doesn't understand one bit of her Guardian powers, outsmarted the great Deceptive Serpent. Maybe I'm not so useless without a Reaper's touch after all. Maybe we really can save Acari.

The thought pulls my attention to where I last saw him. Peering over the serpent, I find him exactly where I left him, Acari pushing himself off Hayliel, and my greatest fear is validated.

She's not moving.

I'm afraid to move, afraid that if the serpent breaks eye contact with the mirror, its power over us will return. But I need to get to Hayliel.

Suddenly, I remember how she acted when I covered her eyes. Even breaking that contact didn't bring her out of the mirror's trance.

I chuck the mirror into the ground, reckless but hopeful that it's large enough that some of the mirror will still show, and I race over to my friends. The serpent shrieks behind us, but I don't look at it. I only stare at Hayliel's limp form.

The swirl on her neck tells me I'm too late. She's gone. She's gone, and I wasn't here to do anything about it.

"What happened?" I ask, voice cracking, wondering if maybe the serpent reached her while I was in my haze. Everything is gray still, like a fog that has yet to clear.

Until I see his crow already perched atop Hayliel's body, its beak wide, ready to feast, and it dawns on me then why a Reaper would be here with us.

My hands slam into Acari's shoulders, and he tumbles back onto the ground beside her.

"What did you do?" I snarl, heart shattering at the very thought that he was sent here to kill her.

They had known each other, Hayliel, a loyal friend who had already crossed half of Tayaraan just to try to save him. The Divine Owlena must be cruel for this to be Hayliel's fate. In the same thought, I blame the Councilspirits too, every Reaper and Shade I've ever known, all of them.

But the blame that hurts the most, is the blame I cast at myself.

Acari is only here because of me. The Councilspirits only sent him here to teach me a lesson.

Blinking, hands buried in mud, Acari stammers. "I didn't—I didn't mean to. Sh-she just grabbed my face. Like she knew me."

Biting back tears, I stare down at Hayliel's dead body as the crow eats her soul, helpless to stop it. Since I'm not a Reaper anymore, I don't see her soul actually leave, and there's something about that, the not knowing for certain that she's dead and gone, that leaves me uneasy.

But it's just false hope. I know that. I've been around death long enough to tell when someone is still alive and when they're...not.

Slowly, Acari stands to his feet again. He stands beside me to watch his crow until the job is done, and I allow myself the comfort of his presence. After all, what use would it be to misdirect my anger at him anyway? He's just a pawn in this.

Suddenly, he spins on his heels. Hand outstretched, he storms back toward the serpent that's still screeching and writhing just like Hayliel had done in the tower when I covered her eyes.

"What are you doing?" I ask him, but when it's obvious he's not listening to me, I jog after him.

The way he carries himself, the solidity of his shoulders, the tightness of his clenched fists, it's not difficult to guess what he's thinking of doing. In his own way, he's grieving too, and casting blame where he believes it belongs.

And from Acari's perspective, the only reason Hayliel is dead is because of the Deceptive Serpent.

25

ENTANGLED

ACARI

Before I get very far, Sinisa's hand falls on my shoulder. She cautions me, gently, "Don't."

Incredulous, I turn away from my determined trajectory and blink at Sinisa. "It's going to try to kill us. Either I kill it now before it finds us again, or it dies sinking its fangs into me and tasting Reaper blood. I know Veltuur can heal me and everything, but I'd kind of prefer not to be bitten."

Unblinking, she says, "It's the last of its kind. You can't kill it."

And just like that, no further argument is necessary. It is forbidden for Reapers to claim the soul of a creature if it would bring that species to extinction. More than forbidden. It's the most unethical thing any of us could do, and no Reaper would dare cross that line.

As if on command, the snake twists its head back, narrowing its eyes at us. Fear sinks its teeth into me, but there's nothing I can do about it. I should step aside and let it finish its meal. Maybe if we did, maybe it would just take her friend and go.

All I know is if I'm standing beside Sinisa when it strikes, not only will the creature die, but so will she.

"I don't care," I tell her. "I'm not letting you die. Not after everything you've done for me."

I tug my shoulder free from her grasp and resume my stride.

But to my surprise, instead of unhinging its jaw and snapping at us, the serpent twists back around and slithers away, unraveling the clearing around us as it drags the length of its body back into the water to disappear. In time, the ground stops quaking. The usual sounds of the swamp return in full, the birds that chirp from the canopy, the stigrees buzzing in the air, the occasional croak of a frog or toad.

"You...really would've killed it? Just to save me?" Sinisa asks, and her voice fills me with a hundred fluttering wings.

"I—Well I just meant..." I keep my gaze fixed to the dark waters, telling myself that I just want to make sure the creature stays gone, rather than admitting I'm afraid she'll see the pink rising in my cheeks. "You know, you saved me—or at least you tried to, so I should probably try to save you too."

A soft laugh, like the whisper of the wind. "I'm still trying to save you."

Confused, I scowl at the water, but I'm too afraid to ask her what she means. When I'm certain the serpent is not going to return, I turn around to face her and instead notice the woman on the ground. "Who was she?"

Sighing, Sinisa turns alongside me. She's quiet for a long moment, like she's trying to decide just how much to tell me. Before I can beg her for the honest truth, she gives it freely. "She was your handmaiden. I think you two cared about each other a lot."

Stiffly, I nod. "I didn't mean to kill her. I was trying to shove her out of the way before the serpent could eat her."

"I know," Sinisa says, reaching out to touch my shoulder again. But when both of our gazes drift to her hand, she pulls it away self-consciously, clutching it instead against her breast.

That's when I notice the key hanging from her neck.

The one that's shining like moonlight is trapped inside it, ready to burst out.

"You're—you're glowing," I say, finger outstretched.

Sinisa examines the luminescent piece of jewelry with wide eyes.

"And you, young Reaper," a raspy voice growls from somewhere out of sight, "are done here."

I'd recognize that voice anywhere, but I'm honestly surprised to know that Nerul has been released from the Wraiths so quickly.

I find Sinisa's eyes, gray and foreboding, just before I'm snatched back to Veltuur.

26

TRIBUNAL

ACARI

Knees slamming into stone, we arrive in the Pit of Judgment a moment later. Above me, the Councilspirits voices are shrill and frenzied.

"I have returned with the Reaper in question." Nerul's voice rings out over all of them as he gestures to me like a putrid slug on the floor.

Suddenly aware of my father's judgmental eyes in the crow beside me, I push myself to my feet and dust off my legs.

"Disobedient wretch!" Nymane shrieks. "We should've kept you in Veltuur where we could keep an eye on you, instead of letting you run freely in Tayaraan, pretending to be king."

The other Councilspirits nod and utter their agreement, and I realize why I've been brought here. This is about my crow—my father. One could argue I didn't *disobey* anything directly, but I'm not about to make that argument. I knew what I was doing when I sent my father-crow away so I could secure the memory tree leaves. I knew they didn't want me doing it, but I did it anyway.

And although in most ways I don't regret my choice, the shaking of my bones says that at least part of me does. Part of me is not prepared to face the consequences of whatever torment the Wraiths have waiting for me.

"Where is Leumas anyway? He should be here to witness the shortcomings of his protégé."

The Councilspirits glance between themselves, and for the first time I notice that two of the thrones are empty, instead of the usual one. Seeing them both without a Councilspirit, reminds me of something I read earlier, about the Festival of Wings, or perhaps the Divine Altúyur, but just as the thought comes, it's gone again. I'm too frightened to focus on anything but what is about to happen to me.

I've never seen the Councilspirits so irate before. Nymane's skin has never looked more cracked as she seethes. Pillox's melted flesh seems to boil with new rage. Even Gazara, a Councilspirit who has always mostly appeared impassive due to the quaint mossy, mushroom beds that cover her arms and I suspect the rest of her body, sours at the sight of me.

This can't *just* be about disobeying an order that was never actually given. And it doesn't take me long to think of other reasons why I might be here.

Leumas had sent me to Kallinei Swamp for a girl. While I was there, not only did I end the lives of about a dozen black willows, cottonwoods, and shrubs, I also inadvertently claimed the soul of a girl who, judging from the hysterics in the room, I'm guessing was the wrong one.

"No matter," the bloated one, Bhascht, croaks, his lips slick with saliva. "The tribunal will continue. Leumas may join us when he is ready."

"I agree," sneers Nerul, but when the Councilspirits hiss down at him, he corrects himself with a bow. "Forgive me, Councilspirits. I know it is not my place. I simply meant that this Reaper is out of control and he needs immediate reprimand, lest things continue in the chaotic ways that they have."

This appeases most of them. All but Nymane settle back into their thrones, the dim light of the candles and the glowing abyss flies casting dark shadows across their twisted, horrific faces.

Nymane clacks her long, yellowed nails together. "You make a fair point, Shade Nerul. Gazara, do you have the record? Let us hear of the chaos this young Reaper has caused."

The woman across from her stands, teeth so long that they protrude from her mouth in either direction. Sludge drips from her hair when she reaches over to retrieve a scroll. The mushrooms on her knuckles jiggle when she hands it to Pillox beside her.

"The unsanctioned death of a fern," the man rasps slowly, like every word is a battle with his lungs. "The unsanctioned death of a mangrove tree. The unsanctioned death—"

"Get to it, Pillox," Nymane warns, her teeth grating against each other.

He skims down to the bottom of his short list—which didn't really warrant an entire scroll, I think—and reads off the final thing written.

"The unsanctioned death of a mortal girl."

The whole chamber grows quiet, my thoughts a vortex.

It's true then. Leumas sent me to the swamp to kill Sinisa. I didn't want to believe it, but then again, I suppose it makes sense. Why else would Leumas give me a *special* mission, if it wasn't to kill the very girl so entangled in my life already?

"Moving straight past the absurdity of the King of Oakfall taking an evening stroll through the Kallinei Swamp instead of fulfilling his kingly duties at Court," Nymane begins. "I cannot seem to wrap my head around why you, a pathetic Reaper, would believe it was your choice to choose the mortal lives in which you take."

All her talk about me being in the swamp when I should've been elsewhere confuses me. It's like she, and the others, have no idea about the *special* mission they supposedly had sent me on.

Not for the first time, I assess Leumas' empty throne.

"Forgive me, Councilspirits, but I am confused. Leumas sent me to the Kallinei Swamp. He summoned me to Veltuur and said that the Council had a special assignment for me there, a girl." I gesture to *my father*, my traitorous mind nearly making those words stumble from my lips. "You can ask my crow. I did not go there on a whim. I went because I thought I was serving the realm."

The Council deliberates among themselves, Nerul glowering beside me.

Finally, Nymane stands, clasping her porcelain hands together inside her billowing, crimson robes. Her smile is sickening. "For now, Reaper Acari, you may go. It seems we need to have a word with Councilspirit Leumas before we may proceed."

Relief washes over me. "Th-thank you, Councilspirits. Should I just report back in the morning for my usual contracts?"

"My apologies, Reaper Acari," she tuts, her abyss eyes mocking me. "I thought I had made myself clear. You will not be returning to the mortal realm. Tayaraan is no place for a young Reaper, and since we have matters to discuss with Councilspirit Leumas, the best place for you is to stay close."

This time, I'm too skeptical to utter my thanks, too aware of the ominous undertones of her words. When I glance at Nerul beside me and find him grinning like the crescent moon, my fears are confirmed.

Shadows slide down the walls of the stone chamber. They creep across the floor, arms unbound by bodies. I shuffle backward into the podium, only to turn to find the dark shapes are descending from there as well. Desperate for an escape, I spin around in the center of the room, my breaths shallow and frantic, until a black pool surrounds me.

The hairs on my arms stand on end as I stare into the inky blackness, waiting.

Then the claws reach out. They pounce, digging into my shoulders, thighs, and neck, until every inch of me is in their grasp. I scream when they pull me under, into a place darker than night, a place where only nightmares dwell.

NOT A NEKO, NOT A KEY

SINISA

"You're glowing." Acari points, bringing my attention to the key around my neck that is, in fact, illuminated.

I stare at it and marvel. No iron key I've ever seen has been able to do such a thing, but I shouldn't be surprised. This isn't just a regular key. It's said to unlock the gate to Veltuur. It's possible that it's glowing because the gate is somewhere close.

"And you, young Reaper"—a voice hisses from the trees—"are done here."

Before I can see where the familiar voice is coming from, I snap my gaze back to Acari's. Fear resides there, blooming as heavy as his widening pupils. I want to tell him that it doesn't matter that a Shade has come for him because I am so close to being able to free him on my own, but before I can summon the words, he disappears.

The light from the neko key flashes not a moment later, clearing the smoke in a blinding burst of light. The key rises from my chest. It pulls away from me like someone is tugging on the other end, like someone is trying to rip it away from me. The leather rope sears into the back of my neck, burning me, being tugged with such force that I stumble forward.

I go willingly to avoid falling, but my hands fly to the back of my neck, fumbling for the tie that is keeping the forsaken necklace around me. But the knot is too solid. It's survived years of sea salt and wear until the knot itself has coalesced into a single nub rather than two separate pieces that can be untied.

The key tugs me forward, one step, two, ten. I spy the mirror I spiked into the earth as it shimmers in the dimming sun. Afraid I'm about to topple over anyway and be dragged face-first through the entire swamp, I throw myself toward it. Frantic, I pry the shard from the mud and wedge it between my throat and the leather. With one quick tug, I slice the leather rope from my neck.

The neko key flies ahead. It twirls and summersaults in the air like it's dancing to celebrate its freedom.

The glow inside it grows brighter still, forcing me to shield my eyes. With my gaze to the muddy moss beneath my hands, the key makes one final burst of light. The tendrils of it fade, and only when something heavy thumps onto the swamp floor in front of me do I look up.

"Who are you?" I ask the tall man standing where the key had been hovering.

He's not just *tall*; he's towering. Although thin in stature, the man no doubt has to crouch and shield his head when he walks through doors.

It's not until he stretches out his arms to examine them that I see the long, black wings attached there. His legs, too, are not like normal legs. They're covered in small, soft green feathers except for a thin line of maroon banded around his knees. It matches the details of his black tunic and the outlandish hair sticking up from his head.

His face might be the only normal thing about him. Brown eyes, a strong jaw, nothing that would suggest he's anything other than human.

Only, he is not. He just sprang to life from a key I've had dangling around my neck for days. If I didn't know what a neko was, I might foolishly think he is one. But nekos have whiskers, not wings, and they are covered in fur, not feathers.

I know who he is, and even if part of me feels like it can't be possible, it is the only answer.

Standing before me is one of the Divine Altúyur.

The strange man pats his chest with the hands at the ends of his wings. He gives himself a thorough examination before looking at me with a lopsided grin. "Funny you should ask who I am," he says, chuckling. "I don't actually know."

Horrified and uncertain, I gape up at him from where I've landed in the mud. Slowly, without taking my eyes off the anomaly before me, I start to pull myself up. "How are you here? What just happened? What do you mean you don't know who you are?" My rambling questions remind me of Acari.

Another laugh flutters from the Altúyur's throat. "I really don't know any of those answers. I keep thinking, *Everyone has a name, so you should too*, but then no name comes to me. I think, *I didn't just appear here, I had to have come here somehow*, but I honestly can't remember anything that led up to this moment. I don't even think I know where I am. Or what day it is. Or year. Or month, for that matter."

He goes on, bemusing himself with each new thing he discovers that he doesn't know.

While he blathers, I wipe what I can of the mud off my clothes. I leave him where he stands, to walk back to the mirror that seems far too dangerous and invaluable to leave here. After grabbing the hem of my dune-colored chemise, I start to tear another strip of cloth off and wrap it around the mirror.

Ashamedly, it's only then that I remember the body growing cold beside me.

Forcing myself to turn around to face her is one of the hardest things I've ever done. I fight myself with every step I take toward her. I don't want to look at Hayliel; I don't want to see her like this, all lifeless and...gone. But I'm too practical for my own good. Her body will eventually rot here. The Deceptive Serpent might even return to finish her off before her flesh has a chance to decay on its own, and although I'd rather not look at her, rather remember her as she was, there's no point in leaving her with anything that could still be valuable to me and the journey that I still have to finish.

I close my eyes and grab the pouch of rupees she kept on her. Hurriedly I stand and turn my back to her still body, tucking the pouch away.

She deserves better than to be left in a swamp, but I can't give it to her. When this is all done, I can't drag her all the way back to the Guardian camp. I have no skills in making a pyre, no fire to light it anyway. The practical thing would be to leave her here for the animals to have her.

But it feels so wrong.

Growling at my bleeding heart, I grab below her arms and start to drag her body across the marsh and into deeper waters. She floats, at first, like I'm steering a boat out to sea. But the deeper we go, the more space her limbs have to sink. They weigh her down, taking the rest of her legs first, then her torso and chest. Finally, the water reaches up to her neck, to the rune of death that's pressed just above her clavicle. And then, her head submerges.

I turn away as the bubbles signal her lungs are filling, and I walk back to where I left the Altúyur.

"I don't know how old I am. I don't know my birthday. I don't know where I was born, or..." The strange man continues rattling off to himself, seemingly unaware that I had left him or that I just disposed of a body, a friend.

"I know who are," I say, cutting him off before he can talk us both to death. "Or at least, I know *what* you are. You're one of the Divine Altúyur."

He frowns, mulling it over before repeating it to himself. "Divine Altúyur. Huh. Never heard of it."

"That can't be true," I say, scowling. "They're kind of important in this realm. The mortals worship you for the gifts you bestow upon them. Depending on which of the Altúyur you are, you—"

The sentence dies on my tongue and my eyes widen when I see what's at his feet. Or rather, what's below them. A door.

I'd almost forgotten what he'd been just moments before: the neko key, the means by which I'm meant to open the gate to Veltuur, the only one in all of Tayaraan.

At my gawking, he grows self-conscious. "What? What is it?"

"By the dove," I breathe, staggering toward him.

When he sees me looking down at his feet, he exclaims, "A door!" and takes a step back.

Together we lean over the arched doorway, tucked between algae-ridden limestones and mud.

"How peculiar, a door leading down. I can't imagine where it goes," he wonders, and I glare up at him. Not because he's done anything wrong, but because...because I guess I feel like he shouldn't be here. I should be discovering this door with Hayliel, and for him to be alongside me instead feels like a violation, like I'm replacing her.

I remind myself that it's not his fault that he doesn't know who he is. Once upon a time, not too long ago, I, too, had no recollection of my past. I can't blame him for being curious, and just because I'd rather be alone right now, I can't blame him for sticking around the only person he's found so far.

With a begrudging sigh, I decide to explain to him why we're here. "The prophecy said you were the key to Veltuur. When I first found you, you *were* a key. I thought you'd open a lock or something, not just make the gate appear."

The Altúyur taps his lips, the long feathers from his arm shielding half of his face. "Veltuur, you say? I think I know this place."

"I wouldn't be surprised. It's the underrealm. The place where Wraiths, Reapers, Councilspirits, and the souls of the dead reside."

The Altúyur grimaces, a shiver running through him. He points at the door emphatically. "I'm not going in there. I've just appeared here, like I've been reborn." A new thought occurs to him then, one that makes his eyes widen with horror. "For all I know, I was already dead and you're just trying to make me go back there."

I roll my eyes. "I don't care where you go. I just need you to open the door. You're the key—literally, before you appeared, you were an actual key that I thought I needed to use on this door whenever I found it."

Keeping his distance, he peers over. "I don't see a keyhole."

I look down, notice the brass handle that's meant to be pulled, and find no key above it. Frowning, I crouch lower. If I didn't need a key this entire time, then why did Gem's prophecy send us to the cave to begin with? If we didn't stop to retrieve the key, Rory and Dethoc would still be alive. Hayliel might still be alive.

I reach down for the handle, fingers clasping around the slimy brass, and pull.

The door resists like it's made of stone.

I replant my feet, widening my stance and adding another hand to the mix, and yank again. Still, the door remains closed.

"Will you just try?" I ask the Altúyur, stepping backward. "I'll stay out of reach, that way you'll know I'm not going to shove you inside. I just, I need to get in there. You don't understand what I've been through. Please, will you do this?"

He taps his mouth again for a moment before beaming. "Okay!"

Caution thrown to the wind, he returns to the door. He cocks his head to examine it, a movement that makes him appear even more birdlike than he already does. I wish I knew which of the Altúyur he was, but even growing up, I never paid much attention to the Divine Teachings. When I still lived with my parents, I was too young to care, and once I was at the orphanage, we no longer spent much time toward devotions. Offerings were expensive, as were costumes for the different celebrations, so we never got to partake.

About the only two Altúyur I remember are Dovenia and Pecolock, and judging from his colors alone, I don't think he's either.

As I watch him squat down to grab the handle, my thumbs slide into my belt. It's then that I remember the pouch I have tied to my hip. If I give him a memory leaf, he might be able to remember who he is.

He heaves and pulls, the door creaking beneath the weight of the water, before finally giving way. It unhinges with a groan, swamp water cascading down the door on either side.

With a wail, he scuffles back again, eyeing me suspiciously.

The look he gives me is all too familiar, reminding me of what it was like to be a Reaper. I never have liked being looked at like that.

"Here," I say, tossing him the pouch.

"What's this?" he asks guardedly, catching the bag before it can land in the mud.

"There are memory leaves inside. If you eat one and focus on yourself, on something you remember about yourself, it should tell you who you are."

While he's still examining the pouch, I round the base of the door, plant one boot on either side, and stare into the abyss below. The water has parted, leaving nothing between me and the gateway. Nothing but darkness is below, calling out to me like it's been awaiting my return.

Over my shoulder, I say to him, "Just don't leave until I'm out. I don't know if the door will lock if you're not here."

Without waiting for an answer, I hop, clomping my boots together, and jump into the black abyss.

The sensation of falling stops as soon as I'm inside. Instead, I feel like I'm floating. Fog laps at my face and body, engulfing me in fumes that I've missed dearly. Even though I know I should hate this place, hate what the Council did to me, I can't help but feel at home the second I'm here. I missed the dampness in the air, the chill of the night that never ends, the ethereal peace of eternal isolation.

I'm not sure when it happens, but eventually my feet find solid ground. Trees surround me on every side, and I'm suddenly struck by how much Veltuur resembles the swamp I've just left. To those who haven't spent years living among trees, they might all look the same, but to me, now that I've noticed it, I can't unsee the similarities. I can't believe I didn't see them sooner.

The tree Hayliel and I passed on our way into the clearing, I should've recognized it. The dead branches that claw through the canopy, the mangled roots. This is the tree that sheltered me for the past three years, the one that gave me a place to call home, a place to belong. Up above, with the daylight shining down on it, and with leaves sprouting from its branches, it looked so different. But now I see it for what it is.

"You came," says a voice from the shadows. "I knew you would."

Though it's familiar and I recognize that it belongs to someone I once thought of as a mentor and friend, hearing it now shatters the false sense of comfort I was allowing myself to fall into.

Slowly, I turn to face Leumas, surprised to find him staring upon me fondly, instead of glaring at me like the traitor he must think I am. I glance through the thicket of trees, in search of the other Councilspirits or Wraiths that I suspect are accompanying him, but I find none.

"What do you mean, you knew I'd come?" I ask warily.

He limps forward, red cloak trailing behind him in the fog. "You were prophesized," he says.

Frowning, I try to clarify. "You mean the prophecy that led me here to save Acari?"

He shakes his head. "I'm afraid the prince cannot be saved. Not yet, anyway, but I've done what I can to lay the groundwork to help with that later. However, saving him is not prophesized. You have a far greater purpose here."

"You're talking about me destroying Veltuur," I utter before glaring at him. "I'm not doing anything until Acari is back in Tayaraan where he belongs. He shouldn't be a Reaper."

"There is a lot about the realms that should and shouldn't be, but that is for fate to decide. Not us. Who are we to judge who the young king should or shouldn't be?" Leumas slinks closer still, like he's hovering instead of walking. "I assure you, young Acari has a role to play in this, as well. Let him play it, and maybe, *maybe* he will be saved. But you, I have waited millennia for you."

"Well then, you've waited for nothing," I snarl. "I don't know how to destroy this place. I don't know how to be a Guardian, let alone a *prophesized* one."

He holds up an ashen hand. "I do not wish for you to end the underrealm."

"But you said..." I let the sentence die as I consider him. I'm missing something, something big, and I can feel it heavy in the air like a storm approaching.

Leumas continues. "This realm was once a beautiful place before Veltuur overtook it."

My eyes widen with a brew of surprise and shock and confusion. "What are you saying? Veltuur is a...is a..."

His knowing nod is staggering and I have to resist the urge to prop myself against a tree. Veltuur is a living being. All this time, I never knew. No one knew. The mortals have certainly never mentioned it, nor have any of the Reapers, or Shades, or—

The empty throne.

I always wondered who was meant to sit there, and why they never showed their face, but now it makes sense. That throne can only belong to Veltuur.

Leumas leans forward, staring into my eyes with regret for whatever else he's about to tell me. "You, dear Sinisa Strigidae, are meant to defeat him. It was foretold, long ago. But first, we need you to free the Divine Altúyur that Veltuur imprisoned. I believe you've already begun."

If it wasn't for the Altúyur I think I met, the one I left behind in Kallinei Swamp, I doubt I'd believe a word Leumas was saying. It sounds ridiculous. Farfetched. The legends and fables of storybooks.

And yet, my gaze floats to the stormy sky above me, as if I'll find the door there and the Altúyur who was once a key looking down upon me, waiting for me.

Instead, all I see are the black branches etching through the gray sky. I wonder what this place used to be like, before Veltuur's reign. I wonder why Veltuur trapped them, what they want with this realm and Tayaraan, how long they've been here.

"What happened to the Altúyur?" I ask.

Leumas sighs. "Unfortunately, we don't have the time for me to tell you the full story. Veltuur and the rest of the Council know that I've been guiding both you and the boy, and they are coming for me. I can't hide from them much longer, and you should not be here when they arrive. But I won't be able to communicate with you once they come, so heed me now."

The underrealm quakes beneath us then. Dread spikes through my heart.

"A long time ago," Leumas continues. "The Altúyur lived freely amongst the mortals. There were nine of them: Macawna, Quetzi, Owlena, Lorik, Pecolock, Sungema, Iracara, Dovenia, and Veltuur."

Staggering on another rumble through the underrealm, I catch myself on my tree and blink, horrified at Leumas. "Veltuur is a Divine Altúyur?"

Leumas nods, but is too fearful to lose his stride. "He trapped the others, where they've remained throughout the ages, and consequently put the realms out of balance. Sungema will explain the details, as she holds the memory of it all. She's the reason no one remembers what happened to the Altúyur, why no one remembers who Veltuur is, who the Prophets are, or the Guardians. Free her, and she will answer all of your questions and will guide you in defeating Veltuur. But you must go now. The Councilspirits will be here soon."

The very fog at our feet begins to writhe. A roar carries through the forest.

"What about you?" I ask, and then realize an even greater priority. "What about Acari?"

"I hope to see you at the end of this, but I cannot leave yet. The Wraiths have your prince and I must—"

"They what?" Fear strikes through me, lightning hot. "You have to take me to him. I can't just leave him here, Leumas. You have to understand."

"You must. The fate of the realms depends on you releasing the Altúyur from their prisons."

"Then take me to Acari. Let me speak to him. I'm not leaving until I do."

Leumas squints at me from behind his bald brow. "You always were stubborn."

"I prefer *determined*."

With a wave of his hand, the red cloak hanging loosely from his arm, Leumas fazes us away. It takes me a moment to realize that the darkness isn't going to dissolve. Down here, where the Wraiths reside, nothing but blackness can penetrate these walls.

"Hello?" I hear Acari's voice echo in the void. "Is s-someone there?"

"It's me! It's Sinisa," I say, following the sound of his voice. "I've come to get you out of here."

"Stop!" he yells, startling me stiff. "Don't come closer. I might accidentally... You might..." he sighs, and when I finally realize what he's afraid of, I don't make him say it. One wrong move, one slight graze, and his power would kill me.

I focus instead on what I need to say, the reason I've crossed half of Tayaraan and traveled to the underrealm. Not to defeat Veltuur. Not to save the Altúyur. But to free Acari.

"You don't have to be a Reaper, you know? If you take the memory leaves, then you'll know—"

"I already took them," he says, solemnly. "I know what you were trying to show me. And I thank you for that. But I-I can't do it yet. I can't let him go."

My brow furrows. "Why not? You could be rid of him forever. You could be rid of this place. I know it's hard; trust me, I know. But I promise, it's worth it."

"You don't understand..."

Guffawing, I take another step forward. "I do understand though. I was a Reaper too. I had a crow just like you, and I had to release him. You forget that I was in the same situation that you're in—"

"No, you weren't!" The words sound harsh on his usually welcoming voice. "Your crow wasn't your father. It was some man who did inexplicable things to you, who you killed because you thought he deserved to die. And I'm not saying he didn't. But my crow is not a stranger. He's not some bruiser or debaucher; he was my father. A man I tried impressing my whole life. A man who always, *always* found a reason to be disappointed by me. A man who sent a Reaper after my own sister."

Staggering back, all I can do is blink, dumbfounded and numb.

"Killing him now means losing any opportunity of ever showing him that I could be great. It means he would never see what I can do on the throne and what I plan to do for people like my sister."

I bow my head and try steeling myself to the pain lancing through me. It took so much for me to get here. It took so many lives—Rory's, and Dethoc's, and Hayliel's—and it was all for nothing if Acari is choosing to stay.

This time when the underrealm quakes again, the entire floor seems to shift. Cracks break through the dirt, hissing with steam as they creep their way toward us.

"You must go, now," Leumas says in my ear.

I whip around, horror filling my eyes, but even with a face as milk white as his, I do not see him.

"Who's that?" Acari asks.

Leumas ignores him. "Find Sungema. She will help you with the others. Leave the boy to me and the seeds you've already planted."

"I can't just leave him—"

"You must! For now. The realms depend on it. I promise, I will look after him but you must go."

Gritting my teeth, it's all I can do not to argue further, but Acari's words replay in my mind and I realize he's never sounded more certain. There's no changing his mind. Not anytime soon, anyways. And though I don't know who Veltuur is and why the underrealm is quaking with rage, I know I don't want to find out.

"How do I find her?" I ask, trying to wedge the sorrow that feels like a knife out of my throat. "Sungema. Where is she?"

"Find who?" Acari asks, still in the dark, but I have to ignore him. It would be too heartbreaking to do anything else.

"You already have found her," Leumas says cryptically. "She bestows the gift of remembrance. Use what you know, and you will realize you already know where she is trapped."

I glance over my shoulder one last time to where Acari is calling to us, to the mission I have failed so miserably.

"Farewell, Sinisa Strigidae," Leumas utters. "May you be the salvation of us all."

28

THE PROPHESIZED ONE

SINISA

The underrealm blurs around me, wind smacking against my face from every direction until Kallinei Swamp swallows the darkness.

Above ground, back in the mortal realm, without Acari, I feel lost. Confused. Disappointed. My body hangs heavier than usual, like I'm carrying the dead bodies of my fallen friends on my back.

"Oh!" the Altúyur exclaims, jumping at my reemergence. "You're back! Did you find what you were looking for?"

My sorrowful eyes drift to the door beside me. "No," I say flatly.

"That's awful news. Will you be going back then?" he asks, and when he does, he sounds so sure that it could be a possibility, that I almost laugh.

"No, I don't think I'm welcome there anymore."

Sadness at the thought trickles its way through me, but before it can become a raging river, I rebuild the dam around my heart. I fortify myself, remind myself that Aulow had said it can take time for a Reaper to come around, and that although Acari has decided to stay for now, he can still change his mind. He is not lost yet.

Feeling a little more emboldened, I straighten when I say to the Altúyur, "But I haven't given up."

"Terrific!" he exclaims, hands slamming together in one resounding clap. "What do we do now then?"

Peculiarly, I stare at the creature before me. It's desire to blindly fasten itself to my side is both baffling and admittedly endearing. If I'm to free Sungema though, the Altúyur of memory, I suppose it makes sense for him to stay with me, that way maybe she can return to him his identity.

"Did you eat a leaf?" I ask, remembering that I'd already given him a means of doing so when I gave him the pouch of memory leaves before entering Veltuur. But before he can answer, sudden realization comes over me. "That's it! Leumas said I already knew where Sungema was trapped. He reminded me that she oversaw all memories. She has to be the memory tree. It's the only thing in all of Tayaraan that helps you recall your past."

"I'm sorry, what are we talking about?"

"Sungema, the Divine Altúyur of Memory."

He squints, thinking. "I don't think I know her. And no, I didn't eat the leaves. I wasn't sure if it was a trick or not."

"It wasn't a trick, but it doesn't matter. There's another way to get your memory back. A better way, I believe."

Reaching out my hand, I ask for the pouch. He tucks it closer to him at first, hesitating for a moment before reluctantly handing it to me.

"Are you sure there's another way?" he asks, eyes cast downward.

Nodding, I ask, "Can you fly with those things?"

He looks them over, the black feathers shimmering just like a crow's—though I try not to think about it. I'm not sure I will ever be able to trust a single crow again, but I want to trust this bizarre half-bird humanoid.

"I don't know," he answers, sounding mildly amused. "We can test them out though!"

He spreads his wings out wide, a gust of wind blowing across the space between us. He gives them a single, mighty flap, testing the feel of them. With a satisfied grin, he jumps, tucks his legs under him, and flaps his wings again. And again.

The mighty strokes carry him higher and higher, the wind from the force of them so powerful that I have to shield my eyes.

When I'm no longer being pummeled in the face by his draft, I glance up to find him hovering high in the sky, and from what I can glimpse behind the thick canopy, he's a natural in the clouds.

"It looks like I can!" he yells down to me.

With a halfhearted chuckle, I smile back. This will make our return to Halaud Palace a lot quicker.

29

VELTUUR

ACARI

Although I don't see Sinisa leave, I feel her absence all the same. Regret fills the void she leaves behind. It's not like I wanted to stay in this dreary, increasingly disturbing, isolating realm of the dead. It's not like I want my father-crow hovering over me anymore.

But part of me can't let him go yet, even if it meant being able to leave with Sinisa, a woman who I know has already sacrificed so much for me.

Someday, I hope to repay her. But, considering I find myself alone in this black dungeon, it might be awhile.

Shadows flicker on the already darkened walls. Claws reach out from them, sharp and glistening despite the absence of light. Creatures, horrendous and gruesome, everywhere.

Horror looms in the vast darkness around me, though no Wraiths have come forth to begin my torturing. Unless the wait is part of it. Not knowing when they will begin, or how bad it'll be, is fraying my nerves so greatly that I might as well be standing above a pit of knives.

For all I know, I am.

Any second now, the black floor could peel away and I could

fall to my demise, whether it be knives, or fire, or a great, big, gaping maw full of row upon row of sharpened teeth.

I shake my head, trying to rid it of my ever-concerning fears.

The longer I wait, the more I start to doubt whether I made the right choices. What would've happened if I hadn't told the Council about Leumas? Would I have just received a slap on the wrist, or would the Wraiths already be torturing me? What if I had tried to do as Sinisa asked and forgive my father-crow and be rid of this place once and for all?

A hand reaches out from the nothingness. At first, I can't see anything, I just feel it as it grips ahold of my tunic and pulls me forward. But the farther I'm dragged, the more light seeps into the darkness, until I can see the hand holding me. Its skin is red and raw, as if someone has dragged a knife over its fingers hundreds of times.

Finally, the trees of Veltuur blink into view, as do the six Councilspirits.

And someone else. Someone new and utterly terrifying.

He is a creature of nightmares, a human half-formed in the pit of hideous. Still clutching my red tunic, the man's ribbed chest is just as raw and wrinkled as his hand, like the shaved underbelly of a chicken. Where his mouth and nose should be, a grotesque claw protrudes from the center of his face, clamping tightly to another that grows out of his jaw.

His black and beady eyes hold me firm, but it's the sound of his wings as they unfold that send a shiver skittering down my spine. Quivering where I stand, his oily wings reflecting nothing but death and misery, something awakens inside my mind and tells me that I know exactly who I'm staring at.

When the Councilspirits bow, I follow suit.

The ground thunders with each of his steps as he makes his way back to the Council.

Frozen in terror, I dare lift my head as far as it will go until I find the talons attached to his legs.

"Rise," he says, the air rippling with power.

Though staggering, I'm quick to obey him.

When he gestures to me, black wings lining his arms, I flinch. "This is the Reaper?"

"Yes, Veltuur," Nymane answers, stepping forward only briefly before resuming her place among the other Councilspirits. She bows her hooded head again.

Veltuur turns to me, his empty eyes on mine. "I'm told Leumas sent you to aid Sinisa in fulfilling the prophecy."

"I—I don't know anything about a prophecy. I thought he sent me to claim a girl—I mean, the soul of a girl. I did. I—I killed one in the swamp—"

When Veltuur snarls, I snap my jaw closed and sink into myself even more.

"The traitor was overheard speaking to Sinisa of Sungema. He said she contains the memories of the past. What do you know of her?"

"I—I know nothing of her. Other than her being the Divine Altúyur of Memory." I recall the hushed conversation I overheard Sinisa sharing with Leumas though, just moments before they fled. "He reminded her of Sungema's gift and told her she already knew where to find her..." With a sudden flash of understanding, it hits me. "There's a memory tree! In the Forbidden Garden at the palace. It gives people back their memories. That could be it."

I realize my treachery only after I've blabbed. And though I do feel guilty and don't want to cause Sinisa any harm, the second I start to doubt whether I should've said anything, Veltuur's beak parts in the most hideous, gruesome grin, and I shudder back into my fear.

"Well done, young Reaper." Turning back around, Veltuur addresses the Councilspirits. "She cannot free Sungema."

"Of course, Your Greatness. We will send every Reaper and Shade at our disposal to the palace to ensure that she doesn't," Nymane offers.

"No. There is still a balance to uphold and that would draw too much unwanted attention." Veltuur returns his focus to me, and it takes everything in me not to cower. "You will go. It will not be suspicious if the king should arrive to the palace."

Behind Veltuur, I see Nymane's jaw unhinge, see the daggers her eyes fling at me. As terrified as I am of getting on her bad side, Veltuur's seems far worse. Not to mention, if Nymane had it her way, I'd be trapped with the Wraiths for eons. This might be my only way to return to Tayaraan, to resume my throne, and to fulfill the promise I've made to avenge myself and Gem.

"W-what do you want me to do?" I ask him.

"Reach the memory tree before Sinisa does," he commands, voice like the hissing steam of a geyser. "And kill her."

"You want me to...kill the memory tree? But...it's the last of its kind. Isn't that against our laws?"

Veltuur stares at me with eyes unblinking, the forest eerily quiet around us. "A Reaper has not the power to kill an Altúyur. We are immortal. Immune. Forever shall we walk the realms." When I stare stupidly in return, he elaborates. "No, young Reaper, you cannot slay Sungema. I wish for you to kill the girl before she can fulfill the prophecy."

Frowning, I worry at my lip. "You...you want me to kill Sinisa."

He's about to unfurl his wings and cast me out of the realm, when Nymane steps forward.

"Almighty Veltuur, might I offer a suggestion?"

"Speak freely," he answers.

Her bow deepens. "We should consider sending a Shade with the young Reaper. He is still new and has already proven troublesome." She pauses to glare at me. "I recommend Shade Nerul. He was assigned to mentor Reaper Acari upon initiation so the two of them have already worked closely together and Shade Nerul is already familiar with his uncooperative ways."

"Then is it not also his fault that his Reaper has been troublesome?" Veltuur counters. He lets the question hang over Nymane, weighing her down until she's almost folded in half. But just as she starts to slink back to her place, he continues. "Very well. Let Shade Nerul accompany Reaper Acari, to ensure that all goes as planned."

With a final flick of his long wing, his voice booms. "Now go."

To be continued in
Fate of the Vulture
PREORDER NOW!

Thank you for reading *Heart of the Sungem*!

Leave a Review
Help other readers find this dark saga by leaving a review on
Amazon, Goodreads, Bookbub, or any other reading website. Even
a simple "I loved it!" can really help!

ARC Team
If you're someone who loves leaving reviews and you're excited by
the idea of having early access to all of my books, check out my
website for more information on how to join my ARC Team: www.
jessacawillis.com/ARC

To be continued

<u>Social Media</u>

And last but not least, if you'd like to stay connected, you can find my social media links here: https://linktr.ee/jessaca_with_an_a

PRIMORDIALS OF SHADOWTHORN
Epic Dark Fantasy Romance

Ruled by tyrants. Hunted by demons.
This vengeful huntress is ready to fight back.

When Halira's parents are slaughtered by the horrifying demons that plague her lands, she joins the Shadow Crusade, a legion of warriors determined to slay the last living Primordial, end its reign of darkness, and destroy demon-kind once and for all.

But as her training begins, Halira soon discovers a secret about the forgotten magic that once thrived throughout the lands, one that could threaten her very survival.

Will Halira be the savior her country needs, or will her own dark secret force her to hide in the shadows?

~Check out the Primordials of Shadowthorn series on Amazon~

THE AWAKENED SERIES
NA/YA Supernatural Apocalyptic

Supernatural powers destroyed the world...
Now four unlikely heroes have to save it.

The world ended two years ago. They called it the Awakening: the supernatural event that gave some people powers and left others normal. Nations went to war and millions died.

Sean was one of the first to Awaken, but it wasn't until he walked in on his brother's brutal murder that he learned of the darker nature of his power: blood calls to him, and he to it. And in that moment, he showed his brother's murderers no mercy.

Now Sean must fight to keep his inner demons in check, and his path to redemption begins with the establishment of a sanctuary for people like him, people with powers: the Awakened.

But not even in the apocalypse are the Awakened safe...

Can Sean and three strangers unite the remnants of mankind when everything else has fallen apart? Can they face the darkest horror this new world has yet to offer?

~Check out The Awakened Quadrilogy on Amazon~

ACKNOWLEDGMENTS

This is the part of the story where recognition is shared with those behind the scenes, the ones that many forget about.

A special thanks to my brother, Michael—as always—for coming to my aid whenever I hit a roadblock. If I had known while we were growing up how much you were going to save my books' asses, I might've been nicer to you.

Other members of my family deserve some recognition as well: my partner, James, who always supports my writing by making sure I have time to do it; To my mom, Julie, who has bought every book I've published; To my son, Kieran, who motivates and inspires me to chase this dream every single day.

Thank you to Luminescence Covers by Claire Holt for the breath-taking covers—and for putting up with all of my post-graphic questions.

Thank you to my fabulous editor, Sandra Ogle (Reedsy) whom I will always be grateful for! This is also the first book that I worked on with proofreader, Kate Anderson, who does fantastic work! You two are lifesavers and I really am always eager to work with you.

Lastly, thank you to all of the readers, bloggers, bookstagrammers, fans, friends, and colleagues who have eagerly devoured these books so far. Knowing that you're enjoying this story and connecting with Sinisa and Acari is always in the back of my mind as I'm working on these books. I wouldn't be able to do any of this without your support, so thank you, so very, very much.

ABOUT THE AUTHOR

Jessaca is a fantasy author with an inclination toward the epic, dark, and adventure sub-genres. She studied social work for both her undergrad and graduate degrees and often incorporates themes from her education (i.e. family dynamics, mental health, systems of oppression) into her writing. She is a self-proclaimed nerd who loves cosplay, video games, and comics, and if you live in the PNW, you just might catch her in cosplay at one of the local comic conventions!

Made in the USA
Middletown, DE
21 December 2021

56857348R00148